More Five-Star Praise for the
Nationally Bestselling Mysteries
of Diane Mott Davidson

"The Julia Child of mystery writers."
—*Colorado Springs Gazette Telegraph*

"Mouthwatering." —*The Denver Post*

"Hearty fare for those who like their murder with a bit
of nosh on the side."
—*Publishers Weekly*

"A surprisingly tart and savory reading experience."
—*The Washington Post Book World*

"If devouring Diane Mott Davidson's newest whodunit
in a single sitting is any reliable indicator, then this was
a delicious hit." —*Los Angeles Times*

"You don't have to be a cook or a mystery fan to love Diane
Mott Davidson's books. But if you're either—her tempting
recipes and elaborate plots add up to a literary feast!"
—*The San Diego Union-Tribune*

"Mixes recipes and mayhem to perfection."
—*Sunday Denver Post*

"Davidson is one of the few authors who has been able to
seamlessly stir in culinary scenes without losing the focus of
the mystery . . . [she] has made the culinary mystery more
than just a passing phase."
—*Sun-Sentinel,* Fort Lauderdale

"Goldy and her collection of friends and family continue to
mix up dandy mysteries and add tempting recipes to the
readers' cookbooks at the same time."
—*The Dallas Morning News*

Catering
to
Nobody

Diane Mott

Davidson

BANTAM BOOKS
New York Toronto London Sydney Auckland

CATERING TO NOBODY
A Bantam Book
PUBLISHING HISTORY

Ballantine paperback edition / October 1992

Bantam paperback edition / March 2002

ISBN 978-0-553-58470-7

Published simultaneously in the United States and Canada

Bantam Books are published by Bantam Books, a division of Random
House, Inc. Its trademark, consisting of the words "Bantam Books" and
the portrayal of a rooster, is Registered in U.S. Patent and Trademark
Office and in other countries. Marca Registrada. Bantam Books, New
York, New York.

PRINTED IN THE UNITED STATES OF AMERICA

OPM   10   9

ACKNOWLEDGMENTS

The author wishes to acknowledge the assistance of the following people: Jim Davidson; Jeffrey Davidson; Sandra Dijkstra; Katherine Goodwin; John William Schenk, J. William's Catering, Bergen Park, Colorado; John B. Newkirk, D.Sc.; William Harbridge; Charles Blakeslee; Emerson Harvey, M.D.; John Hutto, M.D.; Alan Rapaport, M.D.; Doug Palczynski, R.Ph.; Deidre Elliot, Karen Sbrockey, and Elizabeth Green; Kitty Hirs and the writing group that assembled at her house; and Investigator Richard Millsapps, Jefferson County Sheriff's Department, Golden, Colorado.

INTRODUCTION

Catering a wake was not my idea of fun, Goldy the caterer reflects as she shapes dill-speckled bread dough into pillow-shaped rolls. Thus Goldy announces herself at the outset of *Catering to Nobody*. She has no inkling as to how the events at that wake will close down her business and force her to investigate a murder. Nor did *I* have any inkling that Goldy would become a member of my family, a person who speaks her mind, writes me letters, and embarks on culinary and sleuthing expeditions that I find both scary and amazing.

Some years ago, I pulled over onto the shoulder of one of our narrow mountain roads. About twenty yards away, a pickup looked as if it had vaulted into the enormous roadside meadow, and then stalled. Its front wheels were precariously perched over a creekbank. Wanting to see if the driver needed help, I approached. "Is anyone in there?" I called. "Do you need help?" When I was six feet away, a mane of frizzy blond hair came into view. The head with the hair was stuck at an impossible horizontal angle. My body chilled; I could not find my voice. I raced back to my car and hit the accelerator hard. (This was before the widespread use of cell phones.) At home four minutes later, I phoned the Jefferson County Sheriff's Department (a fabulous, dedicated group of law enforcement officers). I explained what I'd seen, then begged them to call me back once they knew what had happened. The young woman driver was okay, a cop told me later. She'd spun the truck's wheels and lost control. She was on some kind of medication (!), and she'd blacked out.

I was relieved the woman was not dead or injured. Still, I chastised myself. *Goldy,* I thought, *would have done much better*.

Goldy's background emerged from my years of volunteer work. Back then, I was continually startled by the number of middle- and upper-class women—women who labored beside me in volunteering—who were physically abused by their husbands. (In the years before the arrest and trial of O.J. Simpson, this demographic aspect of domestic abuse was not well known.) The idea for Goldy came out of what I call the "emotional refrigerator." The emotional refrigerator provides ingredients for books, and foremost among these was this caterer who survives abuse, dumps her cruel husband, and *thrives*. When life handed Goldy the lemon of Doctor John Richard Korman, she determined to make not only lemonade, but also lemon meringue pie, lemon bars, lemon pound cake, lemon sorbet. . . . To the surprise of the small town of Aspen Meadow, Goldy abandoned the role of rich doctor's wife, and put her considerable energies into starting the town's first catering business. Goldy also does her best to raise her much-loved son, Arch, who begins the saga here at age eleven. (As I work on the eleventh Goldy book, Arch is fifteen and just beginning to come out of his emotional and physical timidity.) In *Catering to Nobody*, Goldy has not yet gone back to the church, nor has she figured out where her social life might be heading. But she knows what she's good at—cooking—and she's determined to make her new catering business a success. She doesn't yet know she'll be good at sleuthing . . . but she figures that out!

The first response to the manuscript was mixed. Scores of editors rejected it. Virginia Rich had written three culinary mysteries in the early eighties, but she had been dead for several years. Who would buy a culinary mystery in 1989? When my wonderful agent, Sandra Dijkstra, pointed out to editors that no one—not a single author—had ever had a caterer (who offered recipes!) as a main character, the response was equally negative. Even more damning, the fact that Goldy had survived spousal abuse was seen as "too dark." The recipes were viewed as "intrusive." I felt strongly that both were necessary to explain who Goldy was, so the excellent Hope Dellon of St. Martin's Press, who bought the book, allowed them to stay.

Catering to Nobody, published in 1990 along with hundreds of other new hardcover mysteries, received a 4500-copy first print run. A press release was the only publicity, and so my agent urged me to do my own publicity. I balked, telling her, "Episcopalians don't do publicity." But she convinced me.

I printed up a card for Dungeon Bars, one of the recipes in the book, and sent it to bookstores. I went on the road with three other members of Sisters In Crime, and we did our presentations at a dozen bookstores. To each store, I took platters of Dungeon Bars. If readers liked the cookie, I figured, they might buy the book.

Twelve years after it was first published, *Catering to Nobody* has sold over a million copies, in this country and overseas. I was ecstatic when Bantam Books bought the rights to reprint the book in this new paperback edition. With Bantam, I am blessed to have not only the brilliant Kate Miciak as an editor, but also an entire team of diligent artists, publicists, salespeople, and businesspeople working to ensure that each Goldy book is more successful than the last. For this, too, I am thankful.

Why do people feel connected to Goldy? Despite *Catering to Nobody*'s original publication as a "women's book," the marvelous mail I've received about it is equally split between men and women. These readers identify with Goldy, they are pulling for Arch, they *despise* the Jerk, or they just love cooking . . . or reading about it!

And so on to the other characters and recipes.

Regarding the Jerk: Doctor John Richard Korman strode into my mind with all his arrogance, money, good looks, and apparent invulnerability intact. He is not based on any one man. He is every egotistical clergyman, nasty boss, spiteful boyfriend, arrogant doctor, cruel professor, malevolent friend, wicked husband, *etc.*, that any one of us could ever have—all rolled into a tall, blond, glib, athletic, powerful, much-admired man—the *übermensch* we love to hate.

(Just please don't send me any more mail asking me to kill him. My agent won't let me. After hearing this, one Colorado librarian suggested, "Well, could you *maim* him?")

Regarding Arch: My husband and I have three sons, all of whom have provided "Arch material" over the years. Still, not one of our sons wears glasses; they wouldn't be caught dead in Arch-style clothes; they find his various science, art, and literary projects bizarre. Arch is just Arch.

Regarding Tom: Women frequently ask me, "Where did you *get* him?" No matter what my response, the follow-up question is: "Do you know any single men who are *like* Tom?" No, sorry, I don't. Like Arch, Tom is a composite. He is a good, kind, knowledgeable man—in those ways, he is very similiar to my husband (who is not the Jerk . . . please don't ask him anymore, it upsets him). Tom also possesses a single-minded dedication to law enforcement, like the wonderfully helpful Sergeant Richard Millsapps of the Jefferson County Sheriff's Department. Most importantly, though, Tom—with his charisma, his caring, his love of cooking, and his great affection for Goldy—just knocked on the door of my mind when I was structuring the first crime scene in *Catering to Nobody*. When I opened the door to Tom, he strode in and took charge.

Marla, Goldy's best friend and the other ex-wife of the Jerk, did not knock on my mental entryway. She blasted through it, her ample brown hair twinkling with precious-gem barrettes, her equally ample body swathed in expensive seasonal clothes, her voice exuberant as she delivered gossip, opinions, and advice. She flopped onto an instantly imagined kitchen chair, snagged a handful of cookies, and informed me she was rich as blazes. Moreover, she announced, she was here to stay.

The only other ongoing series character, Julian Teller, is introduced in the book that followed *Catering to Nobody*, *Dying For Chocolate*. Unlike Goldy, Marla, Tom, and Arch, I had no idea Julian Teller would be such a strong presence in the life of Goldy's extended family. But when I sent Julian off to college, I received such a barrage of complaining letters, I brought him back. Julian, like the others, is here to stay.

Regarding the recipes: People often ask me where I "get" them. The answer is, from tasting, experimenting, trials, and many, many errors. Most of the recipes are ones I've worked on, reworked, and experimented with since my husband and I were married in 1969. At that time, I had to start from scratch, since I had no idea of how to cook or even how to *learn* to cook. I put our first steak into the oven at 350°—for an hour. That was what you did with everything else, I figured, so why not? And bless my husband—he proclaimed the resultant leather delicious. (I do much better now.)

With the other recipes in Goldy's books, I sometimes will taste a dish at a restaurant, or some delicacy made by my phenomenally talented catering mentor, John William Schenk, and then try repeatedly to replicate it. This works until the family cries, "Enough!" (They finally announced, when I'd served them weeks of variations on "Julian's Cheese Manicotti"—from *Dying for Chocolate*—"No more manicotti! Ever!")

My sisters, Lucy Mott Faison and Sally Mott Freeman, and my brother, Bill Mott, Jr., have given me wonderful ideas and done much low-altitude testing and tasting, for which I am deeply grateful. Lucy has produced an endless stream of Goldy's cookies, cakes, and muffins, and given all of them to her neighbors, her friends, and her son Will's teachers at the Gilman School in Baltimore. In Bethesda, Maryland, Sally—herself a superb cook; some day I hope to learn to make her incredible chutney—and her sons Christopher and Bobby have been my unflagging publicists. (Some Episcopalians *are* good at publicity, after all!) And Billy, a tireless vice-president at Goldman Sachs, has not only given me numerous insights into the business world, he is also a fabulous cook who helps his wife, Cathie, cook for their children Torry, Gracie, Billy, and Olivia. It was Billy who came up with the terrific idea to grill "Snowboarder's Pork Tenderloin" (from *Tough Cookie*). (It's great, try it!) Needless to say, I am deeply grateful to my siblings, their spouses, and all their wonderful children.

Finally, I wish to all you readers, that you enjoy Bantam's new paperback edition of *Catering to Nobody*. Since (again, unexpectedly) the recipes emerged as one of readers' favorite aspects of the Goldy books, four new ones appear here. I have extensively revamped the honey-spice cookie, renamed it *Honey-I'm-Home Ginger Snaps*, and placed the recipes in a new format. I hope you enjoy them all, and will fix them for someone you love.

Good reading, and bon appétit!

DIANE MOTT DAVIDSON,
October 2001

COLD BUFFET FOR FORTY

Poached salmon

◆

Mayonnaise mixed with wild Maine blueberries

◆

Asparagus vinaigrette with minced tomatoes

◆

Wild rice salad

◆

Herb rolls and honey muffins

◆

Strawberry shortcake buffet

◆

Vouvray, lemonade, coffee and tea

CHAPTER 1

Catering a wake was not my idea of fun.

First of all, there was the short notice. A person died. Three days later there was a funeral. In this case the body had been discovered on a Monday, autopsy Tuesday, funeral Saturday, seven days after the presumed day of death. In Colorado we didn't call the buffet after the funeral a wake. But whether you called it a reception or coming over for a bite to eat afterward, it still meant food for forty mourners.

I dumped a mound of risen dough as soft as flesh onto the oak countertop. Eating, I reflected, was a way of denying death.

I had known her. I did not want to think about it now. My fingers modeled soft dough around dill sprigs, then dropped the little rolls onto a baking sheet, where they looked like rows of miniature green-and-white sofa pillows. This was the last two dozen. I rubbed bits of yeasty mixture off my hands and let cold water gush over them.

A professional caterer has to keep her mind on the job,

not the reason for the job. October was generally a slow month for parties in Aspen Meadow. Despite the fact that Goldilocks' Catering, Where Everything Is Just Right! provided the town's only professional food service, making a living here was always a precarious enterprise. Like it or not, I needed the income from this postfuneral meal.

Still. I would rather have had Laura Smiley alive. She had been Arch's fifth-grade teacher last year. She also had taught him third, when he was recovering from the divorce. They had become special friends, had worked on games and outdoor projects. They had written letters over the summers. I could picture Laura Smiley with my son, her arm around his slender shoulders, her cascade of brown-blond curls just touching the top of his head.

Psychologists and social workers had come into the elementary school to work with the students after the news of Ms. Smiley's death broke on Monday. Arch had not spoken much about it. I did not know what the counselors had said to him, nor he to them. All during the week he had come home from school, taken snack food into his room, and closed the door. Sometimes I could hear him on the phone, acting as dungeon master or playing television trivia games. Perhaps losing Ms. Smiley was not much on his mind. It was hard to tell.

But now because of her death we had this job, which would help pay the bills for October. Laura Smiley's aunt from Illinois, acting in place of parents long dead, had ordered the food and sent me an express mail cheque for eight hundred dollars. This covered my second problem, usually my first, and that was *money*.

Above the steel hand-washing sink, one of several required by the county for commercial food service, the booking calendar showed only two parties between tomorrow, October tenth, and the thirty-first. Clearing four hundred dollars on each of those plus four hundred for tomorrow's buffet would take us to the Halloween-to-

Christmas season, where I made almost enough money to get Arch and me through May. Long ago I had learned to stop depending on regular child support payments from Arch's father, even if he did have an ob-gyn practice with an income as dependable as procreation. The payments were invariably wrong and invariably late. But arguments between us were bad for Arch and dangerous for me. Peace was worth a lower income. I stared grimly at the calendar. Lots of parties between Halloween and Christmas. That was the ticket to financial security.

Problem number three after short notice and money was getting all the supplies for a job. My meat and produce supplier was doing an extra run for me because she, too, had known the financial strains of single motherhood. Her truck was supposed to be rumbling up from Denver right now bringing a salmon and out-of-season asparagus and strawberries. After she delivered them, she'd give me a lecture on going out. She'd say, It's not that tough to have fun.

But tough was like a roll in the microwave. I didn't have time for a harangue about my social life because in addition to needing the supplies, I'd just used the last of the honey to make the rolls. This meant the muffins were on hold. The local honey supplier was a handsome fellow named Pomeroy, lusted after by every unattached woman in the county, a fact my supplier usually did not fail to mention. Unfortunately Pomeroy had said he wouldn't be able to get over for a while to resupply my stock. The unusually warm weather had brought out a predator that had raided one of the hives. And he had his hands full.

Of what, I had wanted to say, but hadn't. Sugar would do for the muffins.

The phone rang.

"Goldilocks' Catering," I said into the receiver, "where everything is just—"

"Spare me the greeting, Goldy," came the voice of

Alicia, my supplier. "I called Northwest Seafood. Fish's all yours."

"You're great."

She mm-hmmed and then said nothing.

I said, "What is it?"

"How well did you know this Laura?"

"She was Arch's teacher. For a couple of grades."

"Young?"

"Early forties," I said. "She acted young." I paused. "I knew her."

She grunted and said she would be up in an hour.

I opened the refrigerator, a walk-in needed for the business. John Richard Korman, my ex-husband, had found the cost of this item ridiculous. Ditto the van and the required new sinks and shelves to store food above insect level. Other purchases out of my sixty-thousand-dollar divorce settlement had included a six-burner stove, extra oven and freezer, and enough cooking equipment to outfit Sears. Retrofitting our old house off Aspen Meadow's Main Street had not been terribly difficult.

What *had* been difficult was hanging up on John Richard's alternately shrieking and pleading voice, and then finally getting the locks changed when he had shown up repeatedly to do one of two things. At first, even though we were separated, he would try to seduce me. Sometimes successfully, I was ashamed to admit. Or he would start a fight to demonstrate his opposition to my financial independence. And by *demonstrate*, I don't mean like Gandhi.

In the walk-in I reached for the butter, eggs, and cream. I backed out and whacked the door with my foot, then regarded my balancing act in the mirror-black surface. Blond curly hair. Freckles on a face unbruised for three years. Brown eyes. These stared back at me, saying, Don't think about it now, just cook. At thirty I was doing okay, single but with good friends, and only slightly pudgy from all the fancy cooking that made the living for Arch and me.

But I was preparing a wake for someone I'd known. Early forties. Also single. Had been.

For the dessert shortcakes I used an old trick: make giant scones. Another thing I'd learned in this business: involve the clients with the food. Make the spread good to look at, smell, touch, taste. Gauge action by needs. At a bridal shower, don't give the guests much to do with the food since they're already involved with the presents. But keeping people active at a wake was essential. Being busy, like working, allayed grief. By splitting cakes and heaping on berries and cream, the mourners could start to get their minds off death.

Getting one's mind off it. Not easy.

Laura had smiled broadly and flourished papers with Arch's drawings of mountain wildlife at our parent conferences, which I'd always attended alone, as John Richard couldn't be bothered. Arch is so talented, Laura had said, one of the most unusual students I've ever had. It's too bad he doesn't have more friends.

The food processor blade whirred and bit through the butter and flour. Soon the kitchen would smell divine. Arch could have a hot scone when he came in from school. Maybe he would eat it in the kitchen instead of heading off to his room.

The phone rang again.

"Goldilocks'—" I began, but was interrupted.

"Shut up, it's me!" shouted Marla Korman, John Richard's other ex-wife, now a good friend of mine. "Arch home yet?"

I strained to see out the window that overlooked Main Street, then listened for the bus. Yellow aspen leaves as bright as lemon disks shook in the warm breeze. No children's shouts announced the bus's afternoon rounds. Instead there was only the roar of a motorcycle and the rushing sound of Cottonwood Creek, already frigid with October snow melt from the high mountains.

I said, "Not yet. Ten minutes or so."

"I've been shopping," Marla said, "because I don't want to think about Laura. The stores are empty now that the tourists have gone. They didn't leave much."

"Maybe we didn't have much in the first place," I said.

"This place," wailed Marla.

I poured a cup of coffee and steeled myself for the coming barrage of complaints. The town would be the warm-up for the ex-husband.

She said, "How demoralizing to live in a terminally quaint western village."

I made sympathetic noises.

"Of course, I don't know why I would need a size sixteen cowgirl dress anyway," Marla complained, "since I'm not coming to this shindig tomorrow. The Jerk's going to be there, isn't he?"

"He certainly is," I said. "But I'm leaving the rolling pin at home."

Bad joke, but we chuckled anyway. The Jerk was what Marla had dubbed our mutual ex, for his personality and his initials, J.R.K. Marla so intensely disliked seeing John Richard that it was hard to understand why she talked about him so much. Seven months after my divorce was final, John Richard ended a fling with a married woman who sang in the church choir and wedded Marla's bulk and wealth. They were divorced fifteen months later and she and I promptly became partners in anger. But before that point Marla's disgust with his extramarital antics had ballooned her up another thirty pounds, weight she'd used to good advantage when he came at her with a rolling pin. She had managed to heave him into a hanging plant, dislocating his shoulder.

I looked down at my right thumb, which still would not bend properly after John Richard had broken it in three places with a hammer.

"That rolling pin," Marla was saying between giggles, "that damn rolling pin. You could use it to fix him green tomato pie."

Without thinking, I looked at the menu. Tomatoes. Damn. Amid all the other grousing he had done, John Richard had been at pains to remind me of his allergies to chocolate and tomatoes. I was planning to mince some of the latter and sprinkle the red bits on the asparagus vinaigrette, for color. John Richard would have to get mushrooms if I didn't want to make him sick. Oh, I thought as I poured my coffee down the sink and finished mixing the scones, the adjustments we make after divorce.

Marla had stopped laughing. "I have news," she announced. "He's bringing his new girlfriend . . ."

I shook my head and began to spoon mounds of batter onto cookie sheets.

"Think of it," Marla went on, "you could poison both of them."

"Wouldn't you just love that," I muttered.

"On second thought, maybe one death is enough for a while," said Marla. "Since the funeral's tomorrow, I guess our women's group won't meet tonight."

"I'm swamped," I said truthfully. "How about later in the month?"

"Don't know if I can wait that long. I need to order some cookies."

I said, "Can we talk about it later? I'm awful busy right now." I wedged the phone between my chin and shoulder and scraped the last of the scone-shortcake batter out. It made a sucking noise before plopping on the sheet.

"The cookies can wait. My pantries are full, anyway. You're getting upset because we've been talking about you-know-who. Sorry."

"Not to worry," I said. "If I hadn't wanted a family so badly, I'd never have made the mistake of marrying him in the first place."

Marla sighed. "Oh God, think of Laura. She didn't even have the chance to get married."

I checked inside the proofing box; the dill rolls had risen. I snapped the other oven button to Preheat.

I said, "I am thinking about it. I am thinking about her. I'm fixing all the food, aren't I?"

"Where's your housemate? What's her name, Patty Sue? Can't she help you? What about Arch? You going to draft him to serve?"

"Patty Sue will help tomorrow," I said. "She's at the doctor now. Korman senior. Arch is going to have to help. I hate to do that to him since he was so close to Laura. Plus the aunt decided to have this reception over at Laura's house, all the worse. Just a sec." I grunted. I was thrusting my free hand through my dry goods shelves. "Oh my God," I said, "I've let my supplies get too low, even if this is the slow season. I'm out of honey *and* sugar."

"No honey and no sugar," observed Marla. "You're not doing very well. And as Laura would have said, you're not acting too *sweet* either, Goldy. I'll call when you're in a better mood. Let me know how the *affair* goes." She suppressed a laugh. "Laura would think it was all a big joke, you know. She'd say, Man, this party is *dead*."

"Goodbye, Marla."

The front door swept open and let in a gust of aspen-sweet October air. Arch traipsed into the kitchen and threw his backpack onto one of the counters before heading for the refrigerator.

I said, "How'd it go today?"

He groaned. "Terrible. As usual."

He turned his small, earnest eleven-year-old face full of freckles and brown hair and tortoise-shell glasses to me.

He said, "Larry and Sean attacked me. They said I was stupid for still going around on Halloween. They say I'm stupid about everything, and they're the stupid ones. Halloween isn't even here yet!" He shook his head, disgusted. "They said it was like believing in Santa Claus. Look, they tore my shirt." He fingered a rip in the blue-and-red flannel.

"Hmm."

He gave me a grim look. "And don't tell me all that stuff about turning the other cheek because I already tried that and it doesn't work. I'm going to have to think of something else."

I said, "Sorry. Want a hot biscuit in two minutes?"

"Can't." His voice wrapped around the open refrigerator door. "Todd's calling as soon as he gets home. We're doing a role-playing game and then TV trivia. I've been reading a book about the old shows all week." He emerged clutching a pitcher of peppermint tea, his favorite. "Don't worry. I'll use the other phone line in case any clients call in."

He smiled, and I wanted to hug him, ripped plaid shirt and all. But he was at the age where this made him uncomfortable, so I just lifted one eyebrow at the tea.

"You use the last of my sugar in that?"

"I had to use something," he said in defense. "I needed it."

I shook my head and began to mince scallions for my Wild Man's Wild Rice Salad, so named because *men* usually turn the other cheek to rice. The rich scent of baking scones filled the kitchen. Arch loaded a plate with oatmeal cookies, a sure sign he was not going to stay and chat.

"Listen up," I said. "You remember I need you to help tomorrow?" He nodded. "Your job now, please," I went on as I handed him two dollar bills, "is to pop on down to the convenience store and get me another bag of sugar. And don't open it for a sweet fix on the way home. I have to have it for the muffins and strawberries and lemonade."

He groaned dramatically and clomped out, yelling something over his shoulder about Todd calling back in half an hour.

I washed the food processor and started on Goldy's Marvelous Mayonnaise. When Todd rang I gave him the message. Halfway through drizzling in the safflower oil for the mayo, Alicia banged through the front door. With all the

Goldy's Marvelous Mayonnaise

1 large egg, purchased from a
   salmonella-free source
1 tablespoon fresh lemon juice
1 tablespoon white wine vinegar
1/2 teaspoon dry mustard
1/2 teaspoon salt
1 cup safflower oil

Put the egg, juice, vinegar, mustard,
and salt in a food processor fitted with
a metal blade. Process until well
blended, about 30 to 40 seonds.

Place the oil in a small pitcher and,
with the machine running, dribble it
into the egg mixture in a thin stream.
When all the oil has been added, turn
off the processor and scrape the mayonnaise from the bowl and the blade
into a small bowl that can be tightly
covered. Keep the mixture chilled. It
is best to use homemade mayonnaise
within 24 hours.

Makes 1 cup

Wild Man's
Wild Rice Salad

$\frac{1}{2}$ cup raw wild rice
2 cups chicken or vegetable broth
2 tablespoons mayonnaise
1 tablespoon tarragon vinegar
$\frac{1}{2}$ teaspoon Dijon mustard (or
    more, if desired)
1 tablespoon olive oil
2 scallions, finely chopped
3 radishes, diced
1 small tomato, drained, seeded,
    and diced
$\frac{1}{3}$ cup jicama, peeled and diced
1 cup baby spinach leaves, well
    washed and drained, plus extra
    for lining platter
Salt and pepper to taste

The night before you are to serve the
salad, thoroughly rinse the rice, place
it in a glass bowl, and completely cover
the kernels with water. Allow the rice
to soak overnight.

The next morning, carefully strain the rice and discard the water. In a large pan, bring the broth to a boil and add the rice. Cover the pan and immediately lower the heat to the lowest setting. Allow the rice to cook, covered, about 1 hour to $1\frac{1}{4}$ hours, or until the kernels have puffed and taste done (i.e., they are not chewy or hard). Drain the rice and measure it. You should have between $1\frac{3}{4}$ and 2 cups cooked rice. Spread the kernels out on two plates to cool *completely*. For the salad, the kernels must be dry and cool. Pat the kernels dry with paper towels, if necessary.

In a small bowl, combine the mayonnaise, vinegar, and mustard, and whisk well. Add the oil in a thin stream, whisking all the while, until you have a smooth, blended dressing. In a medium-sized bowl, gently combine the cool rice kernels with the scallions, radishes, tomato, jicama, and spinach. Pour the dressing over this mixture and mix very gently. Taste and correct the seasoning. Chill at least 2 hours

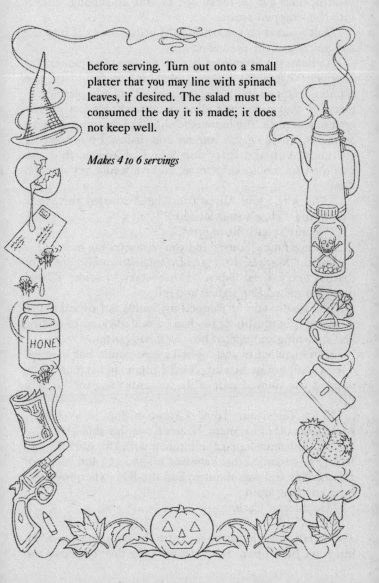

before serving. Turn out onto a small platter that you may line with spinach leaves, if desired. The salad must be consumed the day it is made; it does not keep well.

Makes 4 to 6 servings

interruptions I'd be lucky not to end up mixing vinegar into the whipped cream.

"Let's put it on the counter," I yelled over the buzzing and gulping of the processor.

We heaved a Styrofoam box up next to the mountain of chopped vegetables for the salad. Inside would be the salmon, wrapped in plastic and packed in ice. I planned to poach it that night and slice the strawberries, whip the cream, and make the lemonade all in the morning. Laura's aunt was providing the Vouvray and dishes. I was bringing the cups. Arch and Patty Sue, who had lived with us for two months, would help serve, and we would get through this.

"That's it," said Alicia after she'd downed the scone I'd offered. "How's your love life?"

"No news that's fit to print."

She eyed me. "Something you're not telling me?"

I said, "Maybe." In a gossipy small town one does not discuss one's social hopes. "Don't worry," I said. "I'll get out eventually." She sighed and left.

The silvery salmon slapped my hands as I rinsed it and wrapped it in muslin. It too had been dedicated to mating and spawning and look at how far *it* had gotten.

Arch marched in and lobbed a two-pound bag of sugar onto a chair before heading for the phone in his room. The opened bag snowed part of its contents onto the kitchen floor.

"The Television Trivia Championship is at hand," Arch, ignorant of his mess, hollered over his shoulder.

The rolls enveloped the kitchen with the smell of dill. In a large ceramic bowl I sloshed oil and egg and sugar for the muffins and was about to add the flour when my business line rang again.

"Goldilocks' Catering—"

"Stop."

Marla again. I began to measure the flour into the bowl, but some blew up my nose and onto the floor on top of the sugar. New powder on top of packed powder. Soon we could ski in the kitchen.

"What now?" I said.

"Don't tell me you haven't heard the *latest*."

"How could I? I just talked to you within the last hour."

"*He* is *marrying* this girl."

I set the bowl down.

"Goldy, did you hear me?"

I reached for the mushrooms.

"Goldy, do you believe this?"

I said, "Hmm."

"Well, my dear," she demanded shrilly, "what are we going to do?"

"Feel sorry for her. Not give tomatoes to him," I answered as I began to mince.

"Anyway," continued Marla, "the thought of a third daughter-in-law was too much for Vonette. She got drunk, I mean really *gone*, and Fritz called the cops and had her hauled down to Furman County detox."

"Not again," I said as bits of mushroom fell from the side of my knife. "Did someone go get her?"

"Yes, she's home, doing better. She'll be at the wake tomorrow. Fritz, for all that silver fox routine, isn't exactly what you'd call compassionate. Must run in the family."

I said, "Should I try to keep Vonette away from the Vouvray?"

"No way," said Marla with a snort. "I can't believe that in your eight years with John Richard, you never saw Vonette's flask. She keeps it in her purse. You must be blind."

"I am not blind," I replied before hanging up, "but I will be broke if I can't finish the food for this party."

With the mushrooms minced and wrapped and the muffins steaming in the oven, I headed down the hall toward Arch's room, sugar bag in hand.

"Do you realize the mess you made by tearing into this?" I demanded after knocking and entering and offering the bag as evidence. He told Todd to hang on and cupped his hand over the phone.

"Please, Mom," he said as he held up a book, something about TV facts. "Let me talk. Besides, I didn't do that. See," he said as he tongued forward a wet pink mass, "I had bubble gum."

I cocked my head at him. "Arch, alibis are like food service. They have to do more than look good and hold up. They have to be palatable. And yours," I added, "doesn't even look good."

"Sorry, Mom," he said. "Really. I'll clean it up."

I wanted to open his head and look in, to see what he was really thinking, how he was dealing with everything. I wanted to say, Are you okay? And have him say, Yeah, Mom.

"Don't bother," I said. "I swept it. Just be more careful, all right?"

He nodded solemnly and said nothing. And then I turned away. I did not know what the right grieving behavior should be from a boy whose favorite teacher ever, Laura Smiley, had only six days before slashed her wrists and bled to death.

CHAPTER 2

I'm starving," said Patty Sue as she tiptoed into the kitchen in a ruffled pink housecoat the next morning. I finished slicing the strawberries and offered her a bowl. A lanky twenty-year-old who had a twig-like figure and the metabolism of an athlete, Patty Sue Williams had been my roommate since August tenth at Vonette Korman's request.

"She just doesn't have anywhere to live while she's here, Goldy honey," my ex-mother-in-law had said, "and she needs Fritz to treat her medical problems. Take her in for a while. Give her a job. She's never done anything out there in eastern Colorado except live with her folks. This gal wants to learn, Goldy. You can teach her."

This I had come to doubt, I reflected as I pushed down on lemon halves to ream out their juice for the lemonade. Patty Sue had been so sheltered by her parents that her approach to any new endeavor was timidity, confusion, or both. She had attended a local community college "for a while," she said vaguely, as if that, like everything else in her life, had not quite panned out. When she first arrived she had told me all about herself, including the fact that she was a virgin. Dr. Fritz Korman, John Richard's father and the other half of Korman and Korman Ob-Gyn, was treating Patty Sue for amenorrhea. Which meant she hadn't had a menstrual cycle for the last year.

"This is a bad thing?" Marla had asked at the last meeting of Amour Anonymous, our women's group.

"It needs to be treated," I replied. "Her doctor out in Fort Morgan sent her to Fritz, who claims to be some kind of specialist with it. It's serious enough that Patty Sue's mother let her come out and live with me, although she calls once a week to make sure I'm not corrupting her."

"Not a chance of that, I'm afraid," Marla said. "Maybe we could bring her into the group as a special assignment."

I doubted if Patty Sue would have recognized herself in any of the literature about love-addicted women, which the Amour Anonymous group reads religiously. Sometimes I wondered if she recognized herself as anything. She was tall, lovely, and unsophisticated to the point of never having operated a dishwasher. She wanted to learn to drive a car but was intimidated by crown roast of pork. At first she had been quite eager to learn the catering business. She had made cementlike loaves of bread and overcooked hamburgers with the brightest of smiles. But just when she started mastering the skills, she had detoured into a state of distraction.

In September she'd started avoiding my eyes and my questions. Perhaps she was thinking about her sickness. It was strange because she didn't *look* sick. In fact, physical fitness was her one obsession. She had even asked that her first wages as a caterer's helper go to adding her to my athletic club membership. Despite the mood shift, which she unfortunately could not blame on PMS, she still worked out at the gym. But her energy had become feverish instead of enthusiastic. And her cooking abilities, such as they were, had gone to hell.

"That was great," Patty Sue said now as she licked her fingers from the strawberries. "This kitchen always smells super."

I set the bowl aside and broke three eggs into an iron skillet, then went back to squeezing lemons until it was time for the over-easy part. These days, nothing was easy for Patty Sue *until* it was over. My attempts in the last two weeks to teach her to cook anything more complicated than toast, much less eggs, had not gone well. Words like *marinate* and *braise* were beyond her. I had asked if she was homesick. She'd said no, and gone on to leave the top off the food processor when she worked with flour, generating small blizzards.

So I had put her to work serving to pay for her rent, food, and right to exercise indoors. For Laura Smiley's wake she was in charge of the strawberry shortcake buffet. This would mean little beyond keeping a platter stacked with scones and replenishing bowls with sliced strawberries and whipped cream.

"Where's Arch?" I asked as I placed little glasses of orange juice next to each placemat.

Patty Sue said, "On the phone, I think."

Since she obviously was not going to get him, I started down the hall to his room. On the way I glanced at the drawings of mountain flowers he had done last spring. Laura had encouraged his artwork after he'd produced the sketches of high-country animals. These delicate pen-and-ink works were of bluebell, fireweed, daisy, lady's slipper— all part of a project on nectar producers. Arch had chewed his tongue and furrowed his brow while drawing the details of tendrils and stamens.

Arch was the other problem-in-residence. Never gregarious, he had seemed even more isolated since the beginning of school. Twice he had come home with a black eye and a note from the principal saying he had been in a fight. I knew better than to pry. Or worse, rescue. I just wanted to understand what was going on.

Since Laura's death he had become even more with-drawn. Whenever I was near he spoke on the phone in a hushed tone. His eyes glazed more and more in indiffer-ence, as if he were taking lessons from Patty Sue. Our days of counting spoons, of telling stories, of loitering next to the hill of pumpkins at the grocery store to choose just the right one for a jack-o'-lantern—these were over. Immersed in fantasy role-playing games, he prepared and embarked on elaborate paper adventures, the purpose of which eluded me. As I edged away from the drawings and ap-proached his room I could hear the authoritative voice he invariably used when directing one of these adventures. I slid his door open.

". . . and since you have trespassed the space in front of their lair," he announced, "you will be attacked by a low-flying straight line of stringrays—"

"Arch!" I stuck my head into his room. "Hate to inter-rupt. Breakfast."

He looked up at me from his neatly made bed. He was already wearing his white shirt and black pants. Soon he would cover this outfit with one of our white chef's aprons.

"To be continued," he said, and hung up. Behind the glasses his eyes were inscrutable.

"You're all right?" I said, half statement, half question.

"I'm not hungry," he said with straight-lipped calm. "For eggs or anything. Let's just go."

And so we did. Patty Sue ate all the eggs. We packed the van and set out.

The air was cool but calm, quite different from the snarling frost-blowing beast an October day could be. At eight thousand feet above sea level, snow and cakes fell unexpectedly. After eleven years I'd learned how to adjust the recipes, but driving the van through storms and over ice remains a challenge. This day the aspen leaves moved languidly as the van sputtered out of the driveway's dust. Above, the sky was deep blue and cloudless, as if nature were holding her breath before the first storms. Starting the descent to Main Street, we passed a vacant lot and had a glimpse of the far distance.

"Oh," said Patty Sue, "what is that?"

She was pointing to the town's namesake, *the* Aspen Meadow, now a large patch of gold in a green-and-brown quilt of trees about seven miles away. This patchwork of fall color nestled at the base of mountains already blanketed with white. I explained to her that that area was known as the Aspen Meadow Wildlife Preserve. There, I added as we turned onto Main Street, the forest was so thick that during dry spells even hikers were barred entry, for fear of forest fire.

"Arch knows all about the Aspen Meadow," I announced, hoping to invite him out of his silence. "He's done drawings as part of his school work."

"You do?" said Patty Sue as she turned to face him. "You have?"

"Oh, I guess," said Arch in a flat voice. "The Webelos hike in for the last pack meeting of the year," he said. "The woods are real deep. We see a lot of deer and elk and foxes and stuff like that. But to get in you have to go down a long dirt road. Fritz fishes the upper Cottonwood in the summer, and Pomeroy Locraft raises bees." He thought for a moment and then explained to Patty Sue, "I used to help Pom with the hives, last spring when I was studying bees."

"And flowers," I added.

"Did you get stung?" Patty Sue asked. "Did you catch fish?"

"I caught some trout," said Arch. He thought for a minute. "The bees never stung me." I looked at him in the mirror. He was shaking his head at Patty Sue, as if he were twenty and she eleven. He explained, "You learn how to be careful. Pomeroy taught me stuff like wearing white around the bees." Arch sighed. "He taught me a lot."

"This Pomeroy," I said to anticipate Patty Sue's next

question, "teaches driver ed over at the high school and does the apiary in the summer. Pomeroy is also recently divorced." I stopped at Main Street's one red light and smiled at my housemate. "A new single person in town can be an interesting part of the landscape, too."

"Oh," said Patty Sue.

"Will Dad be at Ms. Smiley's?" asked Arch.

"Yep," I said, and pushed the van's grinding gears into first. "Vonette and Fritz, too. Plus all the teachers from the schools."

Patty Sue said, "I've never seen a dead person."

"Don't worry," I assured her, "we're not going to the church at all. Plus it's not that kind of wake. They'll have the funeral and the interment while we're setting up. All we'll see is live people."

Patty Sue paused and then said suddenly, "I never knew anyone who killed herself."

I did not answer but glanced again at Arch in the rearview mirror. He was looking out the window, but sensed my eyes.

"It's okay, Mom," he said. "You can talk about it."

"All I know is," I said quietly, "what I've heard. She was out doing errands Saturday morning. One week ago today. On Monday she didn't show up for school and didn't call in. They got a substitute." I coaxed the van into second and turned onto Homestead Drive before going on. "Apparently one of the teachers came over at lunchtime to check on her and to bring some papers that needed correcting. The door was open. Laura was in the bathtub. Dead. Razor in her hand and dried blood all over, I guess. No note, but no sign of a fight or anything. There was an autopsy." I cleared my throat. "I think that's routine. Anyway, the guy said suicide." I paused. "Except that it just seems so sad. Premature."

I glanced at Arch. He was intent on the view out the window. The van released another cloud of dust as we turned onto Piney Circle, a dirt road where wood-paneled houses peeked out from behind stands of ponderosa and lodgepole pine.

"So did you know her?" Patty Sue asked.

Alicia's question. Why did people inquire so suspiciously about your prior acquaintance with a suicide victim? Were they trying to ascertain guilt? If you had known her better, she wouldn't have done this? If you hadn't known her at all, you were off the hook?

"She was Arch's teacher last year and two years ago. I saw her at conferences," I replied. "Sometimes I saw her in exercise class. That's it." I thought for a minute. "She was funny. She could make you laugh talking about how she was going to be a taxing person for the IRS, things like that. And she was a special person for Arch."

I looked again in the mirror. My son was holding his hands over his eyes. I pulled over onto the graveled shoulder and turned to face him.

"Arch," I said. "You don't have to do this. Listen, we can manage with just Patty Sue and myself serving. You don't even have to come at all."

Patty Sue and I sat as Arch sobbed quietly. I handed him a tissue. I shouldn't have talked about Laura Smiley, after all. Arch blew his nose and coughed as people do when they want it to look as if the real problem is sinus congestion, not heartache.

"It's okay," he said. He cleared his throat. "Let's go. Please."

I said, "You really don't have to."

"Yeah," he said, "I do."

We turned off Piney Circle and onto Pine Needle Lane. Whoever had named the streets wanted to remind us we were in the mountains. The lane was a dirt road that would take us to Laura's house. She had lived close to the center of town, in a hilly area once peppered with log cabins. In the Forties, Aspen Meadow had been a rustic retreat from Denver for the well-to-do. Now the largest portion of residents made the hour-long commute to

Denver to work. In Laura's residential area small A-frames and wood-paneled houses built in the Fifties and Sixties were sandwiched between a scattering of remaining cabins. The resulting architectural mishmash made the area not a good investment for the commuters, but a haven for teachers, artists, waiters, and others who could not afford a ritzier neighborhood.

The van shook as we started down the steep, dusty driveway to Laura's bungalow. The aunt from Illinois had flown in and rented a car. It stood outside the open garage, as she had planned to take a limousine to the funeral. She had left us enough room so that I could just edge the van in next to the garage door.

Fortunately the aunt also had remembered to leave the door unlocked. We pushed in with our crates, boxes, foodstuffs, bowls, and cups.

Once inside I took a deep breath. A professional service from Denver had been in to clean. Their assignment included, Laura's aunt had crisply informed me, disinfecting and regrouting the bloodied bathroom tile. This was about the fifth time I'd done a postfuneral meal in the home where a person had died. I shivered in anticipation of any lingering smell or sense of death.

But here there was none. Large bouquets of flowers, florist's mixtures of carnations and gladioli, snapdragons and baby's breath, crowded the counters in the brightly wallpapered kitchen. Only the cinnamon smell from the carnations and the piney scent of disinfectant lingered in the air.

The house was small. We carted our boxes through the garage into the kitchen, which adjoined a larger dining–living room combination. The guests would be parking around the side near the aunt's car. On that side there was a walkway to the front door, which opened into the dining-living area. I surveyed the room to figure out how to set up the tables and arrange the flowers between the plates and food. Like an investigator at a crash site, I did not want to think about the tragedy that had happened here. We had a job to do. The living had to eat.

Nevertheless, pacing off the living room for measurement, I kept expecting to feel some eeriness in the house. What was actually discomfiting was that the whole place seemed so terribly cozy. Two of the living room walls paneled in diagonal beetle-killed wood glowed green-gold in the sunlight. Shelves and cabinets dotted the other walls. There was a wall of photographs. Deep blue carpet covered the area where the floor was not wood. In addition to the photos there were painted pictures of snowy mountains and snowy fields and brooks with snowy banks. Laura's two wing chairs looked newly reupholstered, as did the two old but not antique love seats. The fabric on the furniture and several throw pillows was a print of spring flowers—periwinkle blue, kelly green, sunshine yellow. With the blue rug and rows of wooden shelves and cabinets, the big room was lively with color. Nowhere in sight were the browns and grays and blacks, the filth or lack of care one would expect of a suicidal personality.

The three long tables ordered from Mountainside Rental lay piled like slabs of rock on the blue rug. They would all fit. We pushed the love seats and chairs into conversational groupings, then cracked open the tables and arranged them in a horseshoe shape. Arch unfurled the tablecloths while Patty Sue and I began to unpack the food.

"Listen to this," I said a few moments later. I had just closed the refrigerator and was perusing the homemade magnets and cartoons with which Laura had festooned the door. Arch and Patty Sue were in the living room setting out silverware and plates in the areas between the flower baskets.

I read, " 'This refrigerator is cooler than Dave Brubeck.' Uh-huh. 'A woman should be more than a cute dish in the Cabinet. She should be Secretary of State.' Very funny. 'The only time I COOK is on the highway.' Ha!" I turned to the dining room, where Patty Sue and Arch had begun unraveling extension cords for the coffee machine. "How could a funny person get so depressed?"

After a minute Arch said, "Oh Mom, you know. She was always making jokes. 'A school is for fish,' stuff like that."

"Right," I muttered, then read above the stove: "When is a pig a canine? When it is a hot dog." By the sink: "I went to plumbing school and told them to make me into Farrah Faucet."

Patty Sue joined me. Her face was paler than usual. She said, "I feel kind of spooky. Please tell me again what you want me to do. I mean, when the people get here."

I explained her duties once more, then showed her the bathroom, in case folks asked for directions. To my relief the aunt or the cleaning service had put up an opaque white shower curtain, whose new-plastic smell was overwhelming. It was drawn across the tub. I couldn't help it: I poked my head around the curtain while Patty Sue checked her lipstick in the mirror. The bathtub was spotless. What I had expected to find I did not know. I hustled Patty Sue out to the kitchen to show her where everything would be. Arch was busy slicing lemons to float in the lemonade pitcher.

When Patty Sue was occupied in the living room opening bottles of wine, Arch said to me, "You know Dad has a new girlfriend."

I said, "I know."

I was looking through Laura's pantry for extra sugar in case we needed additional lemonade. I had brought the rest of the new bag, but the warmth of the day made me worry about the possibility of needing more. The only thing I found was some flour she had put in a canister sporting, naturally enough, a painted flower. Since I knew no homonym for sugar, I gave up.

"Maybe she'll be here," said Arch.

"Right," I said. I turned to him. "The girlfriend. Do you care?"

He stared down at the lemons and I was immediately sorry. I knew his warning was meant to prepare *me* for not caring, not him.

"Sorry, hon," I said. "I've just got a lot on my mind."

"Will Vonette be here?" he asked. "I wanted to talk to her yesterday but Fritz said she was sick again."

Arch did not use words like *grammy* or *grandpa* because John Richard and I had never taught him to. He had a child's devotion to his grandmother, who doted on him. Fritz had always been too involved in his practice to pay any more attention to Arch than recognizing him. But Vonette's "being sick" was the euphemism the adults in Arch's life used to refer to her cocktail hour beginning at eleven in the morning. I often wondered if Arch knew, or suspected, the truth.

"Sick again," I repeated as I scanned the kitchen. "Yes, Marla told me that."

"They're coming," called Patty Sue from the other room.

"Quick, slip on your apron, kiddo," I told Arch. "Then go to the front door and greet people. Tell them to leave coats, if they have any, in Laura's bedroom, which is on the other side of the living room." I hesitated. Then I said, "And show them where the bathroom is."

His apron was in place; he raised fearful brown eyes to mine at the word *bathroom*.

I put my hands on his shoulders. "I checked it, and it's all clean."

He said, "I really don't like this. I'm afraid."

And so, for different reasons, was I.

CHAPTER 3

Parsley tendrils brushed the sides of the salmon and the exposed pink backmeat when I set the silver platter down on the long main-course table. I ladled the mayonnaise into a crystal bowl and placed it next to the salmon. Then I carried out the asparagus and the rest, including a packet with the mushrooms I had minced to replace the Jerk's tomatoes. Arch had ushered the first group into Laura's bedroom to leave their coats. The murmur of voices and click of heels on the brick walkway filtered through the air.

Backing up to the kitchen, I gave the room a quick scan before putting on my apron. Catering a reception was much like directing a play: the props and actors all had to be in place before the entertainment could begin.

My hands were shaking, my ears burning. Inexplicably, my right shoulder began to hurt. I had to take mental stock. Pull yourself together, I told myself. But the old fears welled up.

Toward the end of my marriage to John Richard, we had a fight in which I fell backward into an open dishwasher. My right shoulder was slit open by a protruding knife, necessitating stitches and a sling. While I was recovering, but before I could consciously acknowledge how bad things had become, I had a recurrent nightmare of being raped. The man in the nightmare was a famous regional tennis player named John. When the rape was over, a voice would say, "Call the plumber." Then with great clarity one morning I realized that John in the dream was John my spouse, and that it was my life which was draining away.

I filed for divorce, then threw myself into the catering work with the zeal of a lover. Though I'd finally gone back to school when Arch was in first grade to finish a degree in psychology, the food service offered the most immediate potential for financial security. The child support payments, when they came, took care of about a third of the house payment. New recipes, new bookings, keeping accounts, working in the kitchen, and most important, being financially independent of John Richard, all these I relished. My shoulder healed; my work was my love. My nightmare now, when I had one, was that the business would be taken away as my dream of a family life had been.

I took a deep breath. My heart beat in its cavity. John Richard was going to be here and I understood why Marla was staying away. He would act charming, do his handsome guy routine with the women. Then in a few moments he would come up and make some cutting remark. He wouldn't do anything to hurt me, in any event not physically, not here in front of all these people. I pressed my lips together. Go greet the guests, I told myself, but could not.

I looked through the kitchen drawers and found a pack of Kools, lit one, and inhaled deeply. Heavenly. I pondered the walls of the kitchen, which Laura had papered in a pattern of ice cream cones in Neopolitan colors. Just right for a teacher. But at least she smoked. *Smoking is self-destructive. Laura Smiley was self-destructive, remember?*

But she hadn't had an ex-husband showing up to taunt her, I reminded my inner voice.

How do you know what taunted her? asked the voice.

I put out the cigarette and slipped into the living room. Maybe I would just take a look at that wall of photos during my break, see who had been the people in Ms. Smiley's life. But I couldn't take a break if I never started working.

"Trixie," I said to the backside of a tall, muscled woman.

Trixie Jackson finished shaking off her coat and turned around. She was one of the aerobics instructors at Aspen Meadow's athletic club, although I had not seen her for about a year and had put it down to a class-schedule change. She narrowed her eyes at me. I thought, She can smell the cigarette.

"Good to see you," I said. "How was the funeral?"

"Depressing," she replied. She raised an eyebrow at me. "Your ex-husband was there. John Richard."

I resisted asking her if that was what made it depressing and motioned Arch over to take her coat. More people shuffled through the door and their low voices gurgled through the room like water melting a lake of ice. Trixie headed off toward the as-yet unmanned beverage table.

Vonette Korman's shrill voice carried over from outside. "It just makes me so sad," she was saying, "and she was so young and all. Course maybe not that young. Still, though. She was a caring person. And it is sad."

I was caught in a dark bustle of coats, unneeded on this warm day but for the chilling effects of a funeral. Vonette's highly made-up face and brilliant orange-red hair emerged by Trixie and the glasses of white wine. Threading my way back toward the food, I kept an eye on my ex-mother-in-law by pretending to examine the straightness of the tablecloths. And there it was, just as Marla had observed. As quickly and stealthily as any magician, Vonette drew a small leather-covered flask out of her purse and poured a clear liquid into her wineglass. It must have been vodka or gin. Unlike a magician's, her glass contents did not change color, although I imagined it had changed into a martini.

"Mom," came Arch's shrill whisper from nearby. "Now what do you want me to do?"

"Go tend the drinks," I whispered back. "Let them pour their own wine. You just do lemonade and coffee." I looked back at the table. "And tea. That other pot has hot water in it and the Lipton bags are next to it. Sugar and cream are on the table. All you need to do is keep everything going."

He nodded and turned away.

"Please come and have something to eat," I said to a desultory group. And with that the show had begun. When their stomachs were full, the entertainment would be complete. I hoped.

"Well, if it isn't the little food lady," came the all-too-familiar voice. How he had found me so quickly I did not know. "I may not miss much," John Richard said with a laugh, more like a snort, "but sometimes I miss your cooking."

"Really?" I replied. "Funny, I don't miss anything."

I looked up at my ex-husband. Although I had not cared what clothes he'd worn when we were married—he looked like a male model in everything—I had a compulsive interest in assessing his current wardrobe. Perhaps it was the new ostentation. *He wants to look younger.* Or the leather, wool, occasional silk: *he's making lots of money.* If I thought it was polyester, I savored an inner victory: *the practice is failing.* I now glanced from the hand-tooled cowboy boots past the charcoal-colored wool pants to the silk cowboy shirt and Navajo bolo tie. The bolo was held with a silver ring sporting a hunk of turquoise that matched his eyes. John Richard was tall and blond, with broad shoulders and narrow hips. He had more the build of a prizefighter than a doctor. Which, I reflected, was probably appropriate.

He straightened his tie.

He said, "Outfit okay?"

I took a deep breath. I was too angry to admit he looked fabulous. I closed my eyes and feigned boredom.

"Remember," I said, "I'm from New Jersey. There, people wear cowboy clothes up to fourth grade. But suit yourself."

He was walking away. He held his hand up in mock salute. "I'll do that."

I looked at the food spread out on the table, then scanned the room for Patty Sue. She was talking to Pomeroy the beekeeper. At least someone was having a decent conversation with a man. Fritz Korman was sidling up to Patty Sue himself. Didn't he see her enough with the twice-weekly visits? I also noticed Vonette watching Fritz.

Not a student of social interaction, I put myself to work. Besides, I didn't want to seem to be looking for John Richard.

"Come and eat," I invited a new gaggle of people eyeing the salmon. "C'mon, Trix," I said because she was once more near me.

Trixie's right arm—*ripped, shredded, cut,* as they say in the body business—reached for a plate. I lifted salmon flesh from the carcass.

"Asparagus?" I asked her.

"Of course," she said. "But no bread."

"Were you a friend of Laura's?" I asked.

"I knew her," she said vaguely, as I topped her coral-colored mound of fish with a dollop of mayonnaise. Trixie looked at me, dark brown eyes in a face framed with streaked blond hair. She said, "Not too much mayo." She thought for a minute. "Laura used to come to class. Sometimes we talked afterward. She was funny, a little wacko, I thought, but not . . . She never came to the club's parties. She was like you, didn't really go out with men."

I mm-hmmed and averted my eyes to end the conversation. This was not the assessment of my current social life that I wanted John Richard to overhear.

The aunt came up and asked how everything was going, then complimented us on the food, which she had yet to taste. She was a short woman with pale makeup and too-black hair cut severely short around her face.

"Thank you," I said. "Will you be around long?"

She shook her head. "I'm flying back to Chicago tonight. The house is going up for sale Monday. She left her goods to me, but I certainly don't know what to do with them. I'll be back in November to finish things up." She gave me an ingratiating smile. "Your son is just a little darling. And how nice of him to help you with the business."

I nodded and fixed her a plate, then glanced in the direction of Arch, who was talking to John Richard, or rather, being talked to. Arch was nodding, his face full of pain. I could imagine the questions. Did you try out for soccer? Are you going to play football? Have you thought about basketball? Why not? The Jerk had never accepted the fact that his son was not destined for the NFL.

I reassured the moneyed aunt that the catering business was very important to me, as well as to Arch. She gave me a sympathetic look and slid away.

Now I could sense John Richard, hear him, see him shuffling along in what had become a fairly long food line, maybe ten people. With that kind of backup I was now preparing the plates in advance, whether the guests wanted asparagus or not. I heard him again and looked up. He was talking to Fritz. A medical conversation, no doubt. Beside the Jerk was the new girlfriend, a nondescript brunette whom my memory could only vaguely identify as a teacher.

I counted out the plates to John Richard's. Eight. I drew out the mushroom packet. No sense in making him sick with tomatoes, thus risking more wrath, although the thought made me giggle. I sprinkled the mushroom bits on top of John Richard's asparagus vinaigrette and kept going with plate preparation. I looked back at the line. For heaven's sake. The girlfriend had stepped in front of the Jerk, so now she would get the mushrooms and he would still get tomatoes. I clanked the plates into their proper order, and that was my mistake.

John Richard sidled up to the front of the line and again straightened the bolo as he peered at the dishes. Then he raised a thick wrist to dramatically count the number of people in line.

"Okay, Goldy," he said with a deep sigh, as he picked up the plate with the mushrooms. "What are you trying to feed me?"

"It's not for you. It's for your girlfriend. An aphrodisiac. She may need it."

He said, "Then you won't mind if I send this down to a lab and have it analyzed."

"Don't be so paranoid." I grabbed the edge of the plate. "It's just mushrooms instead of tomatoes, because I didn't want you to get sick."

He pulled the plate toward him. The salmon made a precarious slide toward the silk cowboy shirt.

"Will you stop?" I said through clenched teeth. "Just let me get you a new one."

"Like hell," he said. He pulled the plate as I let go. The vinaigrette splashed down the silk.

John Richard cursed.

I met his withering look and said, "Send me the cleaning bill."

He muttered something and moved off.

I wasn't having a very good day.

Patty Sue appeared next to me and complained that no one was ready for dessert yet.

"Take over the food line," I commanded. "I need a break. Funerals for the wrong people depress me."

Once she had taken my place, I stared at the wall of photos. When it was my turn at the coffeepot I let the dark liquid gush into two of the deep Styrofoam cups with my logo on them. One was for me and one was for Vonette, who probably would be needing caffeine about now. But before I could deliver it I saw Fritz Korman chatting with Patty Sue again. This meant Patty Sue had slowed down in serving the food. I strolled back.

"Well hello, Goldy," said my ex-father-in-law with his patented toothy grin. The light shone off strands of white hair carefully combed across his bald pate. His teeth gleamed as he directed his smile back to Patty Sue, the wolf welcoming Red Riding Hood. John Richard had inherited his hulking build from Fritz, which was shown off to good advantage in yet another silk shirt with fringed vest and pants.

I said, "Fritz, you look like you just stepped off the set of 'Bonanza.' "

He chucked me under the chin, unruffled. Fritz was like a man who was perpetually running for office, and he always treated me as if we were old friends or lovers or both.

"Has Patty Sue told you," I began as I set down the cups, "that her father is a doctor, too?"

"Why no," said Fritz, startled.

"But he isn't," said Patty Sue.

"Oh yes," I continued as I again began to flick out creamy glops of mayonnaise onto piles of salmon. "Patty Sue's father, the doctor, works in Washington, D.C. Very important fellow. Proctologist, to be exact."

"What?" said Patty Sue and Fritz in unison.

"The Pentagon proctologist," I rolled on, "who also gives political advice. He tells the generals working on Iran policy, Shove it up there where it hurts."

Success. A confused look passed over Fritz's face before

he walked away. After a minute, Patty Sue started serving again.

"You need to get more mayonnaise from the kitchen," I advised as I handed her the bowl. "Quickly." When she returned I took the lukewarm coffee over to Vonette, who was bending Pomeroy Locraft's ear.

"It just makes me so sad," Vonette was saying, true to form. The sorrier and sadder she felt, the more she drank.

I said, "What makes you so sad?"

"Oh hi, Goldy," she replied. Pomeroy, tall, dark, thirty-ish, and flannel shirted, nodded at me.

Vonette went on. "Did I hear you talking to Fritz about Iran over there? Honey, Fritz doesn't care about foreign policy." A swig. "He didn't even vote for Bush last time." Another swig. "Hell, he's still mad about Nixon going to China."

"What?" said Pomeroy.

"Why?" I asked.

"Oh, you know how mad he gets," she said with a roll of her eyes, "and those Red Chinese, I mean in addition to being Commies"—another swig—"have this forced abortion policy."

Pomeroy shook his head, stood up, and walked away.

"I'm still out of honey," I called after him. He turned. I handed Vonette her coffee and walked over.

Pomeroy was and always had been an enigma to me. Apparently he also gave that impression to the other women in town, who had given him the moniker Ice Man. He had none of the flirtatious mock shyness that John Richard used to such advantage with women.

Arch, on the other hand, adored Pomeroy. Something about his aura of quiet, his life in a remote cabin, his way with the bees, had magnetized my son. Through a whole year of teaching Sunday school I had only rare clues that Arch was absorbing any of the study-of-saints curriculum. Nevertheless, after his spring project working out at the hives, Arch had said Pomeroy was like Saint Francis. He loves all the animals, Arch had said; he understands nature.

So I was interested in Pomeroy in a way that was more than curiosity. I had been unwilling to discuss my interest with Alicia, as I didn't know what kind of chance I had with an icy-tempered beekeeper.

"You walked away from that conversation awful fast," I said to him.

He shook his head. "I don't have to listen to her when she's like that, or when she's talking about that . . . subject. No one has to."

"Oh, well. Besides Vonette, how're you doing?" I asked with a bright smile.

He said, "Why do you care?"

So much for social interchange. I said, "I don't know," and walked back to my ex-mother-in-law.

"How's your coffee, Vonette?" I asked. It was on the table, and it looked untouched. Under the table was the purse that held the flask.

"Think I need it?" she asked, her voice still full of self-pity. Her head of wild red hair shook slightly. I waved my hand at the dessert and beverage tables, where Arch and Patty Sue were now feverishly trying to keep up with the flow of people finished with the main portion of the meal.

"No," I said, "but everyone's lining up for shortcake now, and they'll be wanting coffee, too. I brought you some so you wouldn't have to get up." But of course she needed it. This day was upsetting enough without another trip to detox.

Arch was looking frantic by the coffee machine; I joined him.

"Mom," he said, "I need more lemons. I don't know why everyone wants lemonade all of a sudden."

"I'll do it. Just keep them going with the coffee and wine, if they want it."

Out in the kitchen, I located my manual squeezer and extracted the juice from a dozen lemons, then cut paper-thin slices from two more using a knife from a wall mount. After a few moments Arch came in.

"Now what?" I asked. He was opening cupboards and looking through them.

"Well," he said as he pulled over one of the kitchen chairs to climb up for a better view, "now somebody wants herb tea. All we've got out there is that Lipton stuff." He strained to look in the high cupboards. "So I have to find some."

I left the lemons and joined Arch in his search. In the process I finally found Laura's sugar in a canister with a magazine picture of Sugar Ray Leonard taped on the front. But there was no herb tea.

"See if whoever it is will try this," I said as I handed him Postum. "I'll be out in a minute with the lemonade."

He left. The running water foamed up over the sugar and juice. When I brought the pitcher into the living room, Arch had disappeared again, and there were only a few people left in the food line. I hoped the lemonade shortage would be our last crisis of the day.

Within twenty minutes people were nearly finished with the last of their plates. Conversation settled into small pockets around the room. Quietly I began to gather plates and ashtrays to take out to the kitchen. Clients do not like to have dirty plates around at a party, but they don't want to hear you wash them either. Luckily there was a door between the kitchen and the main room, and I could begin the cleaning unobtrusively.

Hot water and suds were just churning over the silverware when I heard a sound that made me shudder. Someone was moaning.

I turned off the water. From the living room came the same loud sound, the kind of deep groaning you associate with . . .

Associate with . . .

I didn't even want to think. If someone vomited at a function I catered, that would be the end of the business. Or close to it.

I pushed through the door to the other room. The groan became a howl. There was a crowd gathered around the sound, and several people were walking quickly toward me uttering names of things they wanted.

"Water—"

"Phone—"

"Towel—"

My face was suddenly cool with the sweat of fear, as I prayed, *Please not Arch, please let him be all right.* I made my way past tables and chairs as if in slow motion. *Please let my child be okay.* At the outskirts of the crowd I could hear Vonette's high whine, words like *What is it, honey? Oh what is it, honey?*

"Let me through," I begged the people I was elbowing past, darting my head all around to find Arch. The first thing I saw was the jar of Postum on the coffee table. *Let him not be hurt. Let him not be in pain.* The guttural groan of agony did not quit. It was too deep for a child.

I gasped and pleaded to be let through, then at the front of the crowd asked, "What is it?"

Fritz Korman was on the floor. His large frame was writhing on the blue rug. He was holding his stomach. Horror and distress surged through me—Fritz was family, or had been. And he was in terrible agony.

"Get back, get back!" my ex-husband was yelling above the general buzz and the groaning from Fritz, which continued unabated. John Richard was waving his hands to move people away from around Fritz, who was now curled up on his side like a fetus. Arch was tugging on my apron. I clutched him to me.

"What is going on?" I asked into the general melee.

John Richard started screaming as soon as he saw me.

"You did this, you bitch! You poisoned my father! Did you mean it for me and then do him by mistake?"

I could feel my mouth come open, my head shake from side to side.

John Richard shrieked, "You did it, and I'm going to have you nailed!"

CHAPTER 4

At first, I thought some kind of shock had made John Richard accuse me. But after his outburst, he turned his back and refused even to acknowledge my presence. What was worse, debonair, ever-in-control Fritz was not getting any better. All around, people were turning their heads away and murmuring. Someone was phoning for help; others were applying damp cloths and asking questions. Was it the mayonnaise, the cream, the fish? There was nothing for me to do. That was a good thing, since I couldn't have done anything anyway. I felt terrible, and dizzy with a vague sense of guilt . . . Did Fritz have a food allergy, too?

I herded Arch back to the kitchen, found the pack of Kools, and smoked one after another until Patty Sue came out and said Fritz was on his way to the hospital. She added, hesitantly, that John Richard had called the police and they were coming over. Now that my ex-husband had left, I went into the other room. That he would call the police was incredible. What could he possibly have told them? Was he even remotely convincing? Would they believe that I was trying to poison anyone? I, who had, earlier in the afternoon, tried to keep an abusive ex-husband from suffering an allergic reaction to tomatoes? Would they believe me, a caterer? Or would they believe him, a doctor?

I wondered what the food would be like in jail.

Investigator Tom Schulz of the Furman County Sheriff's Department was introduced to us by another cop, whose reverential tone said, Here's God. Schulz loomed large in height and bulk. When he came striding through the door of Laura Smiley's house, shifting his weight from one foot to the other, he looked like one of those old-time movie heroes who use sword and cape to threaten villains, to keep skeptics at bay, to summon up an imposing sense of self-importance. Only the investigator needed neither sword nor cape. He had his size.

In general, I felt powerful with hefty people. They held me in great esteem because I was an expert cook. But within five minutes of watching Investigator Schulz scan the tables, glasses, coffee cups, and the bevy of trembling faces, my confidence melted. He consulted a guest list given to him by Laura's aunt. Then he cocked an authoritative thumb at the first person to be questioned and hiked up his belt as if it were a holster before he banged through the door into the kitchen, the improvised interrogation chamber.

John Richard had insisted on accompanying Fritz in the ambulance to Lutheran Hospital, I had heard. Lutheran was located in Wheat Ridge, a suburb west of Denver that was forty-five minutes from Aspen Meadow. The Denver Poison Center had recommended this course rather than ipecac or any other treatment. The person who had called the Poison Center had made an announcement: within an hour of Fritz's entering the hospital, blood and urine tests would indicate the source of distress.

Vonette sat slumped in one of the wing chairs, overcome. I wanted to go and comfort her, tell her maybe Fritz had stomach flu. But the two uniformed policemen who had arrived with Schulz had commanded us not to touch anything and not to talk to each other.

"Us" at that point was the forty mourners for Laura, now witnesses to exactly what, I still did not know. But I was going to have to find out. I felt sorry for Fritz, anxious for him. He was in pain and possibly in danger. But there was something else. This incident could pose an acute threat to my business. Unfortunately, I could not determine anything when all of us were sitting around looking guilty and being silent, as if this were Adult Detention Hall. One policeman took me aside to say Investigator Schulz had ordered him to call the Colorado Department of Health so that all the food could be seized and analyzed.

Marvelous. What microbes might the Health Department detect? Before I could worry about that, Investigator Schulz called a second person to be questioned, then a third. Some people came out right away: they hadn't seen anything. Patty Sue went in and came out looking confused. Arch and I were last. When it was Arch's turn, Tom Schulz's thumb indicated that he wanted me, too.

"I thought you wanted us individually," I muttered, once we had settled into Laura's red wire kitchen chairs, the kind you used to see in ice cream parlors.

Investigator Schulz adjusted his backside on the too-small chair. He was, I noticed somewhat reluctantly, good-looking as well as charismatic. The other room had been filled with men trying to look macho in their western attire. Tom Schulz was the real thing. Despite his coat, sweater, and tie, he had the commanding aura of a ranch foreman. In the caramel-colored October light filling the kitchen, his hair shone gold-brown. It was cut short, parted on the side, and combed at a jaunty angle above bushy eyebrows. These thick triangles of hair climbed up and dropped down his forehead when he listened or talked. He had a sideways smile that came easily and suggested a sense of humor. His green eyes beheld everything just a moment longer than necessary, as if by concentrating hard enough, he could see through things and people. He grinned widely at me. Fear froze my face.

"Your boy's a minor. Got to have you here when I talk to him." The green eyes regarded me. He added, "By law."

I nodded, but felt sick.

Schulz reached a fleshy palm out to Arch.

"My name is Tom Schulz," he said as he shook Arch's small hand, "and I need to ask you a few questions about what happened here today."

Arch sat in one of the red chairs and straightened his glasses. He said, "Okay."

Schulz took our full names and address. He showed some confusion over my name, Gertrude Bear. I told him with two other Mrs. Kormans in town I had thought my business would do better under my maiden name.

He said, "What's Goldy short for?"

"Nothing, really," I said, feeling my cheeks get hot. "No one's called me Gertrude for twenty-some years. When I was little I had blond hair—"

"Still do," observed Schulz.

"It was just a nickname that stuck. I liked it better than Gertrude, anyway."

He nodded.

I said, "I use Goldilocks for the business. You know, like the story, everything is just right. It's just an ad, connecting me with the food service."

Schulz nodded again. He said he would ask Arch only a few questions before he could leave and it would be my turn. Then he put his notebook away.

He asked, "What grade are you in, Arch?"

"Sixth, sir." Arch's voice was trembling slightly. He

crossed his legs and looked down in his lap before raising his eyes to Schulz.

"Do you play soccer?"

The inevitable subject of sports. A look of pain passed briefly over my nonathletic son's face. This tack for putting Arch at ease would not work.

"No, sir," Arch said.

"What do you like to do? Do you like to play any games?"

"Oh yes," said Arch, brightening.

"Such as?"

"Fantasy role-playing. Have you heard of them? Like Dungeons and Dragons and Top Secret? Do you know about those?"

"A little bit," said Schulz, leaning back in the chair. "How do they work? Do you play them with your friends?"

"Well, you roll different kinds of dice," Arch began with characteristic enthusiasm, "like ten-sided, twenty-sided, or thirty-sided, see, to figure out what character you're going to be. Then you decide on the attributes. Well, I mean, you roll the dice again to see about that stuff. There are charts and things for the different abilities. For the characters, I mean." He looked at Schulz sympathetically, not unlike the way he had looked at Patty Sue on the drive over. "It can get pretty complicated," he said.

"Mm-hmm. Then what do you do?"

"Well," said Arch, "then you, like, go on adventures."

I thought this must be boring for a police officer, but he repeated, "Adventures."

"Yeah," said Arch, "with the other characters. You can play with up to five people. Usually I just play with one. One guy will make up the dungeon or whatever it is you're going to do, and then you go through it to see what happens to your character. You use the dice for that, too."

Now Arch was relaxed. Good work, Schulz.

"Do you play with the kids in your class?" asked Schulz.

"Some of them," said Arch. "It's really pretty hard. Most kids aren't interested."

Schulz shifted in the small chair. He reached down and flicked invisible bits of lint off his oatmeal-colored sweater. He asked, "Did you ever play with your grandfather?"

"Oh no," said Arch. "He's much too busy."

"Your grandmother?"

"No. She's sick a lot."

"Your mom? Any other grownups?"

"No." Arch raised his eyes to me apologetically. "My mom's really not interested in it. Neither is my dad. Usually just kids like it. Like my friend Todd Druckman. He's in sixth grade, too." He thought for a moment. He said, "Ms. Smiley was interested in playing."

"Ms. Smiley," said Schulz, "whose house we're in."

"Yeah. She was my teacher last year. She's dead."

"Right. And that's why we're here, isn't it? Because Ms. Smiley died and everybody misses her."

"I guess."

"Do you like to help your mom with her food business? To work on parties like this one?"

Now it was my turn to cross my legs. I couldn't imagine where this was going.

"Well," said Arch slowly, "I don't exactly like it. But I do it when she asks me."

"Like today."

"Yeah."

"Do you think you're good at helping her?"

"Oh yes," said Arch confidently. "I know all about serving."

"What was your job at this party?" Schulz asked.

"The drinks. Coffee, tea, and lemonade. Not the wine," he explained as he pushed the glasses back on his nose, "because I'm too young."

Well, thank God he added that, I thought. At least I didn't break *that* law.

Schulz gave me a brief smile.

"Did you stay over at the coffee machine?" Schulz asked. "The whole time, I mean."

"No. I had to do the lemonade too, see, and we only had two pitchers. So sometimes I had to come out to the kitchen to fill those up."

"Did you see what your grandfather was eating or drinking?"

Arch thought. "I guess Fritz had some of the food, because he came over for a glass of wine. But I didn't see him eat. Later he wanted a cup of coffee. I don't think he likes lemonade."

"Fritz."

"That's what I call him," said Arch. "My grandfather."

"He's always called his grandparents by their first—" I started to explain.

Schulz held his hand up to me.

"Did you see Fritz drink the wine?" asked Schulz. "Did you see what he did with his glass?"

"No," said Arch, "I didn't see either."

"Before Fritz got sick, did he drink anything else?"

"Let's see," said Arch. "Okay, now I remember. We were out of lemonade and my mom was making some in the kitchen. A lot of people had been asking for it. Fritz was, let's see, he was talking to Trixie, the woman who teaches the exercise class, you know? And when she came over for coffee . . ." Arch paused to think. "No, wait a minute, she doesn't drink coffee. I remember now because she wanted lemonade. We didn't have any yet so she asked me if we had any herb tea."

Schulz drew his eyebrows together. He said, "Herb tea."

"Yes, she asked me if we had any herb tea. I said I didn't think so. Then Fritz came over and laughed and said Trixie thought coffee was bad for you. He was, like, laughing and saying Trixie thought a lot of things were bad for you. But he said he would have some anyway. Coffee. So I poured her some hot water and him some coffee. And then Trixie said, Well, could I check and see if Ms. Smiley kept any herb tea in her kitchen. So I came in here to check."

Schulz leaned ever so slightly toward Arch. "Where was Fritz's coffee then? Did he take it from you and start drinking it?"

"No," said Arch slowly. "I put them both, the cups of coffee and hot water, next to each other on the table. Then I came out here to look for the tea."

"The two cups were just sitting there?"

"Right," said Arch. "I thought I'd just be gone a minute, and they had started talking again."

"Did you find any tea?"

"No. I was looking and looking, and Mom was helping me."

Schulz said, "So your mother was in the kitchen then?"

"Yes," said Arch, "she was busy making lemonade. We looked for some tea. Finally she gave me some Postum instead. And then Patty Sue ran out of strawberries and I helped her with that for a while. And then I saw my mom emptying ashtrays and picking up dirty dishes . . . I guess I just forgot about the tea. Anyway, when I came back to the table somebody asked me again for lemonade."

"So how long was it from the time you gave Fritz, or rather, put down Fritz's coffee and the woman's water for tea, and then got back to do lemonade?"

Arch shrugged. "I don't know. A long time, I guess. Twenty minutes? I can't remember. Toward the end of a party, Mom says, you don't have to pay as much attention to the guests. But I did forget the tea." He looked at me. "Sorry."

Schulz stared at Arch. "When you went back out, who asked you for lemonade?"

"Vonette, I think. We still didn't have any, so she said, Well, never mind, she'd have coffee."

"What was the next thing that happened?" asked Schulz.

"I went to the bathroom." Again he looked at me apologetically.

"Did you see Trixie again?"

"No, she was gone before I decided to go to the uh, you know. She never even got the Postum."

"Know what happened to the hot water?"

"What hot water?" Arch wrinkled his nose. "Oh, Trixie's. No."

"Then what?"

"Well, I heard Fritz sort of like moaning. So I came back out to the living room."

"Uh-huh. Now this is important, Arch. Was there anyone else around the drinks table when you came out to the kitchen to look for the tea?"

Arch closed his eyes. "There were lots of people."

"Anybody's face come to mind?"

Arch thought. He said, "No."

"Okay," said Schulz, "now just a few more questions. Besides Trixie, do you remember your grandfather talking to anyone else?"

"Vonette, I think. And my dad."

"Was Fritz arguing with anyone, anything like that?"

Arch sighed. "No. Everybody was just talking about Ms. Smiley, saying how nice she was. That it was really weird that she had killed herself because she was such a, you know, funny person. Nobody was arguing." Arch looked at me from behind his glasses. He lowered his voice. "Except my mom and dad. They were arguing."

I groaned and walked over to the cabinet where I'd put the cigarettes, took another one, and lit it.

"I know about that," said Investigator Schulz. "Do you know what your mom and dad were arguing about, Arch?"

Arch looked back at Schulz. "No. My dad had his new girlfriend here. I think that upset my mom. My mom and dad are divorced, you know."

"I know."

I inhaled deeply on the cigarette and looked through the window at the aspens shaking in the breeze. I imagined dirty laundry hanging out there to air.

Arch said, "May I go now?"

"Just one more question, Arch. Do you know if anyone was mad at Fritz? Mad enough to try to make him sick, say?"

Arch hesitated. "Well, the only person I know who sort of didn't like Fritz . . . well, this sounds kind of dumb. I'm really not sure . . ." He furrowed his forehead and looked at me.

"It's okay," I said. "Just tell Mr. Schulz whatever it is."

"Well," Arch said again, "I don't think Ms. Smiley liked him very much. I don't think she liked Vonette either."

I coughed on the cigarette smoke. This was news to me. I said, "Ms. Smiley? Didn't like Fritz Korman? Or Vonette? How'd she even know them?"

Schulz said, "Mrs. Korman. Miss Bear. Goldy. Please."

"That's what I mean," continued Arch. "I told you it sounded dumb."

"Do you know what she was mad about?" asked Schulz.

"No."

"When did she tell you she didn't like the Kormans?"

Again Arch closed his eyes. "I can't remember. I'm not even sure she was the one who told me."

Investigator Schulz stood up. "Arch, thanks a lot. You've been helpful. I'll give you a card with my number. You keep it in your pocket. If you think of something else, call me."

"My turn?" I asked.

Investigator Schulz looked at me with those penetrating green eyes. An unexpected and unwanted wave of sexual something rolled over me.

Schulz said, "You bet. Just begin by telling me if you saw anything suspicious with the food."

Before I could begin the long explanation about John Richard's tomato allergy, one of the uniformed policemen interrupted us.

"Schulz, you'd better come take a look at this."

Tom Schulz stood up and walked out of the kitchen. This reminded me of the many calls John Richard had received at home, always from females in one sort of pain or another, and only rarely, I found out from the hospital, actual patients.

I shook this off and went out to the living room. The guests had left and two fellows, presumably from the Health Department, were labeling everything and packing the containers into boxes. Schulz was in consultation with his man, their voices lowered.

Outside I could hear Patty Sue laughing, so I went to investigate. She was seated on a wooden bench next to the cluster of aspens in Laura's front yard. Next to her was Pomeroy Locraft.

He was grinning. Seeing him with Patty Sue did not make me feel great. Last spring I had dropped several hints that Pom and Arch and I all go out for pizza or a movie after their worktime. Perhaps I was too subtle. Perhaps Pom was dense, uninterested, or both, which was the way he had acted today. Now he was engaged in a lively conversation with Patty Sue. I had the uncomforting thought that she was at least ten years too young for him.

I walked in their direction through the long dry grass, which the summer heat had burned to gold. Here and there bushes reduced by the fall sun to thorned sticks snared my stockings. Above, fluffs of cloud sailed across a deep blue sky. The air was thick with the sweet mixed smell of decaying aspen leaves and smoke from a wood fire, probably built during the early morning chill. But the day had turned out warm and beautiful, and the calm was disorienting after the turmoil in the house.

"Hi, Mom!" yelled Arch from somewhere I couldn't see.

"Where are you?" I called back.

"Here!" he hollered triumphantly from the middle part of a lodgepole pine near the bench. I absolutely hated seeing Arch climb those feeble-branched evergreens. As if in answer to my worries, he let out a shout.

"Help!" he cried. "I'm falling!"

I could see his body toppling, hear branches snapping. I was too far away but my feet darted forward anyway.

With startling swiftness Pomeroy ran to the bottom of the tree, where he caught Arch by the arm and broke his fall. By the time I got to the pine, the two of them were laughing. I was not amused, as this was the second time in one day that I'd come close to coronary arrest worrying about my child's welfare.

I said, "Thanks, Pom." He had handed Arch his glasses and was brushing bits of bark off Arch's formerly white shirt.

"It's okay," he said, as much to Arch as to me. "Can't blame a kid for wanting to climb a tree, right?"

"No," Arch said.

"Yes," I said.

"Oh, Arch and I are buddies," said Pomeroy with that half smile. "Right, bud?"

Arch nodded and started toward the chokecherry bushes that lined Laura Smiley's driveway.

"Thanks for being nice to him," I said. "Thanks for being a good catcher."

"I like kids."

"So I see."

Pomeroy gave me another embarrassed look—not the pink-red of shyness, but a black-red that glowed from underneath his skin. I could not imagine what was bothering him, so I let it go.

Pomeroy sat back on the bench, then turned to me and

smiled. He had recovered his composure, and the impish smile and splatter of freckles over his pale cheeks gave him the look of a child. But the dark good looks and brown mustache were unmistakably adult, as was the lanky body that spilled over the bench's slats. His brown eyes held mine, and I could not think of what to say next.

He said, "Before we were interrupted, Patty Sue here was telling me she can't drive."

"She's made a few attempts with her father's pickup, I believe," I said.

Patty Sue groaned.

"I was thinking," said Pomeroy. "Maybe she could come to one of my driver-ed classes. At the high school." He gave a slight grin. "There's not much money from the county for this type of thing, and some of my cars are pretty old, but she could still learn."

"Sounds marvelous," I said with false cheer. My ex-husband might have been able to mine the high school faculty for dates. But with Pomeroy stuck on my housemate, it looked as if my chance to find social life from the same place was collapsing with the rapidity of a soufflé. Schulz appeared at the end of the driveway and motioned me back down to the house with that thumb.

I said, "I have to go."

"I'll check on the liability and what not," Pom called after me. "Are you all free Friday afternoons?"

I turned around and put my hand on my hip. "What do you need *me* for?"

He grinned again, wide and sheepish, and I felt some of the frost in my heart melt. Maybe there was hope. He was still good-looking and single. Perhaps his ability to get along with children, witness the relationship with Arch, was merely extended to Patty Sue.

He leaned toward me and said, "Somebody's got to get her a learner's permit and bring her to the high school."

I nodded and traipsed back toward Schulz, who had gone inside.

"Look familiar?" he said as he pointed to one of my Styrofoam cups. "Don't touch," he admonished. "Just peek inside."

I did as ordered and saw an almost empty coffee cup with what looked like about twenty little green pellets on the bottom.

"I don't know," I said.

Schulz grinned at me, a wide face-breaker.

"Miss Goldy," he began. "Excuse me, *Miz*. Your business is closed down until further notice. You served this coffee, you're responsible until I find out otherwise. I wonder if I could come over and ask you some questions tomorrow? I'm a little tied up right now." He motioned to one of his underlings to come retrieve the cup.

"For God's sake," I protested, "what's in the cup?"

He had begun to walk away, but at my question turned back. "Oh," he said, "you just flunked Detection 101. Dr. Korman drank that coffee, but he didn't know what was on the bottom. Looks to me like whoever tried to do him in was using rat poison."

Saturday ended with a whimper after the day's bang. When Pomeroy left, I outlined our suddenly disastrous finances to both Patty Sue and Arch. Patty Sue's rent was her ability to work for the catering business, and without the business both of us would have to do whatever work we could find just to buy groceries and make the November house payment. Arch accepted the suspension of his allowance with a grim silence.

Even our dinner that night was a problem. I reminded Patty Sue and Arch of this as we pulled into our driveway. After a job, we usually feasted on leftovers and odds and ends. Now the leftovers were being analyzed down at the Department of Health.

Arch offered to heat chili in the microwave. I didn't

think things could get a whole lot worse until he pointed to an enormous bouquet of dried flowers on our deck. Damn. One of the arrangements for the funeral or reception had been delivered here by mistake.

But no. The envelope was addressed to me. Inside was an unsigned message.

"Don't worry about Fritz, sweetie pie. He deserves it."

CHAPTER 5

How'd you do it?" my ex-husband demanded over the phone the next morning, Sunday. "Get your dumb-ass roommate to drop the stuff in? You tell her they were sweetening capsules?"

"Oh stop," I said. "Just tell me how Fritz is."

"Not until you answer my question."

"My roommate is a patient of your father's," I reminded him, "and she is living here at your mother's request. She's a lovely girl who respects your father, and does not deserve to be maligned by you."

He started to yell, and I held the phone away from my ear. It was only seven o'clock, but John Richard and I were both early risers. The first year of our marriage this had meant lovemaking and fresh sweet rolls as strokes of sunlight swept the walls of the house. Later the fights merely started earlier; accusations came at sunrise followed by the recriminations and my learning to dodge the frying pan full of hot bacon and grease.

In fact, I thought as I looked around the kitchen while

still holding the screeching voice at arm's length, the first thing I had redecorated after he moved out was this room where I now made my living. I slid my foot against the slick black and white tile that had replaced the brick-colored vinyl flooring. The walls and curtains now glowed with a muted red and white checked print. Think of something else, I told myself as John Richard continued to shriek. Breakfast.

"You there?" the Jerk was saying.

"If you're not going to tell me how Fritz is, then I need to fix breakfast," I said dryly. "Tell me something else, though. Why don't you ever blow up like this in public? Then people would know why we got divorced. Look. You called me. What do you want, anyway?"

"Nothing," he said. "Not a damn thing." He hung up.

I rubbed my temples, removed rolls, bacon, and coffee beans from the freezer, and put my mind on the day ahead. Probably the best thing was that the Broncos were due to play Green Bay, which promised to be an easy win. It was good to have the regular season underway. I disliked the preseason, with its mandatory shrinkage of team size. Getting cut was probably a lot like getting divorced.

During the time before kickoff, I needed to make calls canceling parties and food supplies on order. Talking to the Jerk was like waking up and not being able to shake a nightmare. Even worse, I realized as a sharp pain grabbed my chest, was that the more recent nightmare had come true: my business and I were separated.

I needed to think. Get things in perspective. For openers, there was figuring out what it was the flower sender thought Fritz deserved. Was the flower sender the rat poisoner? The impending questioning from Schulz was another dark cloud on the day's emotional horizon. If the Broncos didn't win, the day would be a complete loss.

First things first. Patty Sue and Arch were still asleep. I steeled myself to make the first call. It would largely determine the tone of the day.

"Vonette," I said brightly to her foggy greeting, "Goldy. Tell me how Fritz is doing."

"Just fine, honey. My God, what time is it?" She groped and muttered. "Yeah, Fritz. Can't imagine what happened to him."

I was sorry to awaken her, but it was the only way I could be sure to catch her sober. I said, "How was the hospital? Did they give him anything?"

"Oh yeah, something. He put up a fuss, good heavens. Don't know what it was he drank after that funeral. Like D-Kon, they said. Does the same thing, or whatever."

"Does what same thing?"

She yawned. "Causes internal bleeding or such like that. But don't worry, he's not bleeding anymore. That stuff hit his ulcer and made him hurt, but he's fine now. You're bigger than any old rodent, I told him. It won't kill you. Goldy, let me call you right back. I need to go make some coffee."

I hung up, ground espresso beans, and filled the cappuccino maker. Vonette's tone was strange. Maybe she was just tired. The machine steamed and gasped. When I was sipping the result, she called back.

I said, "Is he still sick? Is he upset?"

"Aw," she said with a yawn, "he'll stay home today, watch the game, you know, maybe rest for a couple more days. They wanted him to take it easy for a week and I laughed. Lord, I laughed. You know how important that practice is to him, I told those guys down at Lutheran. No way he's going to stay in bed for a week. Doctors can be stubborn, I said."

"Arch was saying something about how you all had known Laura."

"Little Arch," she said. I could feel her smile come over the phone. "I told Fritz to be sure and speak to him but I don't think he did. And then all hell broke loose."

"Did you and Fritz know Laura Smiley for a long time?"

A pause. She said, "A long time ago, we knew her."

"How?"

"Oh," she said, "she kind of worked for us one time. She was a . . . teacher and then a . . . a . . . what do they call it these days? Like a nanny one time. When we went on a vacation."

"When was that?"

There was a longer silence. "You know, Goldy," Vonette said, suddenly perplexed, "I don't want to talk any more right now. I do feel one powerful headache coming on."

This was bad news. The effects of chronic headaches on Vonette had led her past aspirin through Darvon, Valium, Librium, and whatever was the latest miracle cure. She occasionally had such pain, she had told me, that Fritz gave her shots of Demerol. This was in addition to the substantial amounts of alcohol she put away on a daily basis. Why she had not died from these combinations long ago was beyond me; I figured she possessed an incredible tolerance for drugs. I heard her gulp something down, and I knew our conversation about Laura was finished, at least for the moment.

"Let me help out," I offered. "Let me bring your meals over. I mean," I added hastily, "if you want."

"I would, honey," she said in a lower tone, "but you know John Richard is just in such a state about that food from yesterday. Lord! What does Goldy have against Fritz, I asked him. Exactly nothing, that's what." Another yawn. "I said to John Richard, Well, you know, son, there's lots of women thought your daddy was a rat." She giggled. The painkiller was taking effect.

"Vonette," I said before the conversation degenerated further, "I'm coming over on Tuesday, and I'm going to bring Fritz some things to eat I know he likes. Okay?"

She giggled again.

"You can even test them," I said, "and I want to visit with you, anyway. Make sure there are no hard feelings with old Fritz."

Vonette inhaled. She said, "Goldy, honey. Thanks. That

would be sweet. I'll taste them if you want. Hell, nobody cares if *I* die. Just kidding, of course. Laura Smiley had that kind of attitude and it did her in, didn't it? Well, who knows. And you know what else? John Richard will be taking over the whole practice for Fritz for a couple of days anyway, so he won't be around to bother you. You know."

Did I ever. Maybe I should have adopted Marla's attitude and actively avoided John Richard. My life might have been a lot easier. It would be good to have the son out of the way when I chatted with the mother. Though I hated to use Vonette, I needed information she might have. I didn't know what in the world was going on. I had to start somewhere.

"Guess what?" I said. "Those cops are going to close down my operation until this is all cleared up. Maybe you can help me out a little."

"Oh, honey," she said, "I'll give you all the cash you need. It'll just be our little secret."

"No no no. I mean, thanks, really, but I don't mean money. All I want to do is talk to you, about some of the possibilities. Of who could have done this to Fritz."

"Goldy honey, I keep telling you. Fritz is fine. Just let the police handle it." She was quiet for a minute. Then she said, "Do you know what? Maybe nobody did it to him. Maybe somebody did it so's your catering business would be busted. Ever think of that?"

As a matter of fact, I had not. Besides John Richard, who hated me? The flowers from yesterday seemed to indicate I was not the target. No need to confuse Vonette with that, however.

I promised to see her in two days, rang off, and phoned Marla.

"You'll never guess what happened to Fritz Korman," I began.

"Pfft!" she answered. "Old news, sweetie pie. The way I hear it, you're the one tried to do it."

Wait a minute.

"Well, *sweetie pie*," I said, "as a matter of fact, I was wondering if *you* had anything to do with it."

"Don't be ridiculous," said Marla. "I wasn't even there, for God's sake." She began to chew something. "Trixie said the guy from the sheriff's department was good-looking in an oversized mountain-man sort of way. That skinny bitch. She thinks anyone who doesn't look as if they just came out of a refugee camp is overweight." More chewing. "So tell me about this guy."

"What guy?"

"The cop."

"Marla," I said in a voice full of vinegar, "tell me why you called me sweetie pie."

"I don't know. Does it bother you? Think I'm sweet on *you*? I just asked you about a policeman. Schulz, she said his name was."

I gave her a brief description of the investigating officer and then told her about the flowers and their message, with its "sweetie pie."

"Weird," she said.

"Is that all you can think of to say? My whole life's falling apart, for God's sake!"

"Well, *I* didn't send them," she protested. "Did John Richard ever send you flowers?"

"Only when he felt guilty about some fling he was having," I said. "You?"

"No, not after I served him edible nasturtiums."

I said, "Could the Jerk possibly have sent them? I mean, is this guy cracking up or what?" I told her about the tomato allergy, about my innocent substitution of the mushrooms. "When Fritz got sick John Richard had a fit and blamed me. Because of the mushrooms, if you can believe it."

Marla said, "Okay, okay. You are still my good buddy and I am still yours. Everything is going to be all right. Let's think." She stopped to drink something. "The Jerk is pissed off with you. So what else is new? But look at it this way. Maybe he did it. He blames you, makes it look like you, raises a stink. So nobody says, Well now, who spends the most time hanging around Daddy? Catch my drift?"

Another new angle. Everyone had a theory. I couldn't wait to try them out on Schulz. On second thought, I could wait.

"Get him sent to jail, will you?" Marla begged. "I'm getting tired of avoiding him."

After hanging up I considered. Would Schulz have thought of these possibilities? Perhaps not yet.

I spent the remainder of the morning calling the clients whose parties I was supposed to cater in the next month. Canceling felt like pouring money down the drain. Worse, and to my surprise, my clients were all eager to try Denver caterers. Bad news traveled fast. Then I balanced the checkbook. Three hundred ninety dollars. More bad news, even if the November child support payment came on time, which was unlikely. I calculated what it would take to make the next house payment and pay the bills.

I should have majored in math, I'd decided within a week of being single again. The degree in psychology had not only provided the depressing evidence that I had married a violent egotistical narcissist, it had also failed to help in making money.

My fallback during dry periods with the catering business was housecleaning, which paid a reliable eight bucks an hour. If I could book the jobs, Patty Sue and I each were going to have to do three houses a week just to make the November house payment and buy groceries. Luckily, finding needy clients whose houses were a mess was never difficult.

The only questionable debt was monthly dues for the athletic club. Missing this payment meant starting over with the four-hundred-dollar initiation fee, and I certainly didn't want to do that. But the club was a place I needed to get away from the kitchen. Arch enjoyed the pool in summer. I called and got, of all people, Trixie Jackson.

"Oh Trix," I said casually, "I need to speak to Hal."

Hal owned the club; I knew he was the only one in a position to let me barter for the dues.

"He's gone down to the game," she replied. And then, "I can't get over that mess yesterday. Fritz writhing on the floor like a woman in labor. Makes him know what it's like."

To the best of my knowledge, Trixie had no children. How did she know what it was like? "Just tell me when Hal will be back," I said.

"Oh, not until tomorrow. Why? You have a problem with something?"

"Look, Trix," I said, "tell him I want to do something for him to take care of my dues this month. Clean or whatever. Just see what he says."

She agreed. We decided to talk more the next day at the morning aerobics class, which she had taken over from another instructor. After that I called Alicia and canceled all my food for the upcoming month. Arch and Patty Sue began to wander into the kitchen and litter it with cinnamon roll crumbs, cereal boxes, and grease-soaked paper towels from draining the bacon. At one o'clock the doorbell rang.

Investigator Tom Schulz.

He sauntered in. Sensing his first question, I took him silently into the kitchen to look around. He smiled politely at Patty Sue and Arch, nodded at the pots and pans, walls and floors, cabinets and counters, said "Mm-hmm" and "It sure smells good in here," and scanned everything with those green eyes. Next I led him out to the living room, which I had redecorated postdivorce in a riot of yellows and oranges. The eucalyptus in the mysterious dried flower arrangement perfumed the room.

"Nice arrangement," he said.

"A bizarre arrangement," I said, and told him of its sudden appearance and anonymous message. He asked to see the card. I gave it to him and he pocketed it. Then he made a silent visual check of the entire room before settling himself on the lemon-colored couch.

"Miss Goldy," he began, "why don't you start by telling me about your husband? About this allegation of his?"

"My ex-husband," I said, suddenly angry, "is a—" I stopped and looked at my hands. "John Richard Korman," I began again, "is an abusive man. He frightens me. I was trying to give him mushrooms instead of tomatoes, to which he is allergic." I looked at Schulz. "Believe me," I said, "I don't have that much interest in Fritz Korman. He's just an old charmer whose wife is an alc—" I paused. I said, "Not under my jurisdiction, as you cops would say."

Schulz pulled his mouth into a small *o*. He leaned toward me and raised the tentlike eyebrows.

He said, "Just calm down." He leaned back again. "Let's start over. You can begin by offering me a nice cup of espresso and some of those rolls they're eating out in the kitchen. I don't ordinarily take refreshment at a suspect's house, but I'm going to make a large exception, since it smells so good in here."

I complied. Somehow the fact that he was hungry for something I had fixed, and that he trusted something I *would* fix, was encouraging.

He smiled at me between sips and bites.

"This is really nice, this place," he said. "I like this old neighborhood. Has a lot of charm. So do some of the residents." He gave what appeared to be either a judicious wink or a left-eye tic.

What in the world was going on? After a moment I said, "Are you going to ask me some questions or not?"

"Okeydoke." He laboriously wiped each of his fingers on the napkin I had given him. "Just take it easy, okay?"

I nodded.

He said, "Did you put a foreign substance into Fritz Korman's food to make him sick or kill him?"

I looked Investigator Schulz square in his X-ray vision eyes.

"No," I said. "I did not."

"Did you put a foreign substance into John Richard Korman's food to make him sick or kill him?"

I said, "I did not. It would harm my business, which is my sole source of income—"

Schulz chuckled. "It has already harmed your business. It may be the end of your business. Please assure me they weren't funny mushrooms."

"They were the regular kind."

"Good. Health Department report'll be in tomorrow or the day after. That spread sure looked good, too, hated to waste it. Poached salmon. Strawberry shortcake." He took a deep breath and leaned back to hike up his belt. "I've never been to a party you've catered."

"So?"

"Now Miss Goldy, I'm just saying you seem to be a good cook. You've got a reputation to protect."

I said, "The way you say it, it sounds like soliciting."

"There you go again." He closed his eyes, then opened them to look around the room. He stopped to gaze at a bright orange All Saints' Day drawing Arch had done at the beginning of Sunday school class, the one I'd taught. Since Arch did not at that point know about any actual saints, his picture was a cluster of Mom, Dad, Vonette, Fritz, and Mother Teresa. I explained all this to Schulz when he asked about it.

"Interesting," he said. "Now look. You don't need to get uptight. About your business. I'm just saying a good cook is hard to find. You make great cinnamon rolls."

He stopped and worked his jaw for a few moments.

"Now tell me why a good unmarried cook with a reputation to protect would get so upset talking to a cop who's trying to help her out?"

I shook my head. I said, "Sorry. Talking about my ex-husband gets me upset." I took a deep breath. "That's what our argument was about, anyway. The Jerk and no tomatoes. That son of a bitch. Nothing even happened to him."

"Something happened, though."

I looked at Schulz. "I didn't do anything to John Richard. I thought it was inappropriate for him to bring a new girlfriend, his fiancée, mind you, to a reception after the funeral of one of his son's teachers. Plus he walked over and insulted me. Then we fought over the dish with the mushrooms. But that's it."

Schulz swung his body around to the side and crossed his legs. He was wearing tan corduroy slacks and a gray sweater and tie: preppy clothes over his mountain-man body. He lifted his eyebrows and shoulders, opened his hands in question.

I said, "The guys down at the Health Department aren't going to find anything in that trash bag."

"Let's hope not."

I was suddenly exhausted. Worse, I did not like the way Investigator Tom Schulz was making me feel. He made me want to trust him, which did not come easily.

I said, "So am I going to jail or what?"

He shook his head and smiled. "No. But the other incident is something else. We have a policy about attempted poisoning. Sorry, your business will have to stay closed down. For a while. Until we find out about the rodent poison, who did it and why. That's it."

"Please don't do that to me," I begged. My eyes sought his. "My busy season is coming up. Arch and I depend on the November and December income to make it through the next year. The longer I'm closed down, the worse things will get for us financially. I can't make it on housecleaning alone."

He shrugged. "Have to, sorry. At least until this mess with Fritz Korman is cleared up."

"How long will that take?"

"That depends."

I leaned forward. "I can help you. Really. I'm already going over there day after tomorrow to talk to Vonette."

Schulz lifted an eyebrow, tilted his head.

He said, "To talk to Vonette. Listen. When I want help on this case, I'll ask for it."

It was my turn to shrug.

He said, "Okay, Goldy. Do you know who didn't get along with Doctor Korman? Sounds as if you know a lot of people."

"Oh, well," I began. I felt a wave of sympathy for Vonette. How could I be disloyal to her? What could I say? I shook my head.

"Look," I said, "everyone in this town knows Fritz. Most of the people under twenty were delivered by him, for God's sake."

"Know anybody who thought he wasn't a good doctor? Anybody at the party?"

"No."

"Were any of his patients there yesterday?"

I thought. "I think Trixie Jackson is one of his patients. The aerobics instructor."

"Yeah," said Schulz. "I used to see her over at the athletic club. She married?"

"Yes," I said, "she is, I think. I remember seeing her in the Kormans' office. But that was a long while ago, when I was still married." I frowned. A guilty knot tied itself in my stomach. It wasn't up to me to give Trixie's ob-gyn history to Schulz. After the divorce I'd changed doctors; I now went to a female gynecologist in Denver. I didn't keep up with the Kormans' practice.

Schulz said, "Who else?"

"Why don't you just subpoena his records or whatever it's called?" I could hear the exasperation in my voice. A minute ago I had offered to help him. Now I just wanted him to leave.

"Okay," I went on wearily, "Patty Sue Williams. My roommate. He's treating her for amenorrhea. It's in the dictionary. Anyway, her doctor from eastern Colorado sent her out here to be treated by Fritz." I switched to a lower tone. "Believe me," I said, "Fritz might as well be the governor, the way Patty Sue looks up to him. She'd have an anxiety attack before she'd put poison in his coffee."

He tapped his fingers on the mahogany coffee table. "What about the wife?" He looked at the ceiling as if he were turning things over in his mind. "Vonette."

"Look," I said, "you can check all this in your files somewhere. Vonette's an alcoholic. Fritz got her tossed into detox a few nights ago. It happens now and then. But that doesn't mean she tried to do anything to him." I paused. "She doesn't operate that way. When she's upset with Fritz she takes it out on herself. She drinks."

"I'll do the interpreting around here, if you don't mind." He smiled. "What about this Laura person? What's this your son said about her not liking Korman?"

"I'm going to see what Vonette knows about that," I replied. "All I know about Laura is from our teacher-parent conferences last year and two years before, when she was Arch's teacher."

"How did your son feel about Ms. Smiley?"

"They were very close. They used to tell each other jokes, write letters." I paused. "He's very upset about her killing herself. At least, he seems that way."

Schulz cleared his throat. "I've read about those fantasy games," he said. "Some kids can get awfully involved in them. Think they're real."

"Tell me something I don't know."

"Your son was in charge of the coffee and whatnot. He was friends with Ms. Smiley and for some reason thought Fritz Korman was her enemy. He's having trouble dealing with her death, but puts great stock in fantasy games where they use potions and the like. Any chance that could spell trouble for his grandfather?"

I stared at Schulz with my mouth open.

I said, "My son is not a liar."

"He didn't tell me he didn't do it."

"You didn't ask." I felt my ears burning. "Arch!" I called toward the kitchen door. "Arch, the policeman wants to ask you another question!"

Arch stuck his head into the living room.

"What?" he said.

Schulz said nothing. He only looked benevolently at Arch.

"Hon," I said gently, "did you put anything into Fritz's coffee?"

"Huh?"

"Did you"—I began again and opened my eyes wide at him—"put something into Fritz's coffee to make him sick?"

Arch reddened. "No," he replied. "Why? Do you think I did?"

"No," I said in relief, and glanced back at Schulz, who was studying Arch's face. "You can go. Unless Mr. Schulz here has any more questions."

He shook his head. Arch left, and I stood up.

Tom Schulz gave me a long look. This time I felt that the X-ray vision was not directed to seeing what was in my mind. I felt he was looking for something else, but I couldn't quite figure out what.

He said, "Let's keep in touch."

CHAPTER 6

Monday morning arrived gray and chilly. From my bedroom window a nimbus of fog was just visible shrouding the far mountains. Gray fingers of cloud drifted down to caress the yellowed treetops of the Wildlife Preserve. The wooden window stuck in its track when I pulled; eventually it shuddered open and let in a flood of air as cold and sweet as the cherry cider Colorado farmers sell off the backs of their trucks this time of year.

Arch was out of school because it was Columbus Day. Since Fritz was home recovering, Patty Sue would not see him until Wednesday. As the sole person awake, I did not want to have to face the possibility of another first-strike telephone call from John Richard. I closed the window and slipped into a turtleneck and jeans before heading out for the warmth of Aspen Meadow's pastry shop.

The fresh air hit my face like a slap. Perhaps it was not such a good idea to spend money on someone else's cooking, I reflected as my boots crunched over the frosted gravel of the driveway. I headed down Main Street past the Grizzly Bear Restaurant and Darlene's Antiques and Collectibles. But the lure of hot rolls and coffee won out. The walk took twenty minutes. To my relief the small shop held no one I knew.

"Sorry about your business," was the mournful greeting from Murray, the master baker.

I said, "I love living in a small town."

Murray looked puzzled. "Listen," he said defensively, "it's gonna hurt me, too. Somebody kills that doctor, I'll lose half my customers."

I nodded. The shop was on the first floor of a long two-story wood-paneled building. Upstairs, Fritz and John Richard practiced obstetrics and gynecology. It would be a couple of hours before John Richard came in. But within fifteen minutes of his opening, the pastry shop would begin to fill with pregnant women. I knew the pattern: they would eat nothing before weighing in for their appointment. After seeing the doctor they'd waddle down the wooden staircase outside the building and burst into the pastry shop, starved. I often wondered if that was why Murray had located his bakery-haven in this particular spot.

"Don't worry," I said before ordering, "he's going to be just fine, and so is your business."

Soon I was dipping one finger of that western oversized baked good, the Bear Claw, into coffee and reading in last week's *Mountain Journal* of Laura Smiley's death. The new issue would not be out until later in the week, and it would undoubtedly cover the postfuneral fiasco. That was something I could wait for. Now I read of Laura Smiley, the much beloved teacher at Furman Elementary, who had been born in Denver and raised in Aspen Meadow until she went to the University of Illinois. After that she had become an elementary teacher in Carolton, also in Illinois. There was something familiar about that name, that place. After Laura's parents were killed in a drunk driving accident on Highway 285 near Conifer, she had moved back to

the family home, and had been a teacher at Furman
Elementary ever since.

I stared at the picture. Between the black dots of
newsprint, Laura was caught in a sunny grin. Suddenly, the
dots clouded.

You're depressed, I told myself. Drink some coffee. I
looked up at Murray, who gave me his best version of a
sympathetic wink. I held the paper in front of my face.
Ms. Smiley, the *Journal* went on to say, was found by fellow
teacher Janet Heath, autopsy ordered, new deputy coroner
performing. Funeral Saturday, in lieu of flowers, donations
to Pacifists United or the National Organization for Women.
But some people had sent flowers anyway. And not only
to her.

The rest of the article was what I already knew. But the
words "came as a great surprise to her students and those
who had known her" were difficult to handle. I thought
once again of the cheerful punning magnets and paintings
of serene landscapes in Laura's small home.

Out the pastry shop's picture window old wooden
storefronts broke the cloudy view of distant snow-capped
peaks. Most people moved to the mountains for this vista
and for the slower pace. Now Homestead Drive and Main
Street were silent. The only noises were the gentle gush-
ing of Cottonwood Creek and the occasional ding-ding of
cars announcing their presence at a nearby gas station.

Maybe Laura had been looking for serenity when she
stayed in Aspen Meadow after her parents' death. She had
taught third grade at Furman Elementary. Arch had been
in the class; it was the first time I felt a teacher had appre-
ciated him. The beginning of their friendship, she had related at the first parent conference, had come from a
technological advance.

He had come to her shyly one snowy November morn-
ing before school. A neighbor with a new car had driven
Arch along with his own kids to avoid a late bus. At school
Arch had asked Laura how a door could be a jar. A voice in

the neighbor's car had said, "Your door is ajar!" Then she'd told him once she'd eaten a strawberry moose. Kindred spirits. They'd written little jokes and poetry verses to each other, and later letters, and they were partners in laughter even after he went on to fourth grade. The next year, in one of those moves peculiar to elementary school administrations, Laura was transferred to teaching fifth grade. Arch had ended up with her again.

Sometimes I had thought they spent too much time together. He had come home with some peculiar stories. Ms. Smiley had made fun of the President. Well, who didn't. But with a fifth grader? Then when her street wasn't plowed, she told Arch she was going to hire dump trucks to leave a ton of snow in front of the county commissioners' office. When I asked her about these stories, she just laughed them off. It never occurred to me that Laura Smiley was truly off-balance. With the suicide, of course, I had begun to wonder.

And poor Arch. This year he had slammed into the hostile environment of a large sixth grade. He had reacted by becoming more secretive and serious, more committed to the complex fantasy games, more rebellious in the slide to adolescence. He had no teacher who could talk about dumping fantasy snow on newly cruel peers.

I looked down at the newspaper on the table, then back out the window. The sun had burnt off the fog and shone now in a liquid expanse of blue. It was hard to imagine someone looking at the Colorado sky before making that last trip into the bathroom.

Marla broke the silence by plopping into the chair across from me.

She hummed as she spread out her fare, two buttermilk-glazed doughnuts and a cream-filled Long John—the western version of an éclair—and a cup of coffee, which she immediately began to douse with sugar and cream. She stopped humming to give me a baleful look.

"You shouldn't eat alone," she warned. She shook pillowy

jowls that resembled the Pillsbury doughboy's. She had on a sequined sweat suit. Half of her brown frizzy hair was held by a ponytail. The rest spilled out every which way. Her face, however, was perfectly made up. She bit carefully into one of the doughnuts so as not to smear the scarlet lipstick, then went on with her mouth full. "It's like drinking alone. A bad sign, very bad." She dabbed around her mouth with a napkin. "Especially in the morning."

"Then why are you here?" I asked. I took a sip of coffee before biting off another Bear Claw finger.

She narrowed her eyes and munched thoughtfully, then tongued a small glob of cream that had oozed out of the center of the Long John.

"I'm used to eating alone," she replied. "You're not." She looked at the paper spread out in front of me and shook her head again. "Good God. Eating alone and reading about suicide."

"Give me a break, Marla."

"Hey! I'm trying to cheer you up."

I smiled and looked down at her doughnuts. "What are you doing here, anyway?" I asked. "I thought your larder was full."

"Well," she said hesitantly, "you're not going to believe this, but I can't eat at home. Mice."

"Mice?" I said, staring at her.

She gulped her cream-colored coffee again and touched her free hand to the frizzy mass of hair. "Yeah, so what? It's getting cold outside. The mice come in. They're hungry. They scare me. I call an exterminator. Is there something wrong with that? You sure seem to be on edge this morning." She gestured at the paper. "Stop reading about Laura. That'll only make you feel worse."

I frowned at her. She *was* my friend.

I said, "Whoever tried to do in Fritz Korman used rodent poison."

Marla closed her eyes, then opened them. "I didn't do it, Goldy."

"Sorry," I mumbled.

She leaned across the table. "Listen," she said. "I don't even care about Fritz. And neither should you. The more involved in this you become, the more depressed you're going to get. It's like hanging around John Richard. It just makes things worse. Let the police do their job."

"I have to help them," I said. "My business and livelihood are on the line." This would not have occurred to Marla, of course, since she'd made her money the easy way: she inherited it.

She shrugged and tapped a fat finger twinkling with sapphires on the newspaper picture of Laura. "Here's a mystery you should be working on," she said. "Why'd she do it? I have a theory."

"What's that?"

"Unrequited love."

I looked at her blankly. "What?"

Marla returned the blank look and started to mumble vaguely about not being *completely* sure when the shop door flew open, banged against our table, and sent the coffee into a tidal wave across the Formica.

"I figured you were here," Arch announced triumphantly as he marched in with Patty Sue in tow. "You always come here when you don't have any work."

I gave Marla a rueful glance and dropped a pile of napkins on the table's lake of coffee, then got up to refill our cups and pay for whatever Arch wanted. He ordered a sugar twist and juice. Patty Sue, after noticing she hadn't brought any money, ordered a Long John, a cheese Danish, and two cartons of milk.

"How do you stay so thin?" demanded Marla. "I mean didn't they feed you out in eastern Colorado, before you had to come out here to see Fritz, or what?"

"They fed me. And I'm trying to learn to cook," said

Patty Sue in what I viewed as extraordinary understatement. "One time Dad was sick for a long time and then I had to do the cooking because Mom got sick, too. I fixed frozen stuff like Banquet chicken and Sara Lee."

Marla said, "What did she have, scurvy?"

There was no answer. Patty Sue and Arch were staring at Laura's picture in the paper. Patty Sue put down her Danish and looked out the window. I reached for the paper.

"Guess what," I said to distract Arch. "Marla has mice."

"Oh, cool," he said with genuine admiration. "Do you have gerbils, too?"

Marla turned her look of distaste on me.

"Arch," Marla explained as she gestured with her remaining doughnut, "there are good mice and bad mice. Good mice live in cages and children's stories. Bad mice bite and spread disease after they get into your best cookies and crackers and make a mess. Not to mention that after all your cookies are gone, you have to go to local pastry shops and listen to your best friend ask if you're using rodent poison on humans." She paused to swallow some coffee. "And no to the gerbils, too."

Arch nodded. "Did you call the Division of Wildlife to get rid of them?"

Marla and I both found this amusing. The furrows of confusion in Patty Sue's forehead deepened. I was not sure, but it looked as if she was about to cry.

"Arch honey," I said in a voice I hoped was not patronizing, "you call the Division of Wildlife if you have a problem with a bear or a raccoon or a mountain lion. Not for mice and common animals like that."

Arch said, "I don't think you're right, Mom."

Marla glanced at her watch. "Oh," she said, her mouth full of doughnut, "the irony of it all. Time for exercise class."

I nodded. I still needed to find out if Hal was interested in my cleaning offer, so I hustled Patty Sue and Arch along. As they were getting up to leave, I turned to Marla.

"So what's this about Laura?" I asked in a low voice.

"I've seen and heard this and that," Marla whispered.

"Well, tell me."

"Not now," said Marla. She thought. "Let me ask around at the club. That's where I saw something that made me wonder."

"Made you wonder about what?"

"Let me call around, will you, Goldy? I hate to gossip."

Untrue, I thought, as I hastened after her. Marla *adored* gossip.

We took off for the Aspen Meadow Athletic Club, which occupied the bottom two floors of a streamlined brick building full of glass and sharply angled walls. The other four floors of this incongruously contemporary edifice housed First Bank of Colorado, realtors' offices, even our own branch of Merrill Lynch. The building and its residents were a sign of the urban future coming to our little town, a sign that was none too welcome to the small population that had moved here to get away from all that.

Inside, the athletic facility was about as close to yuppie heaven as one could find in Aspen Meadow. Plexiglas walls enclosed clean white racquetball courts; an advanced sound system boomed in the exercise room; Nautilus equipment and weights were judiciously spaced in another room, which had the look of a museum exhibit of modern sculpture. For postworkout relaxation there was a steamroom, sauna, and hot tub in a locker room that would have given pause to the architects of the Roman baths.

A cook feels more comfortable putting fat into things than taking it out or off, so belonging to a fancy gym had always felt strange. As I pushed through the glass door and shuffled across the beige-and-burgundy striped carpet, it was Marla's comment that reminded me of the other reason for feeling out of place here. The club was the one spot in Aspen Meadow where, as if by agreement, all the single people who did not want to resort to either bars or church groups could meet.

I only felt duty bound to exercise, and that not too much. My business had kept me going until a few days ago. Besides splashing in the pool, Arch enjoyed puttering around on the racquetball court, so I also rationalized paying the dues for his sake. But unless some work materialized soon, we would have to quit. I hated to feel poor. It made me resent John Richard even more than usual.

Needless to say, I hadn't taken advantage of the social life available at the club. There was a small voice of uncertainty in my gut, not unlike the interest in Pomeroy. Over the years some of the muscle-bound fellows had asked me out. I had replied in the negative, claiming to myself that I wasn't ready.

But I belonged to the club, and like the woman on a diet who stares at the frozen desserts, I had my wild thoughts.

This feeling did not diminish when Patty Sue, Marla, Arch, and I retrieved our locker keys from Hal, a shaggy-haired jock who had metamorphosed from surf bum to club owner without losing his beachboy gestalt. He was on the phone and whispered he would talk to me later. The place was crowded since it was a holiday. Glancing into the Nautilus room the first person I saw, of course, was Pomeroy Locraft. Not teaching today because the high school was closed, no doubt. He gave us a hearty wave which, since I had never received it before, was probably meant for Patty Sue. She waved back while Arch sauntered over to chat, probably about beekeeping.

In the locker room Marla said, "I don't know if I'm ready for this after two doughnuts and a Long John. What an unfortunately phallic name for an éclair, anyway." She was struggling into peach-colored tights that made her look even more round and fuzzy than she already was.

"Okay, girls," shouted Trixie after we had stretched calves and assorted ligaments, "let's go get 'em!"

This, coupled with the sudden booming of the theme from *Top Gun*, meant the war on cellulite had been declared. I had not had a class from Trixie in quite a while. I wasn't sure I was up to it.

Within the first minute of activity it was abundantly clear that too long a time had elapsed since my last trip to class, no matter who the teacher was. The ruthless bank of mirrors in front of us pointed out every fatty pouch. My thighs, next to Patty Sue's long slender ones, looked as if they were plastered with rice pudding. My stomach was a *bombe glacée*.

"Come on, girls!" exhorted Trixie. "Get that energy up!" She balled her hands into fists and punched at the air below the ceiling. "Go! Go!"

Beside me Patty Sue was lunging and jumping. Pomeroy and Arch were out of sight. I surveyed the rows of women. I did not want to do this, did not want to do this.

The women were like pasta groupings, I decided. The back row of overweight newcomers wiggled laboriously, manicotti in hot water. Next came lasagne, wide-looking one way and thin when they turned. The linguini in front of them possessed the same thin/wide dimensions, only in not so dramatic proportions. Then onward to spaghetti and finally to vermicelli, thin tall tubes like Patty Sue and Trixie. How Patty Sue could eat so much and stay so thin was beyond me. I was an incidental misfit on this row, short and round. An elbow macaroni, maybe.

After class I stretched out on a towel in the steamroom, where I was soon joined by Patty Sue, Marla, and Trixie.

"Glad you're back," said Marla to Trixie.

"Oh," Trixie said loftily, "I've been back for a couple of weeks."

"In fighting shape," I said as we all settled in the dark room with its swirls of steam.

Trixie said, "What's that supposed to mean?"

"Not a damn thing," I said. "What's the matter?"

"Not a damn thing," she said. After a moment she sniffed.

I said, "Did I say something wrong?"

Trixie flipped over. She said, "Just shut up, Goldy."

I said, "What are you so angry about?"

Trixie said, "Since when are you a shrink?"

"Be cool, girls, be cool," said Marla.

I let a silence go by. Then I said, "Would somebody please tell me what is going on?"

"Not now," said Trixie.

There was another uncomfortable silence, in which Patty Sue cleared her throat several times.

"I've been thinking, Trixie," Marla said finally. "Maybe you'd like to come to our group. Tell her about it, Goldy."

I did, but I didn't know why I was doing it. I explained that we ate dessert and talked. If she was having some problems, I said delicately, it sometimes helped to talk them out.

"I'll think about it," said Trixie. "When do you meet?"

"We're meeting on Thursday the twenty-second," I said. "Then we'll meet again on Friday night the thirtieth."

"Um," said Patty Sue, "can I come too?"

"Sure," I said. "Trix?"

"I teach Thursday nights and Saturday mornings," she said, "so maybe the one near Halloween. Martin's going out of town at the end of the month—it's a possibility." She was quiet for a minute. "I'll think about it."

"Such enthusiasm," said Marla. To me she said, "I'm glad the last one's near Halloween. I'll need a heavy sugar fix right before all the little neighborhood goblins arrive and I actually have to give candy *away*."

After dressing I hunted for and found Hal. We stood in back of the desk to talk while he continued to dispense keys. I told him we were desperate for money to pay our dues, and that I had spent some time doing cleaning in addition to cooking, so I was qualified to do both. And he couldn't beat my prices.

"Tell you what," Hal said as he reached down for a key under its tag, "we usually have a Halloween party the thirty-first and just get all the food from a grocery store. Chocolate cookies, pumpkin cake, same old stuff every year. And one of the problems this year is that our cleaning crew comes in only on Sunday when we're closed. Halloween falls on a Saturday, so we need someone, who I thought was going to be me, to clean up after we close on Friday. If you can do the munchies and punch and decoration, plus clean up beforehand, then that'll take care of your dues for October and November."

I told him the county had forbidden me to do catering. For a while.

"Hey," said Hal, as he screwed his tanned face into indignation, "who cares what the county thinks? You're doing this for me. And I'm doing something for you. Ever since I burned my draft card, I haven't worried about the law."

"Just don't advertise the fact that I'm doing it, or I'll catch hell."

"It's a favor," he said. "Don't worry so much! It's bad for your heart."

I did feel sick, but put it down to too many abdominal exercises. We settled on how many people and what kind of food he would like to have—mild Chinese, hot Mexican, and sweet American.

"Sounds like three girls," he said.

I told him the cash flow problem was severe. He trundled off to get me fifty dollars from the cash register for my supplies.

While I waited for him I glanced down at the board with its rows of glistening keys. Keys to lockers were like keys to inner selves, solutions to outer and inner mysteries. But the one enigma in my current life—who had poisoned

Fritz?—was not dangling on the board. Or if it was, I couldn't see it. Whoever did hold the key to the pellets also determined my business future. Why had someone done it? I noticed Fritz's key and my ex-husband's hanging under the K. Why poison someone after a funeral? Especially after the funeral of a suicide?

What had Arch said? That Laura hadn't gotten along with Fritz and Vonette. Carolton, Illinois, the paper had said.

Carolton, Illinois. John Richard and I had driven by that town once on a summer trip. The highway was near where his father had had a practice a long time ago.

I looked around for Hal. He was caught in conversation with a person carrying some weights.

What about Laura and the Kormans' lives before Aspen Meadow? Who knew? Unless . . .

Unless the attempted poisoning of Korman had had something to do with Laura's death. Which would explain why someone would go to the lengths of trying to do him in at her house, after her funeral, with her spirit or whatever there.

And what about Laura's death, anyway? How indisputable was the determination by the coroner's office, I wondered. With no note, what made them say it was suicide?

This wasn't even a theory. This was an insane idea. The police were looking into the coffee poisoning. They had already decided about Laura Smiley's death by her own hand.

But the police would still get their salaries whether or not they were right about a woman's death, whether or not they figured out who was playing pellets-in-the-coffee. The solution to that question directly affected my livelihood. Was I ready to trust Arch's and my income to someone else's intelligence and perseverance?

I was not. Sweat dimpled my scalp. My fingers shivered. Hal was still talking to the guy with the weights. I would not be able to follow up on this inclination right away. I would have to wait. Wait until the club was silent, empty. Still, it would be a start.

With one swift movement I reached down to the keys marked S, and removed one from its hook: Laura Smiley's.

CHAPTER 7

At home that night I stared at the key and wondered if I'd committed a crime. So far, detection was neither enjoyable nor productive. The Grand Marnier I usually saved for cheesecakes gurgled when I poured some into one of my grandmother's liqueur glasses. The taste like smoke and oranges burned all the way down.

I picked up the key and felt its edges bite into my hand. Think. I would have to wait to search Laura's locker, wait for a time when the athletic club was deserted. It would raise more questions than it was worth to be caught pilfering the goods of a dead woman. This was Monday. The best bet would be Saturday, five days away. Given the choice, most folks would rather shop than sweat on a Saturday morning.

The liqueur did nothing to prevent another fitful night. Like most insomniacs, I fell into a deathlike sleep just as the sun was coming up. To my chagrin two interruptions shattered what could have been restful slumber.

The first was a barely remembered encounter with Arch. Before the bus came he had been banging around the house looking for some seeds for . . . milk? That was what had been confusing, what had sent me back to bed. He'd said he needed it for a potion for unbelievers, which seemed even more incredible.

The second rude awakening was from the phone.

"What is it?" I demanded into the receiver.

"Oh-ho, it's the good-natured caterer, I see," said Tom Schulz. "Resting up for housecleaning somewhere? Or do you have time to talk?"

"What can you possibly want at this hour?"

"It's nine o'clock, Goldy. I could want a lot of things."

I sat up in bed, feeling groggy and uncomfortably warm. Either this guy was flirting with me or my paranoia was taking a turn toward the delusional.

"Listen," he was going on, "I was thinking about something your son said. Funny thing about your kid. He ended up being a cooperative and polite person in spite of his parents."

"Schulz," I said. "Please. It's just that I have some cooking to do."

"Really? Who're you cooking for?"

"I am going, as I told you before, over to visit my ex-in-laws. I am taking them a basket of things to eat. This has nothing to do with my business, either, if that's what you're thinking. It's just—" I groped for words. I did not want Schulz to know of my plans to snoop around as well as ask questions. "Just because I am a nice person after all. And this way, if poison turns up in the coffee cake, you'll know I was the one after all."

"Uh-huh. I'd say more like you're going snooping to figure out what's going on by yourself. Spite of what you say, you don't trust the police to do their job. Goldy wants to get her business opened without benefit of law enforcement agencies, is what I'm hearing."

"I could be more helpful than you think."

"Really," he said again, unconvinced. There was a pause. "You're a suspect, you know."

"Yes, but you know I didn't do it. In your heart of hearts."

"My heart of hearts, she says. About which she knows so much."

"Come on, Investigator Schulz."

Another pause. Then he said, "Well. You want to be in on the investigation? I'll give you a chance to do just that."

"Okay, what?"

"A chance, I said. That means we work together. Within the law."

"Uh-oh. Can't take my Uzi when I question witnesses."

He sighed. "There's something you might be able to look into. What your son said about Laura and Fritz and Vonette not getting along? Turns out they all lived in the same town for a while. Fritz and Vonette moved here from Carolton, Illinois, in 1967. Ms. Smiley came out about a year later, when her parents died. Not that that tells us anything, it's just a strange link."

"They knew each other," I said. "I already asked Vonette. Laura babysat for them during a vacation. But that was twenty years ago."

"Still," he said, "it's a link. I'm going to call out there to Carolton and see if I can do a little background checking on Laura Smiley, maybe on the Kormans, too. Ask if there was anybody else from that town who moved here. See if we get any more strange links."

"Like if anyone had a rodent problem twenty years ago."

He chuckled. "One of these days I'm going to tell you why you're so tough."

I chewed the inside of my cheek and didn't answer.

"Anyway," he went on, "I thought you were itching to help out. You could do just that in your little chat with your ex-in-laws today."

"Will do," I said. "And there's something I want to find out. I was wondering if you could talk to the deputy coroner or whoever it was that said Laura was a suicide. I'd like to know why he said it was suicide."

"We'll see." He harrumphed. "I am letting you in on all this," he went on, "because I want to help you. And of course because I care about you. As a taxpayer, of course."

"You care about me because you're a taxpayer or because I'm one?"

"As a taxpayer, you help pay my salary, Goldy," he said with a grin I could hear. "With no income, your taxes will be lower and there goes my salary. Tell you what. How about if we talk more about this over Chinese food tonight? We could compare notes, my treat. Six o'clock at Aspen Meadow's finest Oriental restaurant."

"You mean Aspen Meadow's only Oriental restaurant."

"Aw," he said, "you take all the fun out of everything."

I thought. It would probably be a long time before I had another chance to be taken out to dinner. Still, I wasn't used to it. I might flunk social adeptness.

"It's just dinner," he said. "Come on."

I could make spaghetti for Patty Sue and Arch. I could even walk to the Dragon's Breath, since it was just off Main Street.

I said, "Six o'clock," and hung up.

Nothing equals mixing and baking to clear the head, I thought after I had showered and downed a quart of coffee. Patty Sue had decided to go for a long run, she told me with an unusual amount of explanation, to get in shape for skiing. Fine. The next few hours of cooking in a quiet house stretched out like a dry road after a storm.

The components of Goldilocks' Cheer-Up Basket usually were the following: three different kinds of baked goods, fresh fruit in season, at least two kinds of fancy cheese, a soup or dinner that could be frozen, and a bouquet of flowers.

For the soup I was in luck. I had already made up a quantity of Goldilocks' Gourmet Spinach Soup and frozen it. This recipe had actually derived from a miscalculation in making Julia Child's entrée crêpes stuffed with spinach and mushrooms. Trying to help Arch with some fourth-grade math homework while making the crêpe filling, I had ended up with quadruple the amount I needed for the crêpes. After the initial distress, I had thinned out the cheese and vegetable mixture with chicken broth, and the result had been brilliant. The success pleased customers no end. Periodically I made great quantities of the stuff, without crêpes, just to keep on hand. So Fritz and Vonette could have some.

The senior Kormans were also partial to coffee cakes. I sometimes saw Fritz in the Aspen Meadow pastry shop indulging in an iced cinnamon roll. Unless I phoned her, Vonette never got up early enough to have a normal breakfast, but she loved my cakes anytime. So I hunted up the buttermilk, took some cream cheese out to soften, and made a New England crumb coffee cake flavored with ginger and nutmeg.

The pièce de résistance was Goldy's Dream Cake. This, too, was a cookbook recipe that I had messed up in the most fortuitous manner. I pulled out the ingredients, made a fingerprint in the cream cheese to make sure it had softened, and then peered at the card.

Vonette and Fritz were not going to get one made ahead. Patty Sue and Arch could have the other one for dessert tonight after their spaghetti. Good thing they were both so thin.

I began to measure and mix. It was all like a cake, I thought. This mess with Fritz, the unknowns about Laura. It was like having a large group of ingredients and not knowing how they were all combined.

And what about Schulz? He wanted to trust me, wanted me to help him with the case. After John Richard, I'd grown suspicious of men and their motives. In Amour

Goldy's Dream Cake

Crumb Mixture:

   4 1/2 cups all-purpose flour
   1 1/2 cups sugar
   1 1/2 cups (3 sticks) unsalted butter,
      cut into 1-tablespoon pieces,
      well chilled

Cake:

   1 teaspoon baking powder
   1 teaspoon bakng soda
   1/2 teaspoon salt
   6 cups reserved crumb mixture
   2 large eggs, beaten
   1 1/2 cups sour cream
   2 teaspoons almond extract

Filling:

   1 pound (two 8-ounce packages)
      cream cheese, softened
   1/2 cup sugar
   2 large eggs, beaten
   1/4 teaspoon vanilla extract

1 cup red raspberry preserves,
sieved to remove seeds

Topping:
²/₃ cup raw whole almonds
2 cups reserved crumb mixture

Preheat the oven to 350°F. Butter two
9- or 10-inch springform pans and set
aside.

In the large bowl of a food processor
fitted with a steel blade, blend the
flour and sugar until well combined,
about 5 seconds. With the motor running, quickly drop the butter pieces
through the chute, blending until the
mixture resembles small, sandy crumbs,
less than a minute. Measure out 6 cups
of this mixture for the cake. Measure
the last 2 cups of the mixture for the
toppng and set aside.

For the cake, gently stir the baking
powder, soda, and salt into the 6 cups
of reserved crumb mixture. In a sepa-
rate bowl, mix the beaten eggs with

the sour cream and almond extract, stirring until well combined. Pour the egg mixture over the crumb mixture and stir until smooth and thick. Spread the cake batter over the bottom and up the sides of each of the prepared pans.

For the filling, beat the cream cheese, sugar, eggs, and vanilla extract in the large bowl of an electric mixer until smooth. Spread half of this mixture over the cake batter in each of the prepared pans. Top the cream cheese mixture in each pan with 1/2 cup of the sieved preserves.

For the topping, whirl the raw almonds in a food processor fitted with the steel blade until chunky. Mix the almonds into the 2 cups reserved crumb mixture and sprinkle half of this mixture over the preserves layer in each pan.

Bake the cakes for 45 to 55 minutes. Test with a toothpick for doneness. (All that should adhere to the toothpick is cream cheese and preserves, not cake batter.) Cool the cakes thoroughly on racks, then cover with foil and refrigerate several hours or, even better, overnight. Serve in the morning with coffee, if desired.

Makes 2 large cakes

Anonymous, we sometimes joked about being addicted to hate. We worried that hostility-for-guys was what drew us together. I wanted to be social again, didn't I? I wanted someone to care about me.

Didn't I?

I was just sprinkling on the crumb-and-almond mixture when the buzzer sounded the completion of the crumb cake. After placing it on a cooling rack I saw myself briefly in the reflection of the black refrigerator door. I was actually going out tonight. I would have to do something with my hair and find some garment besides a corduroy skirt. I was going to have to be sociable, and it wasn't even for a client. I was going out with a man I knew liked me. All of a sudden, I felt sick.

Four hours later the van was grinding its way up the steep entrance to the residential area surrounding Aspen Meadow Country Club. To call this club with its half-hearted golf and tennis offerings a *country* club was an overstatement. The A.M.C.C. never would measure up to any of its eastern counterparts, and migrants from Rumson and Chevy Chase and Lake Forest were quick to point this out. But then again, this was the West. Even the idea of a country club had been imported. Eastern snobbery gave Coloradans no end of psychic pain, and the natives produced a multitude of bumper stickers to express their attendant disgust. The most impudent declared, LOVE NEW YORK? TAKE HIWAY 40 EAST!

I looked down at the basket on the seat next to me. The cakes and container of soup glistened in cellophane wrap tied with bows of yellow and orange and brown. A small arrangement of flowers dried from my own garden last year echoed the fall colors. And speaking of bouquets, maybe I'd be able to find out this afternoon what it was Fritz deserved.

"Well now, Goldy honey," Vonette greeted me after the doorbell on the massive front door to their contemporary wood home had bing-bonged à la Big Ben. "Don't you look cute! You got a date or something?"

I winced. Was the fact that I was showered and coifed and sporting a seldom-worn black wool dress so very unusual? So very new?

Vonette's brilliant red hair was more disheveled than usual, but it just might have been the way it clashed with the purple Ultrasuede hostess gown.

She said in a confidential tone, "I got a batch of margaritas going. Want one before you see Fritz?"

I was tempted. I was about to see a doctor whom half the town thought I had tried to kill, and yet who merited something, according to an anonymous flower sender. Moreover, in a few hours I was going out on my first date in five years with the cop investigating the case. If I succumbed to the buzz from the first hit of salt, lime, and tequila, then it would be numerous margaritas later before the thirst left and the headache began. By that time I'd be knee-deep in egg rolls and moo-shu pork with my head swimming like the shreds of yolk in egg drop soup. This dismal prognosis made me ask for coffee.

Vonette, on the other hand, professed no worry about either Oriental cuisine or the hangover to come. I followed her out to the cavernous kitchen. She waved her free hand gaily as she beeped microwave buttons to heat water for coffee. After a long swig of greenish liquid she started to talk.

"I just don't know what to do with him being home. He's fussing and yapping all day about Lord knows what. That John Richard can't see all his patients. That they need him over there. The practice, the practice. Yappety yap. That some doctor on TV is an idiot. Lord! I wished they'd have given him an injection to make him shut up!"

"I know he's dedicated to his work," I said, thinking of Patty Sue and her mandatory twice-weekly appointments. "How soon before he's back in shape?"

"Tomorrow. Thanks be to God." She paused and

looked at my basket for the first time. "Now look what you've brought. Aren't you just so sweet."

I explained the basket's contents and opened the refrigerator to put in the cake with cream cheese. The food of a noncook littered the shelves. Fancy sliced deli ham and smoked salmon, herring in sour cream, and little nibbled packages of Brie and Samsoe and Port Salut vied for space with beer and wine and every imaginable kind of mixer. It again occurred to me, as it had so many times, that John Richard had married a woman who could cook because he had been raised by one who could not.

"May I see Fritz?" I asked.

She nodded. "Just wait here a sec," she said. "Let me go see if he minds. He probably won't, but you know how ornery he can be. He was talking about taking a shower, so it might just be a little bit."

"I'll wait in the study," I announced, and slipped into the paneled room off the kitchen.

When Vonette had padded off, I slowly opened the drawers of the study desk. Take your shower, Fritz. My heart was knocking loudly and I felt cold. Vonette was not returning immediately. The business has to reopen, I said to myself. Schulz doesn't need to know about this. Start investigating.

Apparently Vonette liked to organize as little as she liked to cook. Letters and papers and photographs were crammed into each of the small drawers like dressing in a too-small turkey. I could feel blood pounding in my throat and ears. I did not know what I was looking for or how I would know when I found it.

There wouldn't be time to read any letters or study any bills, but perhaps I could get some names, something like that. Threats, I told myself, people who don't like him. That's what you're looking for. But would something be here? Would a doctor even keep that kind of thing at home? What about his office?

I came to a box of what looked like old photographs.

There was my unmistakable ex-husband, charming in a sailor suit at about age six. And there he was again in front of a birthday cake, about to blow out four candles. Behind him in the picture was an adolescent girl—a babysitter? Then there was another picture of the same girl, by herself this time in one of those old-fashioned stiff photo portraits done in high schools. She wore a bouffant hairdo with the ends of her hair flipped up. In large looping feminine handwriting were the words "Dear Mom, No matter what, I'm still your baby." And unsigned. As I stared at the photo I thought there was something familiar about it, something I couldn't quite place. The girl was not someone I knew or had ever known. It was not Laura Smiley. But I had seen a picture of this face before somewhere, maybe from when I was married to John Richard. Fat chance I'd have of him telling me who it was.

I crept quickly into the kitchen and slid the picture into my purse. I was heating up a fresh cup of water for instant coffee when Vonette wobbled back and leaned on the counter before pouring herself another margarita.

"He's just on the phone right now with John Richard," she said. "Let's give him a couple more minutes. You know how he hates being interrupted."

I nodded and looked at Vonette, whose coppery toopoufed hair shone in the afternoon light. I really knew little about her. When we got together with the senior Kormans at holidays and other times, John Richard had silently ignored his mother as she began to drink and make outrageous statements. Fritz never seemed to be paying much attention to her either. I felt like a one-woman listening team, saying "uh-huh" and "I know what you mean," and wishing I could get her into a residential treatment program for alcoholics. But she had never told me much about anything personal. Her diatribes were against people in the church she didn't like, or what was wrong with the school system, the highway department, or the Republican party.

"Vonette," I said, "do you know who put that stuff into Fritz's coffee?"

She turned away and opened the freezer door of the refrigerator. "Nope," she said without looking at me. "Just like I told that cop." She brought out a can of frozen limeade and started to peel off the plastic tab.

"But you must know who his enemies are," I persisted. "You must know who at the funeral didn't like him."

She dug hard into the frozen concentrate with a metal spoon and said, "Enemies? C'mon, honey. What do you think this is, a war?"

"What about his patients? Please, Vonette," I begged, "help me with this. I can't make enough money to support Arch and myself without the catering business, and the police have shut me down hard. You must know something."

Finally she turned to face me. "Goldy," she said, "I don't. Well, leastwise not that much. And after all that's happened—"

She shrugged and began to run water to dilute the lime concentrate. She said, "I don't really want to know."

"After all *what* has happened, Vonette? You mean Fritz and the rat poison?"

She threw the can of water against the side of the sink. "Goddamn but I've got a headache. If you want to see Fritz, Goldy honey, just go on back. You need money, call me later. But I gotta go lie down now." And she tottered out of the kitchen before I had a chance to say anything.

Great. Something had happened. Thinking about it gave Vonette a headache. And now I had to face Fritz alone. I picked up my basket.

"Well hello, Goldy," said Fritz after I had knocked and been admitted to their enormous bedroom suite done in pink, green, and white. "Or should I say Little Red Riding Hood?"

I didn't know where Vonette had gone to lie down. Fritz was propped up with at least half a dozen pillows behind him. His almost-bald head shone like a baby's bum in the gray light from the television, which had a picture but no volume. The newspaper, a tray with dishes and cups, and the remote control for the television were spread out around his lap. He was wearing pale blue pajamas covered with tiny dark blue fleurs de lis. A French king in repose, sans wig.

I stared at him. He was a good-looking man. There are people who age badly and people like Fritz, who age beautifully. The silver chest hair peeking out from the V of his pajama top matched the silver hair above his ears. His face was radiant with the fine-boned handsomeness that had been inherited by the man I had loved for eight years.

"Just pull up a chair," he said, "and look, you've brought me something. Now John Richard would say I shouldn't eat anything you bring me." He winked after I had settled stiffly on the side of a chaise longue. "You know what I said to him? I said, Son, don't you worry about it. Goldy and I get along just great. Don't we?"

I nodded, described the various things in the basket, and told him about the cake in the refrigerator. He thanked me and then there was a pause while soap opera characters ranted silently on the flickering screen.

"Well," I lied, "Patty Sue says hello."

"Does she?" His eyes sparkled. "Great gal. Marvelous patient. She must be such a help for you."

I didn't want to appear difficult and disagree. "Well," I said finally. "Well, well." I had to get out of here. I was beginning to have a headache myself, and I was meeting Schulz shortly. I smiled at Fritz and said, "So John Richard still thinks I did this to you?"

Fritz sat up straight in bed and screwed up his face into a menacing grimace. He shook his head. His eyebrows formed a bushy line just above his nose, and his mouth was set downward over the clean-cut jaw.

"Don't you worry about this, Goldy, you hear?"

"Okay," I said, moving my knees back and forth. The

wool was making them itch. "I really am sorry this happened to you. I still do think of us as being sort of related." There was an uncomfortable silence. "Maybe I'd better go." I stood up to leave. "Hope you feel better," I said as I opened the bedroom door.

"Don't fret about John Richard," Fritz said with a smile, full of charm. I nodded, speechless again. Fritz's face relaxed suddenly, and he gave a slight laugh. " 'After all, son,' I told him, 'you're the only one standing to gain if I go.' " He laughed again, somewhat wildly.

"Well, bye now," I said as I started down the hall.

"I said, 'Son, look here!' " he yelled after me. " 'Get Goldy out of your mind, will you? If I die, she doesn't inherit the practice. You do!' "

CHAPTER 8

Despite its name, the Dragon's Breath Chinese Restaurant was not strictly Szechuan. In a small town a food place could not afford to alienate those with milder tastes, so the proprietor offered Cantonese dishes in addition to those made with vinegar and mustard and red pepper. This was good, since my own feeling was that spicy cooking was better left to the Mexicans. Whether Tom Schulz had mild tastes I did not know. Asking me out to dinner indicated something to the contrary.

The restaurant's entrance was carved in the shape of a dragon's head. Coming through the mouth-door with its solid inverted-pyramid teeth, I always had a feeling of sympathy for Jonah. During the restaurant's remodeling, so the story went, a local sculptor had created this monstrosity in exchange for a year's free Chinese food. Poor man, I always thought, he must have been terribly hungry.

Inside, sparkling polygonal lights flashed and winked off ornately framed mirrors, pots of glass flowers, and shiny red plastic booths. From the kitchen came the beckoning sizzle of stir-fried meat. The Dragon's Breath, I remembered while threading through the tables, also served wonderful shrimp-stuffed egg rolls and homemade almond cookies. Two years ago I had begged for the almond cookie recipe and received it once the smiling cook understood my question. Then I had pressed candied cherries in the centers instead of almonds and served them to clients at Christmas.

Christmas parties, perish the thought. Much work, more income. And it was in the power of Investigator Tom Schulz to say whether I would be able to start planning for them.

"You're frowning," he said when I slid into the booth opposite him. He smiled with irrepressible pleasure, and did a respectful half stand. Seated again, he sighed.

"Mad already," he said. "That's a bad sign. What's making Miss Goldy irritable now?"

I couldn't help noticing how his gray houndstooth jacket hugged his shoulders, how deftly he moved his bulk around. There was something comforting about his large presence. He unfurled an enormous white napkin to cover a nubby burgundy sweater. It was, I reflected, an unexpectedly attractive outfit for a cop.

"Thinking about the Christmas parties I may not be giving," I said while he poured tea. "Unless you, we, get this poisoning incident cleared up. Maybe you can pinpoint my ex-husband." I told him about the inheritance configuration.

"Don't you think if a doctor really wanted to poison somebody, he'd do it right? And not in front of a bunch of people?" He went on, still grinning. "Tell me about your Christmas parties, so I can work up an appetite. Maybe talking about food will cheer you up."

I described the almond-turned-cherry cookies as well as the fragrant gingerbread houses I modeled after the hostess's own home. I told him I made a lot of money on these affairs, money that I needed.

He said, "I have never seen a woman so worried about her livelihood." Ordinarily I would have taken offense at such a statement, but his green eyes were soft and kind, the tilt of his head sympathetic.

"I have to support Arch and me," I said. "My ex-husband's willingness to pay child support on time is tenuous at best. I need to give parties to survive." I fingered the thick jade-colored glass leaves of the table's centerpiece. "There's something else, though."

"Something else."

"Well." I felt suddenly uncomfortable, as if I were offering an explanation when none was needed. "I love my job. It fills a hole. It's hard to have it taken away. It's like the hole's ripped open."

"It won't be for long," he said in a low voice. "I just have that feeling. Go on about the parties."

"One time," I said, "I actually did do a Christmas party for free. For the church. I was still teaching Sunday school, trying to carry on this normal life. Then John Richard started seeing a soprano in the choir. He even nuzzled up to Miss Vocal Cords during the coffee hour. It was sickening." I stopped talking, sipped tea. "I remember the Sunday school party, though. Making miniature baby Jesuses out of meringue kept me up half the night. The kids loved them."

"So you're a churchgoer?" he asked, surprised.

"Not anymore," I replied, picking up my menu. "Let's get on with this, okay?"

"My goodness, you make it sound like being with me is torture." He smoothed out his sweater and perused the menu. "Why don't I order and surprise you? Give you a break from being in charge of the food."

The sleepless nights, the worry, the cooking for and visiting with the Kormans—all these had made me too tired to argue. About the meal, anyway. The waitress arrived and I asked for sherry. Tom Schulz ordered scotch.

Then our food waiter appeared and Schulz ordered egg rolls, a pu pu platter, hot and sour soup, steamed trout, pork with broccoli and bamboo shoots, moo-shu shrimp, and red-cooked chicken.

I said, "How many more people are coming to dinner?"

Schulz looked at me silently for a minute, then stuck his chin out.

"Just relax. Okay, Goldy?" The perpetual grin. "We're going to have a nice meal. We're going to talk. I like you, but you sure don't make it easy. Try to remember we're trying to help each other."

"Is that so? Well guess what, I wouldn't give you a nickel for the entire Furman County Sheriff's Department."

The drinks arrived and Schulz sipped his scotch.

"Well," he said, "now we're all clear where we stand."

"It's Tuesday," I replied, "and this thing happened Saturday and what have you found out? I need my business reopened and all you have to offer is strange links and barbecued pu pu."

"Take it easy," he said. "Remember our chat with your son saying the Kormans and Laura Smiley didn't get along? I made that call out to Illinois. Turns out Korman senior was not exactly your universally loved medical man. Before he left twenty years ago, that is. Guy I talked to said there's more, but I need to talk to the fellow who was involved in the investigation, and he's gone to a department in another town. Happens to cops in small towns, you know. You arrest a city councilman's son for drunk driving. The next day you start looking for a new job."

I grunted as the banquet of appetizers arrived.

"What was the investigation about?" I asked.

Schulz offered me the plate of egg rolls and I took one. He dipped one in brown sinus-clearing Chinese mustard and crunched his way through it before starting in on the skewered beef.

"Don't know that yet," he said as he pulled his

eyebrows into a line. "Files twenty years old are put on microfilm, then into storage. Have to have clearance and a microfilm operator to look them up. They're working on it, don't worry. They're going to call me back. Our friend Laura Smiley was involved somehow, though. That's all this guy could remember."

"Is that it?"

"Listen. When you do this kind of research, you've got to talk to the detective who worked the case. Even if they read me that file over the phone, it won't tell as much as the cop involved in it could. And I'm going to find him." He ladled out the soup, then said, "There's something else that may be related. Your little friend Trixie has a record for assault. A recent one."

"*What?*"

He shrugged and swallowed some soup, then gestured with the porcelain spoon. "She was fighting with a neighbor over a dog or something. He, the dog, was barking and driving her nuts. That's what she claimed. So she hauled off and threw one rock after another at the animal until it ran under its owner's deck. Then the fellow who owned the dog came flying out shrieking at Trixie and she beaned him with a hunk of quartz the size of a football." He chuckled. "That woman must be damned strong. Poor bastard had to have eighteen stitches."

I had stopped eating. "What in the world happened?"

"Eat your soup before it gets cold. She pleaded guilty and got a suspended sentence. No priors, and she said because she was pregnant she was on edge or some such."

"Pregnant?"

"Her baby was stillborn a month later," he said. "You said you hadn't seen her around for a while and that's why. I talked to her husband. She had high blood pressure, in spite of all that exercising. High blood pressure, excitable temperament, high-risk pregnancy."

So that was what Marla had meant by *You're back*. And Trixie's mood. I wished I'd known. Poor Trixie.

"That's as far as I've gotten," he said. "But I am working on it, just wanted to let you know. Oh look, here comes our waiter."

I sighed. At this rate, we might have the answers to what happened last Saturday by Valentine's Day.

Our food arrived. Schulz astonished me by ladling enormous amounts onto my plate. Then, muttering something that sounded like "wimps," he waved away the chopsticks proffered by the waiter. He nodded to me before attacking his trout. I smiled, remembering John Richard's selfishness with food. If he ever did serve me first, it was always in small portions. Usually, though, he served himself large quantities and then passed me what was left while he started eating.

I looked from my plate to Schulz's.

A look of worry crossed his face. "What's the matter," he said, "don't you like it?"

"It's fine," I said, attempting to get up some pork with chopsticks. "It's great. Really."

He chuckled between mouthfuls. "I'll bet you just cook so much you get tired of food, don't you?"

"Oh no," I said. I speared the pork. "Honestly. I'm just preoccupied."

We ate in silence for a while, making occasional comments on the size and freshness of the fat shrimp, the perfect seasoning of the trout. Again I felt an odd—because unused—trust melting my resistance.

After a while I said, "When I went to visit Fritz and Vonette today, I kind of looked around. I thought I might be able to figure out who their enemies were if I sort of went through their desk."

He washed down his bite with some tea and said, "You sort of went through their desk? When I said you could help, I didn't say you could burgle the place, for God's sake."

I laughed in spite of myself. "Well, listen up, copper," I went on. "I'm going to go through some of Laura Smiley's stuff, too."

"Christ."

"Look," I said, "I appreciate your making long-distance calls to find people who have moved and files that are on microfilm." I smiled. "You even got over your reluctance to bring me in on the case. But I need more if we're going to go forward." Then I asked, as much for myself as for him, "Why do you think I'm having dinner with you?"

"Miss Goldy," he said while pouring me some more tea, "excuse me. I thought we were here at least partially for social reasons."

"Dating a suspect? Is that legal?"

He held the teapot in midair. My face was warm.

He said, "Tell you what. Let me worry about what's legal. I don't go breaking into folks' desks and *stuff*, for instance. But I wouldn't have brought you in, as you call it, unless it was legal. I can share information with you about what the department is doing, if I think it'll aid the investigation."

"So what you're saying is that being with me is social *and* helpful."

He nodded. "Investigators can get information from any source within the law. Which does not include breaking and entering, I might add. It might include keeping closer tabs on your son, however."

I gave him an absolutely sour look.

He finished a bite of pork and shook his head. "Just precautionary. Find out if he's really nuts about these games. Most kids aren't. But maybe there's something he's not telling me, or not telling you." He thought. "There're people involved in this who might talk more easily to you, is all."

"What kind of information do you expect to get from me?"

He shrugged. "Don't mean to offend you, Goldy, but you know how women talk—"

"You're offending me."

"Tell you what," he said, "let me try to make it up to you by taking you out to dinner again."

"No, I don't think so . . ."

"The movies?"

"No . . ."

"Bronco game?"

I hesitated.

"They're looking awfully good this year. Beat Green Bay last Sunday. Department has a pair of tickets. Let me know which Sunday. When you're free, that is."

"Wait," I said. I felt my head swimming. I wasn't ready for all this. I needed to talk to my group. "I am not looking for a social life," I told him. "For now I just want to solve this crime and start making money again."

"Then let's solve it."

"How? We've, I've, got a huge problem, and you're acting like getting some information on this is some long-term project."

He waved to the waiter for our check.

"What do you want to know?" he asked.

I took a deep breath. "Okay. A, someone tried to poison Fritz. B, that same someone did it in Laura Smiley's house after Laura Smiley's funeral. C, nobody seems to know why Laura killed herself and she didn't leave a note to tell us, and D, Laura and the Kormans didn't get along. Now E, you're telling me, this history between them goes way back. So maybe the two events, Laura dying and Fritz being poisoned, are related." I closed my eyes and nodded. It sounded logical, didn't it? "I told you before, it might help to know what that deputy coroner said about Laura Smiley's death. If she didn't leave a note, why are they calling it suicide?"

"My dear," said Schulz as he looked at the bill, "a note doesn't mean squat. I've seen suicide notes that were photocopied, for God's sake. With blood all over the room. I called the deputy coroner. She slashed her wrists, and there was no sign of a struggle, no burglary, nothing. That's what I know. We treat a suicide like a murder until we know differently. In this case, suicide was the deputy coroner's conclusion. Now granted, the guy is new. And before this he was out in some small town on the western slope." Schulz rubbed his temples.

I said, "Well, would you be willing to look into it some more? I mean if you really want to cooperate on this thing. And I'll work your women's angle. Talk it up, find out about Trixie and if the reason she works out with weights is so that she can exercise her aggression on people. Deal?"

He nodded.

"By the way," I said, "did the Health Department find anything?"

"No. It's probably like sending it down to the crime lab." When I looked puzzled, he said, "You've got to tell them, look for this, look for that. If you've got some white powder that's cocaine and you say, Check for heroin, they'll send your coke back to you and say, It's not heroin. Same principle."

I smiled. "Thanks for dinner."

He said, "Hey. Something else. I need to know more about Vonette. Something's wrong there, I don't know what. And you're welcome. Let's do it again soon."

I nodded, although eliciting more information from Vonette was unappealing. I took a fortune cookie from the tray that held the check.

"Look," he said as he ate his cookie and tossed away the fortune, "we may have a bigger problem. Especially if whoever put the stuff in Fritz's coffee is really trying to kill him."

"Why is that?"

"Because," he said patiently, "if somebody's trying to kill him, they're going to try again."

"At least they're not going to do it at one of my catered functions," I replied, then remembered the Halloween party in three weeks. I wasn't actually being paid for it, just getting my club dues. Still. Better not mention that to Schulz, stickler for legality that he was.

"We'll have all this cleared up soon," Schulz said confidently. "Trust the sheriff's department."

I unfolded the paper fortune in my hand.

It said, "Faith is your greatest present need."

Like Schulz, I tossed it.

At home I noticed miserably that the leftover spaghetti mess in the sink matched the red and white decor of the kitchen. Honestly, that Patty Sue. If she could run all afternoon, why couldn't she make a minimal effort to cook or clean? I tried to remember myself at twenty. Had I really never had the big picture of running a house before I had a child? Probably not.

The house was quiet. Before going to bed I crept down the hall to make sure Arch was safely asleep. This had been my habit since he was born. John Richard had given me the title Helicopter Mom: I hovered.

Arch was not asleep but was murmuring excitedly on the phone.

"That sounds great," he was saying. "But what about the potion?"

A pause.

"No, you have to use milkwort for that. It's all that's available for lethal missions." He listened for a moment, and then said, "You mean I'm going to have to find that, too? Don't you know anything about getting rid of opponents?"

Another pause. I felt a tightness in my chest. Blood pounded in my ears.

"Oh, Todd!" said Arch, irritated. "I can't believe I'm going to have to find the weapon *and* do the spell *and* put together the potion. I'm not going to have time for all that."

I knocked forcefully on Arch's partially opened door.

Perhaps it was just the hammering in my head that made the noise thunderous. Then I swung the door open all the way without getting an answer.

He had hung up the phone.

"What is going on?" I demanded.

"Mom," he said. He looked at me, hair disheveled, glasses askew. They seemed incongruous next to his baseball-print flannel pajamas. In his lap were a guidebook and folder for his games. "You're home!" A pause. "Uh, I stayed up."

"Yes," I said, suddenly feeling out of place. "I just came in to see if you were asleep yet. I heard you on the phone. Was it for your game?"

He turned back to the papers in his lap. "Yes," he said impatiently. "But I'll call him back tomorrow."

"Okay," I said. I stood by his door, unable to put words together.

"Mom?"

"Yes?"

He set his mouth in a straight line and folded his arms across his chest.

"Please," he said, "don't sneak up on me like that again."

CHAPTER 9

The next day I managed to book two cleaning jobs in the country club area, one for that day and one for the next. Since Fritz was back on his feet, I took Patty Sue to her appointment and instructed her to walk home while I went off to scrub, scour, and vacuum. I talked minimally to Arch before he left for school. If checking on him was considered sneaking up, then asking questions would be prying. I did elicit the promise that he would take me on a role-playing adventure over the weekend. It was time for me to find out what was going on with these games. Or at least try.

The house to be cleaned was one of those rambling ranch-style structures done in all-western decor right up to the walls hung with harnesses, cowboy hats, sombreros, and horseshoes. Maid service of this ranchette took six hours, which included polishing a coffee table shaped like a flatbed wagon. The worst part was that I kept expecting Dale Evans to pop out from behind one of the numerous bathroom doors. She didn't, and when I was done I was very glad to receive forty-eight dollars in cash.

After making a run to a janitorial supply house in west Denver I picked up some groceries and came home to give Patty Sue her first lesson in housecleaning for fun and profit.

"I'll do whatever you say," she said, but it was without enthusiasm.

"Need to be safe first," I said, as I Magic-Markered my name on the gallon bottle of phenol-based cleaning fluid I would use at the athletic club. Then I drew a skull and crossbones on the plastic bottle's backside. Industrial-strength concentrations were much cheaper than anything in the supermarket, but they were dangerous to have around.

"I really don't know much about cleaning or chemicals," Patty Sue said. She wrinkled her nose at the plastic bottle.

"Look," I said, looking directly in her eyes, "if you want to be independent, the most important thing is to be financially self-supporting. Housecleaning is a way. Not glamorous, but reliable."

"Yes I know, but . . ."

"But what?"

"Oh," she said, turning away, "just never mind. Just teach me about it, go ahead."

Begin with proper dilutions, I began, pointing to the ten-to-one and twenty-to-one lines on the plastic spray bottles. When I finished, she gave me another wordless look, as if I'd taught her how to construct an atomic bomb in twenty minutes. I ignored it and cheerily assigned her Arch's bathroom to practice on. This was a particularly dirty trick. But chiseling off all that dried spaghetti demanded retribution. I disappeared to answer the phone.

"How's my little darling doing?" asked Patty Sue's mother over the crackle of long distance. One of her regular checkup calls.

"She's working hard," I said truthfully. "As a matter of

fact, she's working right now, so can I have her call you back? Collect?"

"Oh yes, of course," said the mother, disappointed. "I was just worried if she was eating and sleeping all right."

It was difficult for me to see if I in fact overprotected Arch. But I could sure see it in other mothers. Would Arch end up like Patty Sue if I kept worrying about him? This was not a question to dwell on.

"She's eating and sleeping fine," I said. "In fact, she's doing lots of both. And exercising, working, and going to the doctor, so everything's just peachy."

"I called the doctor's office to see how she was doing," she said.

"And?"

"They said she's not improving."

"Well," I said, impatient, "these things take time."

"I'm sorry, I don't want to trouble you."

"You're not."

Next I phoned a real estate agent.

"Kathleen," I said breathily when I got through to the one person I knew at Mountain Realty. "I'm interested in buying Laura Smiley's house."

"Oh, Goldy, the kitchen is marvelous," replied Kathleen. "You'll love it."

I knew darn well that the kitchen had minimal counter space and old appliances, but never mind. While Patty Sue grunted and scrubbed and rinsed in Arch's bathroom, Kathleen and I made an appointment to go through the house the next day. She said that since Laura had left the house to her aunt it would be a while before we could close, but I told her not to worry, it would be a while before I had any money.

Next I phoned Marla and asked her to fabricate a real estate emergency for the next morning so I could be rid of Kathleen once we got to Laura's. She gleefully acquiesced. Marla hated real estate agents.

It was still unseasonably warm for October when Patty Sue and I loaded the van the next morning. Overhead the sky was a deep periwinkle blue, as if a celestial housecleaner had spilled a bottle of bluing agent to the four corners of the earth. A few aspen leaves clung to the tops of slender bone-white branches: the last stage of autumnal undress. I swung the van around a corner toward the house Patty Sue was going to clean and wondered if we would have Indian summer through Halloween instead of our usual late-October snow. After I parked, Patty Sue gingerly pulled out all the cleaning equipment while I promised to pick her up in a few hours.

"I heard your ex was getting married again," Kathleen greeted me when I ground the van to a halt at the top of Laura Smiley's driveway. I tried to find my tongue. If Marla had already put in her call, I would be out of luck.

Kathleen was standing beside a silver Mercedes with a REAL ESTATE FOR SALE sign emblazoned on the driver side door. Surely there were better ways of advertising than wrecking a 450 SL. A sudden beeping interrupted my stare. Kathleen slipped back into her car to answer the mobile phone. There was much heated talking. Kathleen set her fine features into a frown.

"Listen," she said when she was back out of the car, "I've got a problem with an appointment from Denver showing up early. How about if I just give you the key and come back to finish showing you the house in about half an hour?" She smiled hopefully, and I blessed dear old Marla.

I knew that Kathleen knew she would get her commission as long as she showed me the house at some point, so I smiled back and nodded, seeing as how I had no intention of ever being the supplier of the commission.

"Oh," she said over the roar of the Mercedes, "one more thing. I told that aunt I'd do a change-of-address form for Laura but things have been so crazy." She rolled her eyes as if this explained everything. "Anyway. I've been taking the mail in and putting it on the kitchen table when I show the house. Take it for me this time, will you?" she hollered.

I nodded as she gunned her engine away. Would I? You bet.

A breeze lifted the black smoke from the Mercedes' tailpipe and dispersed it into a stand of chokecherry bushes heavy with scarlet berries. Once the car was gone the wind was the only noise. It whispered and sighed through the pines and spruces and aspens of the hilly neighborhood. I put the house key into my pocket and walked over to Laura's rural delivery mailbox, the only kind we have in Aspen Meadow besides those at the post office. It creaked open after I pulled on the rusty cover. Inside was a small assortment of bills and ads. No letters.

I looked through the bills. Here were people who thought Laura was still alive. Public Service of Colorado, a dentist whose name I did not recognize, a doctor whose name I did. I put the mail into my purse.

As I started down the sloping driveway to Laura's house, the wind kicked up again and sanded my eyes with dirt. Dread, sudden and unexpected, throttled me. I stopped and stared at the small house with its green-stained paneling and redwood deck.

The wind stopped. Everything was very still.

I pursed my lips and braced myself, then trotted the rest of the way down the driveway. After all, I wasn't the first Goldilocks to go into an empty house. But at the open garage I came up short again. Had this car been here before? It was familiar.

Then I remembered: it was Laura's blue Volvo, which I had seen many times in the elementary school parking lot. It called attention to itself via its blaring bumper stickers: WOMEN MAKE GREAT LEADERS, YOU'RE FOLLOWING ONE and HAVE YOU HUGGED YOUR TEACHER TODAY? and EASY DOES IT. I did not know where the car had been the day of the funeral, but someone had put it back now.

I stepped around it carefully. There were some nicks in the flat blue paint, and the wheels sported a set of new, but muddy, radials. I did not know what I was looking for, except that it did seem odd that someone who wanted to kill herself would prepare for winter with the purchase of new tires. The doors were unlocked, but there was a decal on the window that read This Car Protected by Ungo. I had had one of those alarms installed in the van, just in case a guest at a catered function tried to filch a few dozen filets. On the side window I saw the small piece of plastic with its wire lead. If a thief tried to jam his way in through the window when the car was locked, his eardrums would never survive.

We had had a rash of car thefts in Aspen Meadow over the past six months. The rumor was that a ring of teens took the cars and a smart mechanic managed to get them fenced down in Denver before the cops could catch him. This was another indication of unsuccessful law enforcement from the sheriff's department which I would have to bring to Schulz's attention.

I hugged myself in the cool air of the garage. Outside, the wind whipped and shot through the trees. Time to go into the house. But not yet. The car ought to be able to tell me something. I walked around to the hood. There was a smell of either exhaust or oil in the garage. Odd. If the car had been sitting here for a week, shouldn't things be odorless and blanketed with dust?

But then I noticed that the clay-red mud was fresh and wet, and that it clung to the car's grille as well as the tires. I reached out to touch the hood.

It was warm.

Well, well. I clenched my teeth. Catering was safer than this, and sometimes you couldn't be sure about catering. I needed to be quiet, I knew that. In fact, I needed to skedaddle.

But my feet stayed cemented to the cold garage floor. I

had come here. I was going to go into Laura's house, and in two days I was going to go through Laura's locker. Kathleen had left me at the top of the driveway; if there was someone in the house, that someone probably would be unaware of my arrival. I was going in. And if I saw somebody I would scream bloody murder and apologize later. I could even arm myself, the way they did on TV. Unfortunately there was no .22 slung across my chest, and I was at least fifteen steps from the kitchen and the nearest meat cleaver.

I looked around the garage. There was a large workbench. Maybe the woman who claimed to be a leader had bought herself a nice heavy hammer or wrench or even a drill. My feet made gritty echoes as I tiptoed over.

The bench was large and long and had two shelves above it and one below. Paint thinner, caulking, and a tool box rested on the first shelf. The tool box yielded a small wrench. I was about to enter the house with it when I saw the edge of something else on the top shelf. I reached up.

It was a BB gun. I recognized this type of firearm from the time I had volunteered as a counselor at Arch's Cub Scout day camp. Many local people used them to shoot bothersome blue jays or rabid squirrels. I ducked down to check the shelf underneath, but there was only a large cardboard box marked BB's.

I was not going to load the gun. For one thing I couldn't exactly remember how to do it. It looked menacing enough, a lot like a rifle really, and I would just have to do a good impersonation of Annie Oakley if the need arose.

I crept through the unlocked door to the kitchen but stopped short before heading through to the living room. In that room, someone was rustling papers.

My body went numb. The unloaded BB gun felt cold and inadequate. I backed up noiselessly, grabbed a long knife off a wall mount above the counter, and turned back toward the garage.

The blue Volvo was still there. I locked its doors, jammed the knife into the edge of the window and pushed down with all one hundred twenty pounds.

The alarm split the air. I jerked the knife out and ran back around to the front of the house.

The door between the kitchen and the garage banged open. After a moment the alarm stopped. Whoever was down there had the keys to the car, and wanted the alarm off so as not to attract attention.

From the top of the driveway came an unexpected female voice, followed by a robe and a head of hair neatly rolled in cylinders.

"Hoohoo! Kathleen, is that you, dear?"

The Volvo engine started and revved. From where I was crouched behind a thicket of chokecherry bushes I could not see who was driving. Worse, the driver appeared to be wearing a ski mask.

"Hey!" yelled the robed woman to the car.

The driver ignored her and gunned the Volvo back up the driveway. I wanted to stand to get a better look, but I didn't want the driver to see that I was the one who had set off the alarm.

"Kathleen!" the woman in the driveway was calling again, now that the Volvo had gone. "Are you in there?"

"Excuse me," I said in a loud voice over the chokecherry bushes. "Hello!"

When I had pushed my way through the underbrush and up to her, I learned the caller was Laura's neighbor, Betsy Goldsmith. She had come out because of the noise, but did not know who could be driving Laura's car, or why. Her husband was a pilot, she added, and since they had no children they traveled frequently and didn't really know too much about what was going on in the neighborhood. She did know, however, that her neighbor had died, although she had missed the funeral.

"Do you know who was in that car?" she asked me. "It

looked like Laura's. Why would someone be over here with it now?"

"I really don't know," I said, then added, "and I sure do wish I did."

"Well, it certainly is strange—" she said, then gave me a quizzical look.

"I'm here to see the house," I told her, before introducing myself.

"The caterer!" she said. An embarrassed smile flooded her face, as if she had met a famous person at the Laundromat. "Well, I certainly hope you buy that house. Most people would be spooked, you know. Don't want to live in a house where there's been a death."

"Did you know Laura?" I asked.

"Oh, you know," she said vaguely, "we waved to each other. In winter my husband would help her shovel out, sometimes give her a lift into town when that car of hers wasn't working, which was a lot." She paused. "Maybe that's who it was, her new mechanic. I knew she had someone new working on the car, maybe that person was looking for her."

By looking through her papers?

"Laura and I gave each other cookies at Christmas," Betsy added bleakly.

"She was my son's teacher," I put in.

"Uh-huh, well," she said, starting back up to her house, "nice meeting you." She turned back almost as an afterthought. "You don't know who the new mechanic was, do you?"

"No, sure don't. Say," I began as if it had just occurred to me, "you didn't see Laura right before she died, did you? I'm, just, wondering how she was."

"We were gone that Monday the teacher came over and found her," she said plaintively. "That last time I saw her was—" she thought for a moment "—the Saturday before."

"But that—" I stopped. If Betsy did not know that Saturday was when the deputy coroner had said Laura was supposed to have died, I was not going to remind her and chance getting her spooked.

"I remember," Betsy went on, "because I was out planting bulbs that day, trying to get them in before the cold weather. Laura walked out of her garage." She stopped to point. "She waved to me as she came up the driveway. 'Car broken again?' I called down to her, and she said, 'You bet.' And that was the last time I saw her."

"Did you know where she was going?"

"No," said Betsy. "Errands, probably, since she taught during the week. Then later I heard a car and I figured she'd walked to the new repair place and picked it up. But I guess not if someone's trying to return it now."

I shook my head.

Betsy said, "Oh, well. When I was out planting the bulbs was the last time I saw her. I don't know who her friends were," she added and turned away again.

I tried to think of how to put the next question before she was out of earshot.

"Kind of odd," I said to her back. "You know. You'd think that the cops would have been interested in you hearing a car on Saturday, huh?"

Betsy turned her rollered head and robed body so she could give me a long look. "How come you're so curious? You're more interested than the cops were. Anyway," she said with a final sigh, "I don't think I told them about hearing her come back later in her car. It doesn't matter now, does it? You don't kill yourself because you have a car that's always quitting." And off she trudged to her house, a two-story affair with several decks and a wide expanse of glass.

I walked quickly into Laura's house, through the kitchen and into the living room. There was an opened box sitting on the blue rug. Its flaps stuck out at angles, as if someone had tried to close it in haste.

That'll teach you to break in when I'm trying to break in.
Lucky for me, in a way, that the cops didn't suspect that
Laura's case was a homicide. They could have secured the
house. This way all the burglars in town could drop in at a
moment's notice.

The box contained bundles of letters and postcards to
Laura. I tried to read through at least one in each bundle,
skimming because I knew Kathleen would be back soon.
Some were from vacationing teachers whose names I recognized. Some were from Illinois, from people whose
names were unfamiliar. I pulled out a pad from my purse
and wrote down the names, Singleton and Carey and
Ludmiller and Druckman. There was even a bundle from
the aunt who had paid the funeral expenses. The first letter was full of news of nephews traveling and a house being redone. None of this was helping me with a possible
link between Laura's death and the attempted poisoning
of Fritz Korman, so I piled all the letters back into the box
and pushed it into a cupboard.

Above the cupboard was a shelf of books. Beside it was
the wall of photographs that I had briefly noted during the
funeral reception. Laura's library reflected sociopolitical
issues of the Sixties and Seventies: Susan Brownmiller's
book on rape, works of Tillie Olsen and Adrienne Rich,
Pacifism in the Nuclear Age and, of course, *Our Bodies, Ourselves.*
In addition there were some books on alcoholism, including *One Day at a Time in Al-Anon.* To my surprise there was
also a copy of *The Dungeon Masters Guide,* which I removed
and flipped through. No name on the flyleaf, but I made a
mental note to ask Arch about it.

The photos on the wall were of grinning family groups
and Laura, white teeth, skin tanned to nut brown, and hair
summer-sun bleached. She was either clad in hiking gear
and leaning against a boulder, or posing with the families
by a lake or cabin. Some photos were signed with the same
names I had seen in the box. In the bottom-left corner of
this display was one picture that gave me a jolt.

It was another youthful photograph of the girl whose picture had been in the Kormans' desk. Now I remembered why that picture had looked familiar to me—I had seen it in this house the day of the funeral. I immediately removed it from the wall and slid the picture out of the frame. On the back was written "Love to a teacher who is smiley (ha-ha) no matter what! B. Hollenbeck."

I put this in my purse and tried not to imagine what Investigator Tom Schulz would say about taking things from Laura's house. I trotted into the bedroom to look around there, if only to figure out where someone could stash some rat poison until an opportune moment presented itself at a postfuneral party. The bedroom was small and neat, with dresses and skirts hung in the closet and a crocheted throw folded carefully at the bottom of the bed. The bathroom was next. Its rows of Jhirmack hair products and Vitabath shower gel and body cream indicated a person who wanted to look and smell good. The medicine cabinet yielded some soap and cream samples as well as a prescription bottle announcing itself as Ornade, a cold medicine I used myself in the winter months.

A car was coming down the driveway. I hurried back through the living room to the kitchen. A quick visual check of both those areas showed no evidence of my prying. The knife was missing from the wall mount. Of course, that was because I had dropped it behind the chokecherry bushes. No point in risking picking it up now and engendering questions from Kathleen.

My eye fell on the pile of old mail by the kitchen phone. I sifted through it quickly, but it was only more ads, a few bills, a postcard from the Singletons. Then I remembered my promise to Kathleen and reached into my purse for the mail I had brought in. Outside, I could hear her opening the car door. I glanced again at the three bills that had arrived that day.

The past due Public Service and dentist's bills I ignored. The third was a bill from my ex-husband and Fritz's office. This seemed very odd to me, given Arch's view that Laura did not get along with the Kormans. Maybe she was John Richard's patient. Swallowing hard, I opened the envelope. Inside was a bill for an office visit.

It was the date that gave me a start.

Laura Smiley had done errands and seen Fritz Korman on Saturday, October third.

Afterward, apparently, she had come home and killed herself.

CHAPTER 10

Ineed to talk to you," I said into the phone to Tom Schulz. I was aware that I was gasping for breath, as if I had just finished running a few miles when all I had done was pick up Patty Sue and drive home.

"What about? You having a heart attack or something?"

"Did you talk to the deputy coroner?" I demanded. "Anything new?"

"Yeah, he said that corpse just jumped out of the grave and told him all kinds of new stuff."

"Not funny."

He sighed. "The only thing I found out that I didn't know already was that there was a foreign substance in her stomach when she died. Looks as if she took some Valium before she did it, settle herself down a little bit."

"Valium?" I said quickly. "There wasn't any Valium in her medicine cabinet."

"Oh boy." He snorted. "Not in her medicine cabinet, she says. What else did you figure out *going through her stuff*? Ever occur to you that what you were doing was illegal? Her medicine cabinet. Maybe that's not where she kept it. Think of that, Detective G?"

"Cool it," I said angrily. "This is why I called you. I'll tell you what I found in my search. Another intruder was there when I got there—what do you think of that? I had to scare off burglar number one before I could do my thing. So. Did your fellow check to see if she had a prescription?"

"Just a sec, back up. You just broke into Laura's house and found someone else had broken in, too? You got a description of this person?"

"I didn't break in," I protested. "But the other person drove off in Laura's blue Volvo. Wearing a ski mask."

A groan. He said, "Great. The woman kills herself and nobody finds her for two days and once she's buried her house is like a practice area for B and E."

"You never answered my question about the coroner."

"What are you getting at?" he said in a voice edged with irritation. "You have any suspects yet? No forced entry, no sign of a struggle, no evidence of second-party involvement at all, which is what the deputy coroner concluded, by the way. You think she was murdered maybe by someone driving her car? And not only that, but whoever did her in is interested in killing Korman too, is that your theory?"

"I don't know why there was no forced entry. Could be she invited the person in, I don't know. Maybe it was someone she knew," I said to Schulz's silence. Then I asked, "Were her legs shaved? Did she have hair under her arms?"

"*What?*"

"The story is she killed herself with a razor blade. But she doesn't have any razors. At least, I didn't see any in her medicine cabinet," I added apologetically. "And guess what else? She read some feminist literature. Lots of them, us, don't believe in shaving."

Schulz said, "Well, no wonder she didn't have any

boyfriends." I tapped my foot while he laughed. "Sorry," he said, "this job gives you a strange sense of humor. Look. You can slash your wrists with a credit card if you try. We had one guy down Cottonwood Creek do just that, had a grudge against American Express. She might have bought a razor just to kill herself. She might have kept the Valium in her purse."

"Might have," I said, "might have. She was happy, she was funny, she didn't leave a note, you said so yourself."

"Yeah, I'm beginning to wish I hadn't," he muttered.

"Suicide a big surprise to all," I went on. "And then somebody, for reasons unknown, tries to poison somebody else in Laura's house after Laura's dead. *Somebody*," I added with vehemence, "maybe the same person, goes waltzing into her house looking for something after Laura's dead. And meanwhile my catering operation is down indefinitely." I stopped. Schulz, after all, was not the enemy. I said, "Tell me this. What do you need to reopen an investigation?"

"What investigation are you talking about? The one into that woman's suicide?"

"Of course."

He said, "An investigation is never closed completely unless we get a conviction of some kind. Which of course you don't with a suicide. But if you're talking about ex-huming the body—"

"Maybe I am," I said defiantly. "Maybe that's what we need to get this cleared up."

"I wish I knew how I ever got you into this."

"By closing down my business. By taking me out to dinner. By telling me I could help you. Tell me what you need to exhume the body."

"You need," he went on wearily, "some evidence you didn't have before—"

"A neighbor heard a car at Laura's house the afternoon she's supposed to have died. This was after the neighbor had seen Laura walking into town in the morning. She didn't tell the police because she thought it was Laura coming back with her car. There's more. Laura made an office visit to Fritz Korman the same day." I didn't add how I'd come upon that bit of information. Surely stealing mail was a federal offense.

Schulz took a deep breath as if to signal he needed to get off the phone. He said, "I can talk to the doctor and the neighbor, but it's not enough. You'd have to produce something like death threats against Laura. In writing, mind you. Or come up with some new physical evidence, a diary entry, a weapon, new indications somebody forced their way in. You got any of that?"

I paused. "No."

"Okay then. Let's go back to what we're supposed to be worried about, and that is who put the stuff in Korman's coffee. I found out the name of that particular rat poison. Just One Bite—how about that? I guess just one sip doesn't work. But get this, it takes more than a bite to kill a human. In fact, you could eat ten times your weight and not die. You'd need a liver transplant, but you'd live. Your slick killer of Laura is incredibly stupid when it comes to poison."

"I didn't say it was the same person," I said.

"Something else," said Schulz. "The folks down at the Poison Center say it takes thirty to sixty minutes before somebody drinking that stuff would have a real bad stomachache."

"What does that mean?" I asked. "That it could have been anybody who was around that coffee machine? Which basically means anybody?"

"That's right."

I sighed. "Doesn't exactly narrow the field."

"Goldy? Listen. I got two other homicides I'm working on. They're both higher priority than this. But I'm still trying to locate that guy in Illinois. I'll talk to the doc and the neighbor. Why don't you just take it easy for a day or so," Schulz suggested. "Think about your parties or something."

"I can't," I said. "All my parties have been canceled. Besides, tomorrow I'm going on another adventure. This time into a dungeon."

Without explanation, I hung up.

After the excitement at Laura's, a fantasy-adventure the next night promised to be a piece of cake. Or batch of cookies. Arch's all-night games generally required baked goods to accompany the popcorn and soft drinks and assorted snacks he and his friends needed to fortify themselves for their forays into lands thick with polymorphs and other-worldly creatures. Todd was coming over so we would have a threesome. A bedraggled Patty Sue had come home from a make-up appointment with Fritz (since he'd been out Monday) and begged off from a party with eleven-year-olds by announcing she wanted to sleep the entire weekend. Todd and Arch and I were going to start off with a dinner of hot dogs and homemade baked beans and finish with Arch's favorite sweet for these adventure nights, an oatmeal-raisin concoction I had dubbed Dungeon Bars.

I got out the oats and unsalted butter, then searched for brown and white sugars. Maybe I had made a mistake not to do the fantasy-role bit with Arch before. Had Laura? Had she been closer to him than I was? His behavior had gone from bothersome to worrisome, and he seemed to think I was out to get him.

I reached for the raisins and eggs and tried to remember what I knew about pre-adolescent behavior. It was normal for eleven-year-olds to distance themselves from parents. But as the single active parent, I found this hard to accept. Arch walked away while I was talking to him. He hastily hung up the phone at my approach. He refused to talk about Ms. Smiley. He never showed me his schoolwork anymore. His new teacher, Ms. Heath, was an unknown, except that she was the one who had discovered the body that fateful Monday.

I sighed and looked at my recipe card for Dungeon Bars.

That was the thing about cooking, I thought after mixing up the creamy batter and spreading it in the prepared pan. It was largely predictable. Children, spouses, and the economy were not. Maybe that was why I liked my job. When I had it.

Arch's bus was due shortly so I set the timer and stepped out into the October sunshine to walk to the stop. The air was like cotton. Sunshine splashed over bright orange and black Halloween decorations in the Main Street store windows. After a few minutes the school bus came huffing toward its stop with a great show of black diesel smoke and blinking yellow and red lights.

"Why're you meeting me, Mom?" asked Arch after the bus had chugged away.

"Just wondered how things, you know, if you, well, were ready to play tonight."

He nodded and slung his backpack over his shoulder and started to march home. In earlier years we would have spent some time looking at the accordions of crepe paper in the merchants' windows or talking about what costume he wanted for Halloween, or what candy he was hoping to get in his treats bag. Other times we would have crossed over to the creek to throw stones into the water. Now I exhaled hard to get the sour smell of diesel exhaust out of my lungs, and trudged up the hill after him.

"You know," I said as I dug out a scoop of vanilla ice cream to put on his warm Dungeon Bar, "I've been thinking about—"

"Ms. Smiley," he answered for me.

"Yes, how did you know?"

"What are we having for dinner?" he asked as he cautiously cut his first bite.

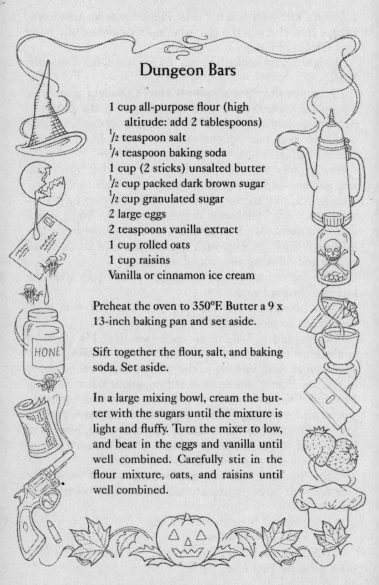

Dungeon Bars

1 cup all-purpose flour (high
    altitude: add 2 tablespoons)
1/2 teaspoon salt
1/4 teaspoon baking soda
1 cup (2 sticks) unsalted butter
1/2 cup packed dark brown sugar
1/2 cup granulated sugar
2 large eggs
2 teaspoons vanilla extract
1 cup rolled oats
1 cup raisins
Vanilla or cinnamon ice cream

Preheat the oven to 350°F. Butter a 9 x
13-inch baking pan and set aside.

Sift together the flour, salt, and baking
soda. Set aside.

In a large mixing bowl, cream the butter with the sugars until the mixture is
light and fluffy. Turn the mixer to low,
and beat in the eggs and vanilla until
well combined. Carefully stir in the
flour mixture, oats, and raisins until
well combined.

Spread in the prepared pan (batter will be thick). Smooth the top. Bake from 20 to 30 minutes, until the batter has puffed and flattened, is brown around the edges, no longer appears wet in the center, and tests done with a toothpick. Cool slightly. While warm, cut into 32 bars. Allow to cool completely on a rack. Serve with best-quality vanilla or cinnamon ice cream.

Makes 32 bars

"Beans and wieners. And don't change the subject. How did you know what I was thinking of?"

"If I eat all my dinner may I have more Dungeon Bars later?" His earnest eyes regarded me.

I said, "Sure. Have you been thinking about Ms. Smiley, too?"

He shook his head and gave a muffled "No."

"What I was thinking about," I began again, "is that it certainly is strange she didn't leave a note or letter or something. Especially since she liked to write letters. To you, for instance."

Arch narrowed his eyes at me, just a little bit, but I got the message. When he had finished his bite he said, "Maybe she did." He paused. "Leave a note."

"Do you know if she did?"

He shrugged.

"Did you know if she was sad? Or upset? Or sick? I need to know, Arch," I added gently, "because it may have something to do with someone giving your grandfather rat poison over at Ms. Smiley's house. That attempted poisoning got my business closed." I paused. "Did you know Ms. Smiley was having problems?"

"Not really."

"Arch," I said, "I found a D and D book over at Ms. Smiley's. Did you ever play with her?"

He shook his head and got up to put his dish in the sink. I thought that pulling teeth had to be easier than this. Without looking at me Arch picked up his bag and started toward his room. Even though I knew, I asked him where he was going.

He turned to me. "I have to go make up your character," he said, "for the adventure."

"What am I going to be?" I asked.

He said, "A thief."

When Todd arrived we ate and cleared the table for combat. We had no board, only a glittering array of multisided dice and Arch's pile of books and papers. He also had some props—a small knife, which represented an authentic crosier for casting spells, scrolled pieces of paper, some marble eggs he had bought on a field trip to the western slope, and a glass of skim milk symbolizing a potion to control the colors of certain dragons.

Arch was in a bad mood. He had spoken sharply to Todd at dinner and yelled at me when I asked if I could help set things up. Giving me sharp sideways glances, he carefully arranged several small metal statues of knights in gallant and aggressive poses.

As dungeon master, Arch was our guide, he crisply informed us. He had created the adventure with its many possibilities. When it was Todd's or my turn he told us what we were doing, where we were going, and what our options were. When we chose an option, we would throw dice to see what happened. It sounded complicated so I poured myself a brandy.

Our characters began in a somewhat downtrodden condition. Taxes, rents, and prices were all high, Arch the dungeon master announced. He brandished a yellowed facsimile of the Declaration of Independence, meant to represent the documentation for these new financial burdens.

"What are *you* doing paying taxes?" I whispered to Todd, who was a high-level cleric.

"Just play the game, Ms. Bear," he replied.

To relieve our difficulties, Arch went on, we were going to have to go into a dangerous forest where the possibility of adventure was high. We were told that after wending our way through the dense array of trees, we had come to a cave. Inside the cave there was the possibility of finding treasure, but only if we could successfully fight the monsters.

I was thinking Freud would have a field day with this when Arch said that I had just encountered six giant water rats, and what did I want to do about it?

"What are my options?" I wanted to know as I poured another brandy.

"Fight or flee," he said solemnly.

I thought. I wanted to ask a number of questions, beginning with "Just how big are these rats?" but then he yelled at me.

"Hurry up, Mom, you're slowing down the game!"

I told him I would fight. This produced a flurry of dice-throwing to match my abilities against the rats' power.

"What happens if I die?" I asked with some timidity while my hit points were being compared to the rats' on a chart from some book. "Do I lose? I mean, am I out of the game?"

Arch said, "There's no such thing as winning and losing in this game, Mom. You might just have a setback. If you die here, the cleric can raise you from the dead."

I looked at Todd, who nodded. Some cleric!

"Do I have a weapon?" I asked.

Arch checked my character's inventory sheet. "Yes," he said, "but you can use other methods. Giant water rats eat any flesh, but the flesh of the electric eel is poisonous to it. So you can crack open a raw alligator egg, which the rats like, and then mix chopped up electric eel into the egg, and the rats will eat it and die." With this lurid explanation, Arch passed me two marble eggs.

I said, "Gross."

"You made that up," Todd protested. "I never read that in any book! Besides, the thief is going to use his knife if you're doing hit points."

"I am the DM," Arch announced. "I can make stuff up."

"Cannot!" protested Todd.

"Shut up!" Arch yelled. He stood and brandished his play knife at Todd.

"What—" I said.

"Shut up, Mom!" Arch's face shook with anger. His knuckles had turned white as he clutched the sword.

"Stop acting that way this minute," I ordered. "Todd is your guest."

"Yeah," said Todd. He pulled his face into a sulk.

"Nobody around here cares about anything I say," said Arch. He glowered at me, and for a horrible moment his eyes bulged with the same look of hatred I had seen so often in his father.

"I care," I said. "Just sit down, okay?"

"I'm the DM," said Arch.

"Nobody's saying you're not," I said.

Fear knotted my stomach. Uneasy silence filled the room for a few moments, until finally Arch put the sword back on the table and sat down.

After some discussion I said I would prefer to use the knife to hunting up electric eels and alligator eggs. To demonstrate this I traded the marble ovoids for the knife-crosier. I was glad to get it away from Arch, in any event. Thanks to the dice I prevailed against the rats. Sheesh! I needed another brandy.

As it turned out the rats were guarding a secret entry to a cave where a princess was being held prisoner. Worse, the princess was immobilized by a spell. On the plus side we learned that the father of the princess was very rich. If the cleric and I could manage to find and free her, we would receive a huge reward in gold pieces from the local king.

Things took a turn for the worse for Todd. He encountered an amulet-sporting lich, a strong anticlerical monster.

"Surely clerics can't carry weapons," I said.

"Only blunt weapons that can't draw blood," said Todd. "And they can cast spells."

"Yeah," said Arch, "no weapons for you."

Todd ignored him and tried to get the initiative on the lich with a dice throw. He lost, and was attacked first. After sustaining some damage to his clerical persona,

Todd asked Arch what the deal was on this heavy-duty monster.

Arch screwed his face into an evil expression that made my flesh crawl. He said, "This lich is seeking vengeance for a wizard whom the king killed in battle." He paused. "It is very powerful. You must approach it from the side, so that it cannot sense your presence. Then you can cast your most harmful spell."

Todd cast a spell of immobilization, the medieval equivalent of a stun gun. We were off again.

"You can't go into that part of the cave," Arch warned when Todd indicated his next move.

"How come?" Todd demanded.

"It'll explode," Arch warned. "It has a special warning device put in by the lich."

"Oh for heaven's sake, Arch," I protested again, "they didn't have explosives in the Middle Ages."

He again wrinkled his face into a malevolent expression. "If you don't want to play, Mom," he said, "you don't have to."

My stomach was still churning, and my mind was feeling the soporific effects of the brandy. I wasn't learning anything, and what I was seeing from Arch was not making me feel any better about his mental health. And while he was calling the plays, it would be impossible to ask questions about Laura Smiley or anything else.

"Mom's going to bed," I said, as if my duties could be lightened by speaking of myself in the third person. I bequeathed to Todd all the gold I had accumulated—on paper, of course—and said I would find out in the morning whether he had succeeded in freeing the princess.

"You boys sure are serious about this," I commented with a yawn.

"Yeah," said Todd, "my mother's making me a thief costume for Halloween. I can't wait."

I turned to Arch. "What about you, son? Want to dress up as the archbishop of Cottonwood Creek?"

"No," said Arch. "I'm going to go as a lich." He said this without looking at me.

"I can see about a costume," I said doubtfully, "if you want. But why do you want to be a monster?"

He shrugged. "You have a lot of power. You can do things you wouldn't be able to do in real life."

CHAPTER 11

The next morning, after dreaming fitfully of alligator eggs and my son pointing a knife at me, I remembered the key I had filched from the athletic club five days before. I doubted that going through Laura's locker could be more productive than going through her house. Still, Arch had correctly role-cast me: I could be a thief.

Arriving at the club brought the horrid realization that the Saturday morning aerobics class was the one for masochists. Attending this class had always led to deep and serious regret. When I sidled into the back row Trixie was leading the pain parade in a high-step double-time run-in-place to the chase scene music from *To Live and Die in L.A.*

"Go! Go!" Trixie shrieked over the din. She was throwing her arms and legs out like a cheerleader fighting off a mugger.

"Best thing for a hangover!" shouted the man next to me as we switched to jumping jacks.

The mirror reflected new unwelcome pillows of flesh in

the worst places. Not rushing around to cater was taking its toll. I went to the wall to stretch ligaments and wished to be dying in L.A. rather than exercising. Back in my spot I began to jog in place. My neighbor (hung over?) responded by increasing the speed of his jumps, which he accompanied with loud grunts.

We flapped arms and kicked legs while Trixie increased the tempo to what could only be described as frenzied. It was like an African tribal dance being filmed by *National Geographic*.

Abruptly the music stopped in midbar. I stopped too, although the maniacs around me kept hopping.

"What is the matter with this thing?" screeched Trixie as she punched buttons on the lifeless stereo. "What! What!"

She picked up one of the weights, a big one.

"Damn you!" she screamed, and heaved the weight at one of the wall-sized mirrors, which shattered with the sound of windows exploding in a small building.

"That's worth at least forty-nine years of bad luck," said Hung-Over.

Trixie ran into the locker room. Hal appeared at the top of the stairs. He looked bewildered, but quickly summoned all the masochists to the outside track. I decided to hit the showers.

In the locker room Trixie was complaining loudly to a group of women in shiny leotards and tights about the stereo system, the club, and life in general. I slipped into the welcome relief of a shower stall. When the crowd dispersed I would check out Laura's locker. But fifteen minutes later the women were still bubbling with subdued chatter about Trixie and her temper tantrum, so I headed for the steam room. There I encountered the becalmed mirror-shatterer herself.

"Trix," I said cautiously as I eased down onto the moist tile steps. "Guess you were a little pissed off back there."

She groaned and turned over. "Guess so," she said.

"Hal's secretary just came down. Breaking the mirror cost me three hundred dollars. Next time it'll be my job."

I muttered something about being in the same boat, a metaphoric fit with the clouds of steam enveloping us. Then I said, "Listen, I don't know how to say this delicately, but I just found out about your baby. I'm sorry. I didn't even know you were pregnant."

She said nothing for a few minutes. Then, "Thanks, Goldy. It's been really hard."

"I'm sorry," I murmured again. In the clouded light I could just see her hand. I took it and squeezed; she squeezed back.

I said, "Want to talk?"

"Maybe sometime. I need to figure out how to break the mirror news to my husband . . . ha ha." She let go of my hand.

"I didn't see your husband at Laura Smiley's house," I said.

She said, "God, it's getting hot in here."

"Really."

"Yeah, Martin," she said vaguely, as if she had just remembered his name. "He was out of town. Doesn't like the thought of death, anyway. Since . . . well."

"Of course," I said, and nodded in the dark mist. I cleared my throat and said, "I went over to Fritz Korman's the other day. He was doing better, went into the office Wednesday."

"Don't mention that man to me."

"Mad at the doctor? Why?"

"Don't call him a doctor," she said evenly as she swung her body around and rearranged herself on the room's tile steps. "Don't exaggerate."

I needed a cold shower. In the last ten minutes heat and moisture had built up in the steam room to almost unbearable proportions. But I couldn't go yet.

"Hey," I said, "I called Fritz's son a husband, and that was the worst exaggeration of my life."

This brought a laugh. She said, "I know I'm being disagreeable. I'm just worried about the cash for the mirror."

"I wrote the book on money worries making you disagreeable. At least no one's asking if I'm premenstrual."

Another harsh laugh.

"Anyway," I added, "if that theory worked, my roommate would be the most agreeable person in the world."

"Also the stupidest," said Trixie acidly, "since she's going to Fritz Korman for treatment."

"How did you know that?"

"She told me, sitting right in here not long ago. She was talking to Laura Smiley about it one time when I came in."

"What? I didn't even know she knew Laura."

Trixie let out a breath. "I'm not saying she knew her, Goldy. I'm just saying that one time she was talking to her. I didn't even hear the whole conversation, since I came in in the middle and had to leave before they finished."

"But what were they talking about? What were they saying?"

"I don't know. They were talking about Fritz. Patty Sue was upset. When I first came in they stopped talking, you know how people do. When I asked them if they wanted me to leave, Laura was, what's the word, cryptic. She said, 'Trixie had the same doctor. She doesn't think too much of him.'"

"Then what?"

Trixie said, "Patty Sue was saying she was sorry she had bothered Laura, and Laura was saying that was okay. I had already dumped all my grievances on Laura once before, and I didn't want to hear any more about Korman. So I got out."

"That's it?"

"I think so. So what?"

I thought for a minute. Then I said, "Well, judging from what happened last Saturday, you weren't the only one dissatisfied with Fritz."

"That doesn't surprise me."

"Of course," I said bitterly, "whoever was upset with him could have managed to give him rat poison someplace besides Laura's funeral."

"Odd that he would even come," said Trixie.

"Why is that?"

"Oh, I don't know. As I said, Laura and I used to talk in here. And usually not with your roommate around. It's hard. With Laura gone, I mean."

"What did you and Laura talk about?"

"Jesus, what is this? Interrogation time?"

"I'm sorry, forgive me," I said. "I'm just interested because of my business being closed down from what happened at her house. Sorry," I said again. I thought I was going to faint from the heat and humidity in the small dark room. The ambient temperature must have been a hundred and twenty. But instead of leaving I cleared my throat and said, "Have you thought any more about coming to our group?"

She moved around on the tiles.

"Tell me again when you're meeting."

"Next week, Thursday, and also Friday night, October thirtieth. I just thought you might enjoy it."

"Well, at least I can enjoy the food, right?" She gave a harsh laugh. Then, "The thirtieth, I guess."

"You'll be glad you did."

She said, "I guess," and stood to leave. The door slammed behind her.

Twenty minutes later I was dried and dressed but still full of questions. While Trixie worked on her hair and makeup I tried to bring up the subject of Laura again, to no avail. When I asked if we could get together before the meeting on the thirtieth she gave me a curious look.

"Just to chat," I said.

"No," she said, then picked up her gym bag and swept out.

The locker room was empty. I groped around in my handbag for the key to Laura's locker. L221. The L stood for Ladies; that much I knew. I wouldn't get over to do the M side until I did my first cleaning job here. For that I could wait.

There was a sudden hush in the locker room. Saturday classes were over before noon. Everyone had left to chop firewood or shop for groceries. This set burgling into high relief, morally speaking.

I put the flat metal key into 221 and turned. Gooseflesh crawled up my neck. The key wouldn't budge. I jiggled it and tried again. The door clanged open.

The inside of the locker door was plastered with homemade signs, and I began to wonder if Laura had a fixation with slogans. "You Can't Find These Muscles on the Seashore." Too much. The uppermost sign was a copy of the Serenity Prayer. She had underlined <u>to change the things I can.</u>

On the top shelf was the usual array of female bath accessories, shampoo, rinse, body lotion. Still no razor, I noticed, and made a mental note to tell Schulz. Not that he would care. My ideas didn't seem to carry much weight with the local constabulary. Behind the toiletries was a paperback, which I imagined from its brittle condition to be reading material Laura took into the sauna. It was a day-by-day meditation book, advocating strength and courage and calm. For what?

Underneath her name in the front of the book were the words *Sundays, noon, Episcopal church.* Thinking of my old parish, I tried to remember what went on at noon on Sundays, after everyone had left. Several times I had stayed to clean the Sunday school room while Arch threw stones into Cottonwood Creek. One time I had gone into the ladies' room to cry when John Richard slipped out with the choir lady. Arch had thrown enough stones into the creek to qualify him for dam construction by the time I came out, red-eyed and sniffly. And there had been a meeting going on, where I remembered several of the people had also been red-eyed and sniffly. What was it? Memory failed.

My hand slid across the cool metal of the shelf. In the far corner there was a piece of paper that was stuck. Perhaps Laura had put a wet bottle of shampoo or damp washcloth up there. It was probably just an old label from soap. Without thinking I pulled, and half of whatever it was came off in my hand.

The torn paper was not a label, and I cursed myself for not trying to extricate it more carefully. It was part of a yellowed article from an old newspaper with a scrawled note: *Show P.S. and T.* I tried to release the rest of the stuck paper from the shelf with my fingernail, but got only illegible bits.

The torn part read:

> ### CAROLTON PHYSICIAN TO MOVE
>
> Local obstetrician Fritz Niebold Korm
> last month on charges of having
> in mistrial, will move his pract
> Sources indicate that Korman
> under investigation by the Il
> Examiners for other alleg
> accusations, Korman sta
> tired of it all," and
> he had received a lic
> been practicing in

The upper left-hand corner said *October 6, 1967.*

I put the book with the notation about Sunday meetings, as well as the article, into my gym bag and headed for the front desk. In 1967 John Richard had been ten years old, so that even if he would be willing to explain this, he probably wouldn't remember. If I could get Vonette sober, she might tell me more. Maybe Schulz had already found out what this was about, though I doubted that. Like the book of advice or the church meeting, or the fact that

Vonette had said that Laura had been a nanny for them, I did not know how this fit.

At the desk I received a note telling me Arch's teacher had tried to reach me at home and had been told to call here, and would I please call her at home during the weekend. Nothing urgent, she'd said, just call at your convenience.

You bet, I thought, but first I had some other business to attend to. I dialed the number for the office of Korman and Korman, asked for an appointment, and was informed that the doctors had left for the weekend. Would I like to see Dr. Korman senior on Monday?

"Yes," I said. "I have to bring Patty Sue Williams in anyway; maybe you could fit me in around that time."

There was a pause.

"I only need to see him for about ten minutes," I said.

"Oh? And what is your problem, Miss Bear? Are you in pain?"

"Chronic. Lower abdomen. I know he'll be able to help me." I said, "There's just so much I can't digest," and hung up.

CHAPTER 12

Show P.S. and T.

Why had Laura Smiley made that note on an article about a mistrial? It had been in her locker; one had to assume that P.S. and T. were available in the athletic club. It was an article about Dr. Fritz Korman, something from two decades before, something which, for a reason I did not know, had relevance for P.S. and T.

I put the article down and tried to call Arch's teacher, Janet Heath, but got her answering machine instead. I stared at the article again.

Trixie (T.?) had said that she and Laura had talked about Korman in the steam room after exercise class. She also had said that Laura and Patty Sue, of all people, had had a tête-à-tête in the same steam room. Time for me to have a little chat with P.S. myself, especially since she was the only woman I knew who was a current patient of Fritz Korman's.

But Patty Sue was out running when I arrived home. When she came back Arch was in and out with Todd so that it was impossible to ask questions. Then she went to bed after we finished the dishes. What was the point of all that exercise if it rendered you constitutionally incapable of staying up past nine at night?

Well, we still lived under the same roof. Sunday morning would do for questions. I dialed Janet Heath again and got her machine again. Another chat set aside for the next morning.

As usual I awoke early. Sunday, with its inevitable doldrums, is the bane of the single person who has been married. For couples and families it is a day of church, picnics, fishing, football games, pizza, and movies. Now the emptiness descended like one of the cold fogs that go creeping through the mountain valleys in winter. The frigid moisture is almost invisible, but you can see the way the icy clouds turn green pines to silver; you can feel the chill seep into your bones.

So I followed my routine. Cooking was the cure for loss. The candy for Arch's Halloween party at Furman Elementary was the next order of business.

A batch of my Terrific Toffee would do for the sixth graders. The candy would keep in the refrigerator for a couple of weeks. I buttered two nine-by-thirteen-inch glass pans and started to melt butter with brown sugar in a big pot. I rummaged through my knife drawer for the candy thermometer, then snapped its long bulb onto the side of the pan.

I stirred, and remembered when Arch was five. We had spent a lot of time playing the game Candyland. This had led to long discussions about how they made all the sweets for that place, which Arch believed existed outside of the game board. The Candyland cement mixer trucks were full of toffee, he insisted, because they could keep it moving all the time. Car engines had little blades to chop up peppermint drops so you could stir them into Christmas fudge. Two years later John Richard moved out, and two months after that dismal Christmas I found a hoard of old

Goldy's Terrific Toffee

2 cups coarsely chopped pecans
2 pounds (8 sticks) unsalted
    butter, plus extra for pans
2 pounds best-quality milk
    chocolate (Lindt)
4 cups packed dark brown sugar

Note: A candy thermometer is essential for this recipe. Making a good toffee is tricky at high altitude, because the traditional soft-crack stage is not reached until the thermometer reaches 300ºF., at which point the toffee is in danger of burning. Therefore, at high altitude, if you are close to 300ºF., detect a burning smell, and stir up a darker substance from the bottom of the pan, stop stirring immediately, remove the toffee from the heat, and quickly pour it into the prepared pans *without scraping the bottom of the cooking pan*. If you have managed not to stir in any of the burnt candy, the toffee will still be delicious. It will be chewier than that made at sea level, but proper refrigeration will maintain a good candy texture.

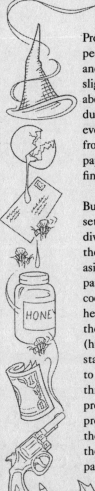

Preheat the oven to 375°F. Spread the pecans in two 9-inch glass pie plates, and roast until the nuts have turned slightly darker and are well toasted, about 10 minutes. Stir once or twice during the roasting process to ensure even browning. Remove the pecans from the oven, spread out to cool on paper towels, and set aside until you finish the toffee.

Butter two 9 x 13-inch glass pans and set aside. Unwrap the chocolate and divide it between two plates. Break all the chocolate into squares and set aside. Using a deep, heavy-bottomed pan, melt the butter with the sugar and cook over medium to medium-high heat, *stirring constantly*, until a candy thermometer hits 285°F. to 290°F. (high altitude: 300°F.), the soft-crack stage. (Candy will be very hot; be sure to protect your skin and clothing through the cooking and pouring processes.) Pour the toffee into the prepared pans and immediately place the squares of chocolate in rows across the toffee (1 pound of chocolate per pan). When the chocolate has soft-

ened, spread it to the edges of the toffee. Sprinkle 1 cup of the toasted
pecans over the chocolate in each pan.
Allow to cool, then cover with foil and
chill.

Using a large, heavy-duty knife, break
the toffee into 1- to 3-inch pieces.

Makes approximately 6 dozen pieces

mint-flavored fudge in one of Arch's drawers. When I asked him about it he said he just kept it there to smell it, so he could pretend he was in Candyland instead of being at home.

The thermometer hit 300°; I poured the bubbling brown stuff into the two pans. Then each pan got a pound bar of chocolate, which I had successfully hidden from Patty Sue. I pushed the bars around over the molten toffee until they melted into soft chocolate lakes. For fancy parties I would have sprinkled minced pecans or filberts on top, but kids were finicky about pimentos, olives, and nuts, so I always omitted them.

"Man," said Patty Sue as she entered the kitchen at ten o'clock, "what smells so great?"

"Toffee for Arch's school Halloween party," I replied. I looked at her. Her face was wan. Her hair, like her general outlook, had dulled since she had arrived in August. She puttered slowly around the kitchen, and I wondered if more could be wrong with her than her cyclical problems.

"Patty Sue," I began, "are you feeling all right?"

She was taking an English muffin out of the toaster.

"Sure," she said without looking at me. "I was just tired after my run yesterday." She spread chokecherry jelly on the muffin, then changed her mind and scraped it off.

I walked over to her and said in a low voice, "Are Dr. Korman's treatments working at all? You don't look very good. Is he giving you iron or any special medication?"

She said, "Yes, he's giving me some pills and no, I'm not normal yet." She sat down heavily on one of the kitchen chairs. "He knows what he's doing. Why would my doctor send me out here if he didn't?"

"I don't know. Why did you talk to Laura Smiley about it?"

She froze in midbite.

I said, "Trixie told me."

She said, "Well, uh . . . ." and then was quiet.

"Patty Sue, I didn't even know you *knew* Laura Smiley."

"I didn't know her."

"You talked to her."

"One time."

"When did this conversation take place? Did she say she wanted to show you an article about Fritz?"

Patty Sue pushed the plate away and began to catch her breath, as if she was about to cry. "I'm sorry," she said, "I'm just so sorry."

"For what?"

She stood up. "Please leave me alone, please, Goldy, I feel really bad."

"About what?"

"About everything," she said with a cough, before running out of the room. She called back, "Please leave me alone!"

"I'm coming with you to the doctor's office tomorrow," I yelled after her.

"Gee, Mom," said a sleepy Arch as he shuffled into the kitchen. "What's going on? What's all the racket about? Are you sick?"

"No. I just told Patty Sue that I'm taking her to her appointment tomorrow, that's all."

He poured himself some cereal. Between bites he said, "You always take her. Maybe after her driving lesson on Friday she'll be able to drive herself and you guys can stop yelling."

I said, "I doubt both."

He ate silently and then rinsed his bowl.

"Just remember," he said in his little-adult voice, "Pomeroy has some old-fashioned kind of driver-ed cars. That's what he told me. You'd better be careful."

I said, "You and Pomeroy had all kinds of conversations, didn't you?" Arch shrugged. "I think what he meant," I went on, "is that his cars are the old driver-ed kind, because he can't get an increase in funds from the school board to set up a more modern instructional program. I read about it in the paper."

"Oh-kay-ay," he said in that singsong cadence associated with *Don't say I didn't warn you*.

I narrowed my eyes at him and said, "I need to make an important phone call."

He nodded and drifted out of the kitchen while I dialed Janet Heath. She didn't sound too happy about being called on Sunday morning, but I was not going to risk another encounter with her answering machine.

"I would like to see you sometime soon," she said stiffly when we had exchanged pleasantries. "About Arch."

I coughed. I said, "Please tell me what's wrong."

"Well, that's what I don't know. I just need to talk to you about some things going on in the classroom. Can you come in this week?"

We settled on Friday before school and hung up. One more thing I just couldn't wait for.

The next morning frost painted the kitchen windows and I had the usual go-round with Arch concerning his outer clothing.

"But it gets so hot in the afternoon," he complained, "and kids make fun of me wearing my coat when they're in sweats."

"So let them," I said. "You won't be sick for Halloween and they will, which is all right because from what you say they don't care about it anyway."

He stomped out muttering something unintelligible.

The van was doing its cough-and-sputter warm-up routine when Patty Sue came skittering out of the house in white lace blouse, white skirt, and matching white tights. No coat for her either. It was no wonder she had health problems. But I couldn't ask her about anything. We had been friends when she first arrived. What had happened?

When I pulled up in front of Korman and Korman, Obstetrics and Gynecology, Patty Sue gave me a puzzled look.

"Did you say you were sick?" she asked.

I sighed. "Yes and no."

Entering K and K, I had always told John Richard, was an experience rivaled only by stepping into the big greenhouse at the Denver Botanic Gardens. Why obstetricians needed a jungle environment for an office was something better left to psychologists. Perhaps the sudden entry into leafiness suggested fecundity. Freud, I had told John Richard to his immense irritation, would have hypothesized something more specific. I avoided the enfolding arms of a stand of Norfolk pine, threaded my way through oversized bamboo plants, and ducked a hanging basket of wandering Jew before arriving at the reception desk.

"Do you have an appointment?" asked the nurse-receptionist.

"Yes," I said breezily. "You just don't recognize me without my safari hat."

"Name?"

"Bear," I said, "as in Goldilocks and the Three—"

"I don't have a chart on you," she said without looking up. "You'll have to fill out new-patient papers." She handed me a clipboard filled with forms that would have given the IRS pause.

"But you don't understand," I said. "John Richard is my—"

I stopped as her withering glance shot through me. Perhaps it would be better not to advertise my presence in this office after a four-year absence. Nor did I feel welcome, given the Jerk's assumption of my guilt in the rat-poison affair. In fact I had better try to avoid him altogether.

"Tell you what," I said conspiratorially, "I'll bet I could find my file back there. Just let me take a look."

"Oh no—" she began, but was interrupted by an extremely distressed patient who had appeared at my side.

"I'm pregnant," whispered a woman to the nurse. Her voice broke. She said, "Unplanned." The patient signaled to her husband, who emerged from behind the foliage.

"You have two options," the nurse started to say as I slid behind the counter's side door.

"And we were so careful," the woman complained.

I surveyed the file cabinets. Inside these formidable gray metal boxes the files were color-coded, I knew. Since more than thirty-six months had elapsed since I had been treated by my ex-husband, I would be classified as inactive. I opened the top drawer, A through I, pink files.

I saw some names I recognized, but no Bear. Were these current? The next drawer, J through S, was more helpful. There was Jackson, T., which would be Trixie, and Korman, M., which would be Marla. She had been married to John Richard more recently than I, and might still be classified as active, although like me she now went to a female gynecologist in Denver. There was also Korman, V.—Vonette. At this juncture I remembered that the last time I had been in the Korman office, I too had been a Korman, so these must be the current or only recently inactive patients.

I skipped the next drawer and opened drawer J through S in the adjoining cabinet, which bulged with green files. Inactive? The unhappily expectant patient at the desk was still bemoaning her fate; her husband was figuring out dates with the nurse. My ex-husband's voice floated out his office door.

If only there were some plants behind the counter. I needed cover.

I turned back to the green files and had a sudden thought. Could Laura Smiley be in here? Would she have been active or inactive? I flipped quickly back to the S pink files: Sandoval, Scalia, Sheffield, Smythe. Back to the green files I went, checking into Slacek, Smalrose, Smart, Smith. No Smiley in either green or pink. Perhaps it had been misfiled. I began with the green H's, where I saw Heath and Hilliard, then the J's, Jacoby, Jermaine, and so on, through K's, where I found Korman, G., and removed it, through the L's, Lapham, Leduc, Locraft, and Ludmiller, when the sudden swift foot of John Richard kicked the file drawer out of my hands so that it crashed into the cabinet.

"You," he said. "What the hell are you doing in here? I mean, besides being nosy?"

"I'm not being nosy," I said. I gritted my teeth and tried to cut him with a glance. From behind the waiting-room bushes faces appeared, like curious pygmies. "I was looking," I said airily, "for my file." I waved it. "Which I found."

Whispers from the waiting room.

John Richard said to the nurse, "Why is she back here?"

The nurse looked at me and back at the Jerk, who was a large hulking blond presence in his white doctor coat.

"She was looking for her file," she said. "I think."

John Richard narrowed his eyes at me again. "I suppose you weaseled your way in here with an appointment?"

I murmured assent, holding my file like a life preserver with one hand, and gesturing to the appointment book with the other. John Richard hunched over the book, and I prayed his pants would split. Then he glared back at me.

"Let me tell you something," he said in a rough whisper. His index finger stabbed the air between us. "I don't know what you're up to here. But you keep out of those confidential files, you little bitch. If you try to harm my father again I'll wring your neck. And listen up. Get yourself another doctor. Don't come back to this office or I'll call the cops."

"I've got another doctor," I said. "But feel free to call the cops. Ah . . . try the one I've been going out with. He shoots people for assault and battery."

John Richard gave me a look with enough steel in it to keep Pittsburgh going for a day. Then he whisked out in a cloud of anger and white coat.

"You can see Dr. Korman now," said the nurse, avoiding my eyes. "The other doctor. Just go on back." She knew she had screwed up.

Patty Sue was nowhere in sight. I assumed she had already seen Fritz, come back out through the plants, and gone downstairs to the pastry shop for a bite to eat. Knowing Patty Sue, it would be more than a bite. I walked quickly past the waiting-room jungle and peered around the corner into the room where they drew blood and refrigerated samples and medications. This was also where they stored all the equipment for "office surgery," their euphemistic term for ridding the uterus of anything unwanted. My guess was that such a procedure would be the next visit for the unexpectedly pregnant patient who had preceded me.

I knew I was also unwanted in this office. I peeked around the corner, unwilling to be removed myself.

The room with the abortion equipment was empty. I walked quietly past.

"Hi, Fritz," I said as I entered his office. "Hope you don't mind my coming in like this."

"Goldy." He looked up at me with a frown. He said, "You know you're not supposed to come in here. Let the nurse put you in one of the examination rooms. Then I'll come see you."

"Oh thanks," I said, and averted my eyes from his tall frame to the office greenery, which resembled the profusion of foliage in the waiting room. There were rows of geraniums on shelves in a built-out window, Swedish and other strains of ivy hanging behind the desk and couch, and tall rubber plants hugging the frame of a door. "Tell me, Fritz," I said, "do you have a repressed desire to be a botanist?"

He smiled. He sat in his chair and swiveled toward me. With his head tilted, his bald pate caught the light and shone like a halo. He said, "Repressed desires? That's shrink talk. Now why don't you go to an examination room and we'll get on with our appointment?"

I sat on the couch, a dark, softly stuffed expanse that exuded the sensual smell and sigh of leather.

"I'm not sick," I said.

He chuckled. "That's not what my son tells me."

"Did you like the cakes?"

He nodded. "Is that why you're here? To talk about food? Because I have other patients to attend to. Ones who are sick."

"I need to talk to you about business. Yours and mine, if that's okay. I won't take long."

He grinned again. His teeth were slightly gray, from age, but when he smiled he filled the room with his aura, a sort of older-movie-star appeal.

He said, "I don't know anything about cooking, Goldy."

"That's okay," I said and looked at a wall of framed degrees and other official-looking papers, then at a table next to the couch where African violets circled some family photographs. In these Vonette and John Richard appeared with the doctor, and there were shots of fishing buddies. There was no sign of the strange girl.

"Fritz." I eyed him solemnly. "You know I didn't put that stuff in your coffee. But the cops have closed down my business until they figure out what's going on. You'd think that would be simple, but it isn't." I told him that I was looking into the histories of some of his former patients who might have something against him.

He said, "So if the catering doesn't work out, you're considering a career with the cops?" Another wide smile. "You know I can't tell you anything about patients. I heard John Richard out there screaming at you for going through the files." He leaned toward me. "They're confidential, Goldy."

"Did Trixie Jackson ever threaten you?" I demanded. "She was real upset about her stillbirth."

He cocked his head and looked at me as if he were dealing with a thick-headed child. "It's a very difficult thing for a prospective mother to take. It's also hard on the doctor."

I gave him a sympathetic look. "I'm sure." I cleared my throat. "How about Laura?"

His face lost expression. "Laura who?"

"Laura Smiley," I said, astonished. Did he really have so many patients with that first name? I said, "Laura whose funeral you attended nine days ago. Who, a long time ago, also lived in Carolton, Illinois." I took a breath. "Who had an appointment with you the day she died."

He shook his head. "You're confused, Goldy, in more ways than one." He stood up, a signal our interview was over. "Do you think Laura Smiley messed with my coffee? She couldn't have put pellets in someone's drink if she was dead, could she? And I told you patient dealings are not open to your misguided prying. Now why don't you go home and cook and let the police do the investigating?"

I stood up but pressed on. "How come there's no file out there on her, if she was a patient?" Fritz shrugged. I said, "Why can't you tell me if or why she was here the day she died? I mean if you or John Richard told her she had cancer or something, then the cops should know."

He stopped by the door I had come in. He said, "She killed herself. That's what the police know. If they want more they can come and ask me themselves. Now it's time for you to go."

"But what about in Illinois? I've found photographs of a girl, a teenager, and then I found an article about you—"

He held the door open.

He said, "Goodbye, Goldy."

CHAPTER 13

I hadn't received any clarification about the torn article in Laura's locker. Not that Fritz would have told me about a mistrial or anything else. He had his reasons for not divulging information. I didn't know what they were, but I doubted confidentiality of files was uppermost in his mind. As I swept and scrubbed and scoured other people's houses that week, I decided my financial rationale for getting information was more important than any of his reasons. Let Fritz clean houses for a while, see how it felt. Unfortunately, I didn't know what my investigation methods were going to be. Yet.

Schulz was no help. In addition to the two homicides he was working on, he'd had another crisis. Some late-season rock climbers had found the body of a biker down Cottonwood Creek Canyon. So he was momentarily tied up sorting out the politics of rival gangs. The department clerk said he'd call me as soon as he could.

The Thursday evening meeting of Amour Anonymous, postponed because of a funeral, was similarly funereal itself, complete with surprise ending.

After cleaning two houses, Patty Sue said she was too tired to attend, but that she'd make the next meeting. Two other women who were occasional attendees called and backed out, so it was just Marla and myself. I made cream puffs and coffee and put out a bottle of dessert sherry.

"I'll eat anything you cook," Marla said when she walked in. "The hell with the health department."

The sight of Marla, grinning broadly and wearing an orange and black jumper—she always dressed in seasonal colors—made my heart soften. She looked like a giant pumpkin. I hugged her.

"I asked for food, not love," her muffled voice said into my shoulder. "We can eat the former and talk about the latter." I let go of her and she held up a package, grinning. "Where's your little guy? I've brought him something."

I called Arch from the nether regions of the house and poured coffee into two cups.

"A whole pack of Hershey bars?" Arch's delighted voice said behind my back. "Gosh, Marla, thanks."

I was about to scold Marla for ruining Arch's teeth when I got a look at his face. It was painted a shiny black.

"What's with the disguise?" I asked, trying to keep my voice light.

"It's part of some work I'm doing," he said seriously. The whites of his eyes shone as he opened them wide. "I'm trying to make our house safer."

"By doing what?" I demanded, but he was gone.

Marla shook her head. "What's with him?"

"Not sure," I said. "But I think he's still pretty spooked about Laura's death."

"Well, who isn't," said Marla. She swallowed the last of her first cream puff and started on another. "And it doesn't help that the dear teacher was a little nutty, either."

"Oh yeah?" I said. "What makes you say that? I mean, I'm beginning to think the same thing. But you get around so much more than I do."

"Oh, you know," she said.

"Marla," I said firmly, "I don't. And every time I try to ask anybody about Laura, the person either starts crying or kicks me off the premises."

"I'd like to see someone try to kick you off any premises."

"Just tell me why you think she was wacko. I really want to know."

"Well, chill out. Good Lord," said Marla. "She would get this bee in her bonnet, I don't know." She sucked the filling out of her third cream puff before delicately biting into it. "I've always wondered about elementary school teachers anyway. They're either slightly off base when they go in or they get that way after five years of ignoring books for grown-ups so they can gobble more third-grade texts."

I said, "Are you talking about teachers in general, or one in particular?"

"Okay, look," said Marla as she extended one of her fleshy arms for the sherry bottle. "Here's an example. We used to both take our cars into that foreign-car repair shop off Main Street. She had that Volvo, I had the Jag. Neither of them were cheap cars to fix, tune up, get parts for, whatever. And I guess she had a lemon or something, or the guy couldn't fix all the problems, but they would always be arguing when I came in. When he would go to check if they'd done all the work, Laura would turn around to me, flick her lighter on, and tell me how she wished she could torch the place. Then she'd light a cigarette and go ha-ha. So I'd ha-ha back. One time she told me she was keeping a list of all the Volvo's problems, and she was going to send it to Ralph Nader in Swedish and put the whole car company out of business."

"Huh?" I said.

"That's what I said, especially when she asked me how to say *piece of shit* in Swedish," Marla went on. "But here's the weird part. The mechanic comes back and she turns all sweet. I mean, a complete switch. Making jokes. And I was sitting there thinking, What the hell's going on here? Then after she paid him and he went back out again, she said, 'You can bet I'm never coming back here.' She said, 'It can't be that difficult to find someone who really knows how to fix cars.' And I guess she did because I never saw her there again."

"Well," I said, "she told Arch the President should paint his skin black and go to South Africa, see what it's really like to live under apartheid."

"Not a bad idea," said Marla with a grunt. "Anyway, is that what Arch is doing tonight? African sympathy ritual?"

The lights flickered.

"I have no idea what he's doing," I said. "But he's been acting odd lately, so I wouldn't put anything past him."

"Do you have something to talk about tonight?" Marla asked. "I mean besides Laura Smiley."

We were quiet while I tried to take the focus off Laura and put it onto myself. The lights flickered again.

"That reminds me," I said. "What about the unrequited love you were claiming for her?"

"I'm checking around. Looking into it. Has to do with the beekeeping Ice Man, though, I can tell you that. I just have to find someone who's been close to him to confirm the rumor."

I said, "Nothing ever works."

Marla wiped her mouth. "Oh, stop complaining." She winked at me. "Tell you what, you can complain now that our two-person meeting is underway. It's your turn, anyway."

I said, "Already?" then sighed while I thought. "I've been kind of bitchy lately, I guess," I said. Marla was silent. "At first I thought it was the business—having it closed down. Or Laura." I looked around. "Arch is acting strange, obviously. And John Richard is getting married—"

"Again," Marla said in disgust.

"Third time's the charm," I said dryly.

More silence.

"I've had this . . . I went out," I said, as if my date had been with a mass murderer. Marla looked noncommittal.

"The last thing I want to do is date," I said. "That's not even the word they use anymore, is it? You go out for dinner and then have casual sex, right? Well, forget that. Except for asking Pomeroy to eat pizza with us, I haven't looked for male companionship at all. And Pom ignored me."

"Hmm," said Marla, in her knowing way. "Part of what I've heard about him is that he is, or was, very hung up on his ex-wife."

"Anyway," I said, "about going out. I did want a relationship. I just didn't want the potential hassle." I drained my sherry glass. "And then along comes this cop. Schulz. My business is a wreck, my eleven-year-old is acting strange, the man I used to love is marrying a geometry teacher, and I'm a prime suspect in attempted murder. This cop comes along, and . . . he likes me! Sheesh!"

Marla said, "You're not that repulsive, silly."

"Fine," I replied. "But I want to be honest, right? I mean, I was dead set against acting nice and sweet and this-could-be-the-start-of-something-great, just to get my business reopened. He's my age, so maybe he doesn't believe in the casual-sex lifestyle. Maybe he doesn't even use the word *lifestyle*."

I stopped to pour myself some coffee.

Marla said, "Do men brood and worry about all these possibilities the way we do? I doubt it. Anyway, what's the bottom line here?"

"I told you," I said. "I'm just afraid that I'm not being very nice to him because I don't know how I feel about him. I wanted Pomeroy, but maybe it was because I knew he would give me the Ice routine. No risk there. But Schulz likes me, he likes Arch, he likes—loves—food. All good."

Marla said, "Pomeroy is unhappily divorced. He lives out in the middle of nowhere. I think he's got a screw-loose. Negative lifestyle, babe."

"That's just great," I said. "Maybe during the three months they worked together, he gave Arch the go-ahead on being weird."

"Look," said Marla, "don't worry about Arch. Don't worry about Pomeroy. If Schulz likes you, go with it. I mean I know we're not supposed to give advice, but this is getting kind of long and involved, my dear, when you haven't even had the second date. You—"

Before she could finish, the lights went out.

"What the hell," I muttered.

"Bring out the candles," Marla demanded. "We're talking about men anyway, might as well make it romantic."

"Hold on. They're back here in the china cabinet," I said, while grunting along on all fours. I felt inside the cabinet, lit a match, and then three candles. A breath of fall air from an open window made shadows move across the walls.

"Hey," she said, "I'm looking at your next door neighbor's house and across the street, and everyone still has power. Looks like you're the unlucky one. I'll take one of these candles out to the kitchen and call Public Service."

"Wait," I said. My own voice trailed off as I listened for another one.

"Mom," came Arch's voice from nearby. "Mom?"

"Arch?" I called. "Do you know what's going on?"

"The thing didn't work!" Arch's voice exploded behind me. He had come into the dining room, but he was hard to see with the black face and the waving light from the candle.

"So what is this," I demanded, "some terrorist routine?"

"Of course not!" he said. "I was trying to hook up an alarm system to our house. One of the stupid fuses blew."

"And why is your face black?"

"That's part of it. Don't you see? You have to be secretive about these things if you really don't want people to know. You get in disguise, then you wire the place up. Don't you even care about living in a safer place?"

"Of course I do," I began, "but—"

"Don't worry about it," he interrupted, and I felt bad for being cross at him. "Todd knows how to replace a fuse. I'll call him and he'll be right over." He took a candle so he could see the phone and disappeared as quickly as he'd come in.

"Good Lord," said Marla. "Maybe we should be seeking a wee bit of professional help."

I didn't say anything because I couldn't think of anything.

"Oh well," said Marla, "where were we?"

I found my voice. "You were telling me, Marla, that I shouldn't be worried about Arch."

CHAPTER 14

The next day was Friday. With the early conference with Arch's teacher, one house to clean, and a driving lesson with Patty Sue and Pom, the day looked as unpromising as the ominous morning clouds spilling like oatmeal over the hills of the Wildlife Preserve. A frost had turned the streets to glass. Foreseeing slippery-road delays meant leaving early, just after I served Arch his French toast.

He talked to me briefly when the soaked bread was beginning to sizzle. I pointed out to him that I was able to cook with electric power thanks to Todd's deftness with fuses. Arch told me he had bought the alarm system from a radio store with his own money, and he was going to return it.

"But what I can't understand," I said when he was pushing the last bite through a puddle of syrup, "is why you thought we needed it."

"Oh Mom, you're giving me such a hard time," he said with his mouth full. He ran off to brush his teeth and gather his things, then came back to announce, "Other people have them, you know. It's not a crime." Then he rushed out to meet Todd before the bus arrived.

Ten minutes later the van skidded and spewed gravel at the entrance to the teachers' parking lot. The vehicle seemed to be as apprehensive as I was at the prospect of a teacher conference.

"Miss Heath?" I asked as I pushed through the sixth-grade door festooned with construction-paper pumpkins. Bats and spiders made from black paper and pipe cleaners hung from the ceiling of the classroom: late October in an elementary school.

Globular blue eyes set in a pale triangular face caught me from across the room, and I walked obediently through the maze of pupils' desks toward the teacher's table. Janet Heath, fettuccine in the aerobics class, was now comfortably ensconced in a billowing black Indian-embroidered tent dress. With her pale blond hair tied up in a ballerina topknot, she had the aspect of a kindly but powerful witch.

We had agreed to a 7:45 meeting to have enough time for a long chat before the students came in. Fixing Arch's breakfast but missing my own now brought on a wave of queasiness.

When I had finished winding my way through under-sized chairs and ducking dangling spiders, I remembered something else. Miss Heath was the one who had found Laura Smiley that fateful Monday afternoon. How she had reacted to finding the body I could not imagine, and did not want to on an empty stomach.

I said, "You wanted to see me."

She gave me an indulgent smile. "Yes."

There was a pause.

"I'm Archibald's mother."

She seemed to be taking me in.

Finally she said, "I know."

"Well," I said, casting my eyes around hopefully for a thermos or other sign of coffee, "here I am."

"I've been worried about the way Arch has been acting in class," she said. "Some of his behavior has been very odd."

I let out an involuntary groan, and Janet Heath gave me a sympathetic look.

She said, "Let's get something hot to drink in the teachers' lounge. They're finishing up a meeting in there, so we can come back here to talk. We'll have plenty of time."

When we came to the smoke-filled faculty lounge, Miss Heath waved at the gray cloud with regal hand motions. I let coffee gush into the biggest Styrofoam cup I could find. Miss Heath fixed chamomile leaf tea, which she strained through a little straw basket, a potionlike beverage to match her outfit.

She took minute sips of her tea as we walked back to the room, then said, "Arch and Laura were close, weren't they?"

"Yes, they were. He used to stay quite a bit after school, just to work on projects, help around the room, so on."

"Yes." More sips of tea. "I have some of the drawings he did for her. They were in with the other things from her desk."

I said, "I'd love to see them, if you don't mind. The drawings, I mean."

We reentered the classroom, more like a cave hung with critters, and I followed her back to her desk. She motioned for me to sit while she shuffled through the desk drawers.

"I've made some toffee for the Halloween party," I said to fill the silence.

Again the ridged brow greeted me as she stopped her search.

She said, "Sugarless?"

"No, afraid not."

She brought a manila envelope out of the desk.

"This is all there was from Ms. Smiley's, Laura's, desk, besides a coffee mug. Arch was helping her with a fifth-grade project on small mammals. It's all in here. I'm sure it's okay for you to take his work. Just leave the rest—I'll have to give it to the principal eventually. Arch does have extraordinary artistic talent, although he rarely uses it in this classroom."

I drew out drawings of raccoons, mice, prairie dogs, skunks. While I was admiring them Miss Heath got up to open a window. I dumped out the rest of what was in the envelope, a grading book, a sheaf of papers with meeting announcements, a teaching aid called "Science in the Classroom," odds and ends. The very last was a small wallet.

I glanced up. Miss Heath was writing Bring Halloween Sheets to Music Class on the board. I opened the wallet.

It contained some pictures of students, a very old photo of what I assumed to be Laura and her parents while they were still alive, some faces signed with familiar names from the box of letters and the wall of photos in her home, and then a jolt. There was a picture of a very young John Richard Korman accompanied by his parents, the much younger Fritz and pre–red-haired Vonette. Standing beside them was the same girl, the same teenager, whose picture had been in Ms. Smiley's living room and in Vonette's desk.

"What's that?" asked Miss Heath. She had returned and was again looking for something on her desk.

"Oh," I said, "I don't mean to be prying. It's just a picture of a family Ms. Smiley and I both know. Knew. I wonder who gave it to her," I said as I slipped the photo out of its plastic folder and flipped it.

An immature female hand, the same as the one on the other two photos, had written "In happier times."

Angry hot blood flowed into my face, and I was wondering just how well Laura Smiley had known my ex-husband's family. She had lived in Aspen Meadow, moved to Illinois, then moved back here after leaving Illinois. What her connection had been to them in that state, besides a vague reference to being a nanny, I did not know.

But questions were beginning to form in my mind. Had the friendship between Laura Smiley and my son been a fluke? Had he truly been so special to her? Had she for some reason sought him out? Or had she resisted becoming friends with him, perhaps because of some unfinished history between herself and the Kormans?

"Well?" said Miss Heath. "Someone you know?"

I stared at her, unable to remember what we'd been talking about. I gathered up Arch's drawings and then slipped the wallet and other papers back into the envelope.

"I'm sorry," I said. "Why don't we just discuss Arch?"

Miss Heath smoothed the skirt of her embroidered dress.

"I am really very worried," she said, "by the way Arch is acting in class. His behavior indicates some kind of distress."

"What kind of behavior?"

"Well," she said as she stood and picked up another sheaf of papers, "let's go over to his desk."

My heart dived. Arch, who was fairly neat at home, never had been one to keep an orderly desk. During parent conferences over the past five years I had always felt compelled to sort through the scrunched-up mess of papers, pencils, crayons, mittens, and overdue library books to bring a little order into the chaos. Today was no exception. The innards of his desk were precariously cantilevered out over his seat. Miss Heath was beginning to talk again, so my cleaning compulsion would have to wait a few minutes, anyway.

"I've been concerned about Arch this whole month,"

she said. "Of course I know all the children were shocked by the loss of Laura Smiley. Many of them had had her for a teacher. The counselors advised us to have them write about their feelings."

She shuffled through a small pile of papers in front of her and handed me one. It was written by one Jane Ross: "I feel sad about Ms. Smiley dying because she was nice to me and she hugged me when my bird died."

Another, from Charlie Johnson: "It's too bad about Ms. Smiley. I feel sad the way I did when my grandmother died. She was old, though."

Clarissa Ludmiller had written, "Today is a very unhappy day because of Ms. Smiley dying. She was funny and she always made us laugh. That's what I will remember about her."

Then Miss Heath handed me Arch's.

It said, "I can't write how I feel about my teacher dying."

I said, "Hmm." I knew all about how important it was to get feelings out. But if he wasn't ready, he wasn't ready.

"Then," Miss Heath went on, "I had them write in their journals, which they hand in from time to time, about someone they absolutely hate. It could even include me."

Now she handed me another student's journal: "The person I hate is my sister. I was so glad when I went to visit my grandparents and she went to camp instead. Grandma bought me a Hershey's Big Block and I didn't have to share it."

Another journal: "The person I hate is the Iutola Koamainee because he hates Americans."

Arch's was next. He wrote, "The person I hate is my grandfather. Not the one in New Jersey, even though he's a bit strange. But my other grandfather has no respect for human life."

"What?" I said aloud. "Fritz delivers babies, for God's sake."

Miss Heath sipped tea and said, "That was my reaction. But I didn't ask him about it because the journals, although I see them, are their own reflections. I always tell them that anything goes." She paused again. "But the most frightening thing to me is the way he's become so involved in these fantasy role-playing games."

I let out a breath. "He is very involved with them," I said lamely.

She went on, oblivious, "He often will stay in at recess to work on a game, or become involved when he has free time." She gestured to the far side of the room, where a fluorescent light was illuminating a large cluster of plants. "He says he's growing milkwort over there for one of his potions." Then came the dreaded words. "It's like an obsession."

"I know," I said. Even the most dim-witted psych major knew that if feelings weren't dealt with they went underground and after a proper incubation period reemerged as neuroses. But an obsession? With potions?

Miss Heath said, "I'm worried about just how serious this is. He's drifted off from his fine school record, and he hangs around with only one friend, Todd Druckman. He's become very touchy."

"He's always been touchy," I offered.

She shook her head.

"I know he's sensitive," she said, "but what I mean is different. In fact what happened last week is what made me think I needed to call you." Another pause, two sips of tea. "The first month of school Arch impressed me as a generous person. He was always there with a pencil or paper clip or whatever for any classmate. But earlier in the week John Hickles started rummaging around in Arch's desk. He was looking for an eraser, he said later. Arch, who was tending to the classroom gerbils over there"—she motioned to a cage next to the fluorescent light—"came running over, shrieking about leaving his stuff alone."

"That's not really typical," I said. "Although he did accuse me of sneaking up on him the other night."

Miss Heath nodded. She said, "Not dealing with feelings, and now sudden outbursts of temper. What do you think about seeing if the school psychologist will have a talk with him?"

This was the second time for this particular suggestion in the last twenty-four hours.

"No," I said, "please. Not yet. Let me try to talk to him a little bit first."

"I really think it's a good idea. I truly think he needs counseling."

"Let me think about it."

"Okay, suit yourself," she said, "but I think you're making a mistake not to set up something right away." There was a long pause, during which she again smoothed her skirt. "All right. Well. Thank you for coming. The kids will be here soon." She got up to cue me that we were done. When I didn't move, she said, "Ah, I have to finish getting the Friday activities ready."

"Please do," I said in a leaden voice, avoiding her eyes. "But," I went on, "I just want to sit here and let all this sink in." I looked down at Arch's paper-crammed desk. "Maybe I'll clean out this mess. Then when Arch or somebody else wants an eraser he won't have to have a temper tantrum."

Miss Heath shrugged. Again she said, "Suit yourself."

I looked at the clock. Eight-thirty. The students wouldn't be coming in until quarter to nine. I could finish by then. Arch was always grateful when I cleaned things up for him, although I tried not to do it too much. Parenting seminars beat you over the head—a term they would never use—with the injunction to let the children be responsible for their own mess.

In any event, I was wondering if there was more to the eraser story than what I'd heard. I pulled the trash can over and sat back down.

Out came the math papers first. They were stapled in several bundles, with Arch's wobbly zeros floating across the lines like jellyfish. I smiled, remembering his first-grade habit of chewing his tongue when he wrote the numbers 1 to 100. Then wadded social studies papers cascaded out, on the subject of drugs and avoiding peer pressure. My groping hands pulled out six erasers and a clump of science worksheets on gerbils and their habitats. Pencils, a mitten, multisided dice. Spelling. Book report. More gerbil info.

And then.

A crumpled envelope. Beige stationery. Something inside, which I didn't look at. Not from school, not from home. I looked at the envelope briefly and then, with the nonchalance that often accompanies being completely stunned, reached for my purse.

The outside of the envelope read, "For Arch, my special friend." In the upper corner, a scrawled "October 2." The handwriting I recognized from numerous other communications—progress reports, comments on book reports, thank-you notes for helping on field trips. I dropped the note in my purse.

The handwriting was Laura Smiley's.

The date was the day before her death.

Perhaps she had left a note, after all.

CHAPTER 15

I walked out of the school building feeling dazed. It was essential that I avoid Arch: my eyes would give me away. Guilt riddled my conscience like bullets. The letter might as well have been burning a hole in my purse. I couldn't read it yet. I needed time to think and I didn't have it. My cleaning assignment on the other side of town was due to start in ten minutes; at noon the owner was having a bridge party.

Waves of children were already surging into the school building. With a growl of defiance, the van started. I slapped it into first gear and took off.

The job was in Aspen Hills, a residential area dominated by boxy contemporary houses that looked as if they'd all been popped ready-made from ice cube trays. In the assigned house I put Laura's letter to my son, her "special friend," out of my mind while I covered the sunken tubs and tiled floors with cleaning solution before starting on the living room. The architect who had designed this particular dwelling had obviously never washed a window in his life. I propped a ladder against the highest of three stories of glass and began to climb up with a bucket containing a squeegee and squirt bottle of ammoniated solution. Below, the ladder teetered on sculptured chartreuse and pink carpeting.

I wondered A, if dropping the solution on the rug would improve its appearance, and B, if my life insurance would be sufficient for Arch should the ladder tumble. To my vertiginous chagrin I noticed that the ceiling was covered, between its rough-cut beams, with the same pink and green carpet. The architect had been impractical; the designer, insane.

After three hours the house from Atlantis was done and I was famished. The pastry shop beckoned: Cornish pasties and tea. The van once again cut a defiant and dusty path through town, but I was thankful for both the trustworthiness of the transport and the warmer weather. Despite early-morning frosts the month was remaining summery and dry. I could do without snow for a while since the blizzard of difficulties in my life was about all I could handle.

The air in the pastry shop was filled with the scent of fresh brownies. I knew Patty Sue would be down after her appointment with Fritz, sometime in the next hour. This would allow me enough time to balance my guilt with my need-to-know, a term they use someplace like the Pentagon. But I did need to digest lunch and Laura's epistle before the driving lesson.

I reached gingerly for the crumpled letter and smoothed it out on the table.

"Correspondence?" said Fritz Korman over my shoulder.

He met my upward stare with a conciliatory nod, then lowered himself into the chair opposite mine. His sudden appearance made me wonder if he'd been watching for me from his office window.

"May I see it?" he asked as he reached for the letter, which I quickly stuffed back into my purse.

"No." I paused. "Why are you so interested? Did the handwriting look familiar?"

He laughed. "Still playing detective, I see. No," he said, "it didn't look familiar. I just thought since you took liberties with my files, you wouldn't mind if I had a look at your letters."

"Right." I dug my fork into one of the pasties. The spicy meat and onion scent steamed out. "Fritz," I said, "do you want to tell me about some mistrial you were involved in?"

"Say," said Fritz, his handsome face suddenly cheery, "doesn't that pasty look and smell good. I believe I'll order something myself. My patients love this place." He winked at me. "Some of them too much. Mind if I join you?"

I shrugged.

"Listen, Goldy," he said when he returned in a few minutes with a plate containing two brownies, "I need to talk to you about something."

"Oh?" I said, cheery myself. "About the time in Illinois? What were the charges?"

"Well." He tilted his head and gave his serious look. "That was all a long time ago, best left in the past. I guess that's why I was surprised when you came barging into the office with all your questions."

I sipped tea, waited. He wasn't touching his brownies.

"I did know Miss Smiley," he said. He closed his eyes and bobbed his head. "Of course. That's why I was at the funeral with the teachers and others who also knew her."

"What was your relationship in Illinois? And did you have contact with her here? I mean beyond the last office visit, of course."

"Now Goldy, you know I take care of women. But that doesn't mean I understand them." He laughed and shook his head. "She showed us this town, Aspen Meadow, one time when we came out on a skiing vacation. She was helping us with our ... family. But we weren't close after ... after we moved out here. We loved Aspen Meadow. When it came time to leave Illinois, we moved here in part because we had loved it when we'd seen it before and in part because at that time Colorado and Illinois had reciprocal licensing procedures for doctors. But Laura ... she ... knew Vonette—"

"Why exactly did you leave Illinois? And why did Laura come to see you the day she died? If she wasn't a patient of yours?"

Fritz stuffed some brownie into his mouth.

"Goldy," he said between chews, "I've told you everything I can. You know I can't talk to you about office matters or anything along those lines." He wiped his mouth and fingers with a paper napkin and then regarded me. His eyes were steely, then soft. "Look," he went on, conciliatory again, "I know you've gotten all involved in this since your business was closed down because of that unfortunate incident at Laura's house."

I looked at him and then puffed up my stomach and chest with air. It was a yoga breathing thing I had learned in the Seventies that was supposed to calm you down. It didn't work.

"Unfortunate," I said, "indeed. It happened to you, and you seem pretty indifferent. What's worse, it just doesn't seem to be getting solved, does it? I keep getting more questions than answers. Pretty weird, huh? Do you know if Laura had medical problems? Emotional problems?"

He pursed his lips, shook his head.

"Goldy," he said, "I don't. She was a troubled girl, woman, that's why she killed herself. We just all need to put losing her behind us. And I sure would like to help you financially through this particular time of stress. Let

Vonette and me give you a couple thousand until you re-open. Okay?"

I shook my head, but he ignored me.

He said, "And I would appreciate it if you would quit worrying about this rat-poison silliness. Just let the police finish their job. They're the ones with the most information. They know what they're doing."

I stood up to clear my place. I said, "As I recall, that was the approach that worked so well with Watergate."

He smiled, stood up, sat down, sighed.

"Tough as nails, that's our Goldy. Now if I had been John Richard, I would have learned how to keep you—"

"Well now, isn't this cozy," said Marla as she waddled up to us. She was wearing a sky-blue sweat suit embroidered with tiny turquoise feathers. Close on her heels fluttered Patty Sue, a vision in rose mohair sweater and white wool slacks. "Is the pastry shop neutral territory? No attempted poisonings allowed? No need for hostilities, it was a joke. Let's see. What are we having? Pasties and chocolate! But I'm interrupting."

"You're not interrupting," I said as I motioned to Patty Sue that we had to leave. Marla pouted. I said to her, "Fritz was just telling me how he doesn't understand women, and he was hoping you could enlighten him."

"Oh Fritz, this just sounds too scrumptious a topic for words," said Marla, seating herself beside him and eyeing his remaining brownie. "I've never enlightened anyone in my life."

On that hopeful note, I guided Patty Sue out of the shop. Pomeroy had instructed me to obtain a learner's permit for her. This proved easy enough at the local office of the Division of Motor Vehicles, because, happily, Patty Sue had learned enough from her handbook to pass the written test.

"I haven't had any lunch," she said, once she was done and we were on the way to the lesson. "Have you?"

She picked up a hot dog and cone at the Dairy Delight next to the high school. We started to walk to class; I held the cone while she worked on the wiener.

"Patty Sue," I began in what I hoped was a mild tone, "could we just try chatting a little bit about Laura Smiley? Please?"

She groaned.

"That reminds me," she said through bites. "Trixie called. From the athletic club. She wanted to know exactly when it was you were going to clean over there, and when we were going to set up the food."

"Right," I said. "Did you all talk about anything else?"

Patty Sue gave me a glassy look. She said, "Not this time," and began on her cone.

"What did you talk about last time?"

"I can't tell you, Goldy."

"Why not?"

"I just can't. It's too . . . dangerous."

Oh give me a break, I thought. I looked around. Pom had said Driver Ed was above the parking lot, next to Dairy Delight. Why the county commissioners had permitted a small commercial zone between two areas of the high school grounds was beyond me. But as with the workings of the police department, I didn't question it.

"No more goodies now," I said firmly to Patty Sue as she gave a longing look back at the giant glass ice cream sculpture. "You don't want to turn into a pillar of salt."

"Huh?"

"You know," I said, "Lot's wife. She looked back when she wasn't supposed to."

"I don't understand what you're talking about."

"Forget it."

One of the boys in my Sunday school class, after hearing this part of the Sodom and Gomorrah story, had said his mom looked back at their house and *she* turned into a telephone pole. Now I gave a longing look back at my van.

I would have preferred being anywhere other than where we were going.

We clambered over a sloped concrete embankment and saw Pomeroy and his students clustered in the middle of the paved expanse ahead. Although the weather had warmed to a cool fifty degrees, the teens standing around in groups wore no sweaters or jackets, but only the uniforms of their group: preppies, punks, or jocks. No hippies, though, and no ideological messages on the shirts. Things had changed.

"There you are," said Pomeroy as he came sauntering up to us. My heart flip-flopped, but I ignored it.

"I have delivered your trainee," I announced. "Now may I go sit over on the embankment while you teach?"

Pom shook his head. "Sorry," he said, "I need you to stay in the car with her. Most of the other kids in the class have been learning to drive for the last six weeks. But Patty Sue here will need more supervision." He smiled at my roommate in her pink and white outfit.

She said, "I'm glad to be learning from a real driving teacher this time."

"You can use my driver-ed car," Pom told me and motioned to a yellow Japanese number on the other side of the lot. "I rigged it up myself so that it's equipped with a brake on your side. That way you can slow things down if you need to. That's old-fashioned driver ed. This is my last class of the day, so when we're done we can go over to Dairy Delight and have hot fudge sundaes. Sound good?"

"It sounds super," said Patty Sue.

He winked at me. "I'll give her the stationary instructions once we get over to the course. You can drive her over," he said, then turned to Patty Sue. "Young lady, you're going to be driving like a pro in no time."

Oh, God. *No time* was what I had for this educational experience.

"Brother," said Patty Sue as she opened the door to the old yellow Civic, "this car sure is little."

"Compared to the van," I said as I slid in on the driver side, "it is."

The teens were trudging across the course marked with fluorescent orange cones toward the Dairy Delight edge of the Driver Ed lot. There, about half of them formed a group to one side while the others disappeared into a line of dark cars with taxi-type signs on top—CAUTION! STUDENT DRIVER!

I had noticed ours didn't have a sign, probably because it was Pom's. Well, who needed a warning about us? I looked at the small windshield and tried to rid myself of a mental image of going through it.

Patty Sue said, "I'm scared. Well, you know what I mean. I wish Pom was the one in here with me." That made two of us. Patty Sue wiggled in her seat. She said, "I feel so cramped."

At that moment Mr. Wonderful was waving and honking to us from his nice big safe-looking Saab.

"First gear!" he called back and made the wagon-ho sign. In Colorado they never let you forget the Old West.

I put the Civic into first and started across the course. I looked over at Patty Sue's feet, which were next to the brake bar. She saw me and tapped the bar. We screeched to a stop.

"What are you doing?" I demanded. "Will you just please put on your seat belt and then hold still?"

"I thought you wanted me to do it," Patty Sue said. "Anyway, my body is too long for this little seat."

I said, "The Japanese are small people."

The Saab chugged along in front of us, and for a moment I had the apprehensive feeling that accompanies the slow incline on a giant roller coaster. When we came up to the class, Pom jumped out. He signaled to the driving teens to repeat the course before heading over toward us. At Pom's request, Patty Sue and I changed places.

"Okay," he said, as he reached across Patty Sue's lap to

restart the car. "You say you've had some driving experience."

"Yes," Patty Sue said hesitantly.

I thought, If she's lying, I'll kill her.

"Do you remember to press in the clutch each time you need to change gears?" Pomeroy was asking. She nodded and he went on. "Then you go a little faster. Do you know how to change gears?"

She nodded again. "I've done it in our driveway at home. Neutral to reverse."

Pom frowned and said, "Why don't you move this seat back a little, Patty Sue? But watch it. When you go back, Goldy here'll come forward. I did it that way for teenage drivers with shorter legs and adult instructors with longer ones. You all are sort of the opposite of that."

I hated it when people referred to my being short. To make up for the coming lack of legroom I put Patty Sue's purse in the back next to *Home Beekeeping* and *Fifth Grade Science in the Classroom, Teachers' Edition.*

Patty Sue grunted and brought her seat back. My face made a sudden spring toward the windshield.

"Not so much!" I howled, but Patty Sue was off.

"Let me know if I'm making you nervous!" she yelled as she gunned the accelerator while we were in first gear. We spurted forward. When I was trying to get comfortable she veered right.

"Gosh, this steers so easily," she cried, as we tilted on two wheels and my door swung open.

"No, no!" I shouted. But she veered left and then right again. Only my seat belt kept me from falling out.

"Brake!" called Pom. "Brake!"

With another screeching turn I was back inside the car and pressing with both feet on the brake bar.

"Damn you!" I yelled at a surprised Patty Sue. "I've got a kid at home to take care of! And at my age I don't care for an extended trip to the hospital and a set of dentures! Now will you calm down, for God's sake?"

"I guess I'm not very good at this," she said, contrite at my sudden rage.

Pom trotted up to us and leaned in on her side.

"Take it easy now, girls."

"Oh shut up!" I said. "Why don't you get in here with Mario Andretti in first gear? See what it's like."

Pom again gave Patty Sue gentle explanations about the gears, clutch, accelerator, and, most important from my point of view, brakes. Getting Patty Sue into a comfortable distance from the steering wheel had meant that my feet were only inches from the brake bar on my side. The students, still standing around in groups, giggled and pointed at us.

"Sorry," Patty Sue said once Pom had sauntered off again. "I guess I just screw up everything."

I felt bad in spite of myself.

"You don't screw up everything," I reassured her as she bumped us along, still in first, to the short middle track of the drivers' course. When she did not answer I surveyed the cones and fences, which had looked like a miniature golf course when we first climbed over the embankment. Now they presented themselves as large and unyielding. Dairy Delight and the cars in the high school parking lot, on the other hand, looked like pieces from a Lionel train set. Laughing, blasé teens zoomed by on both sides of our Honda, downshifting and upshifting and steering around the obstacles as effortlessly as toddlers on trikes.

"I do screw up everything," she said while we were waiting our turn.

"Come on, Patty Sue," I said with false enthusiasm. "You're going to learn to drive, the business is going to be reopened, everything is going to be okay."

"If I had learned to drive when I was supposed to, then

we wouldn't have to be doing this today. And if it weren't for me, your business would be reopened."

Now she really had my attention. We were still stopped, so I said, "What do you mean?"

"Well, you know, my talk with Laura," she said plaintively. "If she hadn't died, then that thing wouldn't have happened at her house."

It was finally our turn, so Patty Sue inched and jerked the Honda along while teens in the passing cars shouted derisively at us. She catapulted us into second and we picked up a little speed.

"Give it a little more gas," Pomeroy called.

Patty Sue obeyed and then said, "I just think if I tell you about it, something bad will happen. Now do I go to fourth?" she asked as she swerved to avoid a cone.

I was gripping the sides of my seat.

I said, "Third. Just concentrate on your driving. We can talk about the rest later."

But she was off and running. "I'm afraid to tell you about Laura!" she wailed. "I'm afraid of what will happen!"

Preoccupied with these thoughts, she pushed the Honda into neutral and the engine gasped. Then she put it into fourth and the car sighed until she stepped on the accelerator again.

"No!" I yelled, as we whizzed by our first set of startled teenagers.

"Downshift!" came Pomeroy's remote voice.

"If I tell you what I told Laura," Patty Sue shouted as her knuckles turned white on the steering wheel, "you might die! That's what happened to her!"

"Don't worry about it now!" I shrieked over the rushing sound the wind was making in our car.

"I don't know how to downshift," Patty Sue called out the window.

"Look out!" I howled as a Volkswagen loomed before us.

Patty Sue swerved wildly and shattered a headlight of the VW. As she turned again my body fell forward, then back, and my feet became jammed underneath the brake bar. I looked out at the timid VW driver, who was stepping gingerly from her car.

I yelled, "My feet are stuck!"

We were speeding headlong toward the ice cream place.

"I can't brake!" yelled Patty Sue. "I'll crush your feet!"

"Take your foot off the accelerator!" I shouted.

She screamed, "Is the accelerator this one?" She pushed down again on the gas.

"No, no, no, no!" came voices far behind us.

Suddenly before us was Dairy Delight, where the tables and chairs were lined up like so many bowling pins. A worker came running out waving a knife. I let go of the dashboard long enough to honk. He leaped out of the way. We hit the plastic chairs and tables with a solid *thunk thunk thunk*. I tried to loosen my feet but could not.

"Why don't you steer?" I cried.

"Where?" Patty Sue screamed. She wrenched the wheel to the left, then gunned the engine again.

We came up behind Dairy Delight. Two attendants were disgorging the remains of three huge ice cream barrels. Before us was a mountain of slop. On the other side of that, I knew, was the cement embankment.

The Honda hit the edge of the ice cream puddle like a water skier going full tilt; the wheels spewed a muddy wave of glop over the attendants. We skidded wildly toward the embankment.

"Oh God," I cried, "no!"

"Help!" called Patty Sue. She began to shriek wildly, then pressed the accelerator again.

I am going to die, I thought as we hit the embankment. But we didn't stop. The Honda climbed. We vaulted the concrete. Below us were the cars in the school lot. Patty Sue passed out.

Unfortunately, I could see our trajectory only too well. We were aiming for a roof, a car roof, that I tried to imagine being soft. A cloud. A trampoline.

But no. When the Honda landed on my van, it collapsed like a beer can.

CHAPTER 16

I really get off on women in hospital gowns," Investigator Tom Schulz said as he patted my knee beneath the white sheet.

The room was slightly fuzzy, but then cleared to pale institutional green walls and a window luminous with the apricot light of sunset. I said to Tom Schulz, "Are you here because I broke a law?"

He gave a low whistle.

"And here I was trying to be sweet and pay you a nice visit. Look. What's wrong with this picture?"

He handed me a photograph, whether made by the police, the school, a bystander, or the *Mountain Journal* I knew not. It showed the yellow Honda perched atop my van. Someone had attached the caption DRIVER ED?

I handed it back to him. "Where are the mountains in the background? There ought to be something pretty about this."

"Your friend didn't try to ski the car, Miss Goldy, she tried to fly it."

A nurse swished in and I checked her name tag. I was at Lutheran Hospital. "Am I all right? Is Patty Sue Williams—"

"You're just banged up," she said. She checked my vital signs and shook her head. "You're lucky you're not dead. And that nothing's broken. Want some pain medication?" I nodded and she went on. "You'll probably only be here tonight. We're just watching you." She smiled. "They said it looks like you'll be discharged in the morning."

Schulz winked at me. "Why don't you let me watch her?"

She ignored him and left.

I closed my eyes and made a mental journey through my body. My head throbbed and my back and hips hurt.

"Do you know about my son?" I asked Schulz. "What time is it?"

"He went to your friend Marla's house. When I heard about an accident at the high school, and that you were in it—" He stopped to shake his head. "I went by your house. Your son had already come home and left you a note. On the door, very bad. Tells criminals you're not home. Anyway, I called the place where he said he was. Talked to that yakkety-yak woman Marla, who says Arch can stay as long as you're in the hospital."

"Thank you," I said. I wasn't just touched by his effort. I was overwhelmed. I said, "That's my ex-husband's second ex-wife you're talking about."

"Well," he said while studying the view out my window, "except for his first wife, the guy shows no taste."

I said, "How's Patty Sue?"

"She got here and asked for your ex-father-in-law. To treat her broken arm."

"But he just does ob-gyn."

"Pardon me, Goldilocks, but your friend isn't very smart. Not to mention that her driving needs a whole lot of work."

"Forgive me for failing to see the humor in this," I said to Schulz. "I do appreciate your efforts, but why are you here, anyway? I thought you were investigating bike gangs."

"I get around," he said. "Radios are a wonderful invention. Not to mention that I was supposed to call you."

I avoided looking at the closet, which I hoped held my purse with Arch's letter from Laura Smiley.

"So you want to talk, or not?" he asked, tapping the sheet.

I said, "I have no job, no car, no helpers, my son is at a friend's house, and I don't have the faintest idea how I'm going to cover the cost of this hospital visit. I'm really not in the mood for talking about the so-called poisoning incident right now."

He clucked his tongue. "Spare me. You were going to check out your ex-mother-in-law and your little friend Trixie and get back to me, remember? I was kind of hoping it would be over pizza tonight. In fact," he went on cheerfully, "I could even go out and get us some right now. Have a supper date right here in the hospital. You like pepperoni?"

My head began its internal thunder again. As if on cue the nurse swept in with a small tray containing what I hoped was an extremely potent narcotic.

"Oh thank you," I said extravagantly, and then to Schulz, "I haven't gotten much out of Vonette. But I will. Trixie, Patty Sue, and Laura Smiley had a conversation in a steamroom close to when Laura died." I took my pill, thought for a minute. "I found an old article about a mistrial back in Illinois. Involving Korman senior. You might want to see what you can dig up. The torn article is by my phone at home. It's what I've been trying to reach you about all week. I'll get it for you as soon as I get out."

"Anything else?"

"That's all I've found out. I don't feel too great," I said

honestly. He *had* been kind to me. And he cared about Arch. I met his gaze. "Thanks again for checking on my son. And on me."

"No sweat," he said. "I'll want that article. Now, have you found out anything about someone named Hollenbeck?"

"I saw the name on a photograph."

"I got the name of the high school in Illinois where Laura Smiley did her internship," he said. "Called out there and talked with the one teacher who was there when our departed friend was there. She remembered a student of Smiley's named Bebe Hollenbeck."

"Can we talk to this student? Can she tell us something?"

"She's been dead for twenty years. But apparently Laura and this gal were very tight."

I said, "Laura kept pictures of her." I thought. "I'll ask Vonette, maybe she'll talk about that time in Illinois."

"Okeydoke." He gave me a wide grin. "You still not sure about going out with me? It's one way for me to keep tabs on you, to make sure you stay safe." He smiled. "If that's possible."

I returned his smile, which was difficult because pain was still knotting up my back. I said, "The athletic club Halloween party. Trick or treat. We can go together, if you'd like."

The nurse gave Schulz an ominous stare, and he left. But not before he had nodded to me. And winked.

"There was another fellow who wanted to see you a little while ago," the nurse said when we were alone. "He went away when he saw you had a visitor, but I imagine he'll be back."

"Please don't tell me it was a doctor."

"I don't think so," said the nurse. "Tall? Good-looking? Claimed he was the one responsible for this mess."

Great. I couldn't wait to throttle that stellar driving instructor, Pomeroy Locraft. Perhaps my window was high enough off the ground so that I could ask the nurse to throw him out.

The nurse was saying, "Do you have someone to pick up you and Miss Williams tomorrow?"

"I'll work something out," I assured her. "Just let me deal with one crisis at a time."

I called Marla; Arch was fine. They were on their way out for burgers after Arch used the last of her Brie to finish constructing an elaborate trap for the resident mice.

Next I called Vonette Korman. It was past five, but she was still coherent. I reminded Vonette that I'd taken in Patty Sue at her request, that Patty Sue was a patient of her husband's, and that it was her son who had treated me so rottenly in the first place that I had to do catering and cleaning in a van that Patty Sue had wrecked. And furthermore, I added before she could do more than make sympathetic murmuring noises, now the two of us were at Lutheran Hospital and we needed her to come and pick us up tomorrow morning. Early.

"That's awful," said Vonette.

"Right," I said. My door was opening again; I needed to get off the phone. "And may I borrow one of your cars, Vonette? I've got to get around somehow."

She mumbled something about seeing what she could do and I hung up.

A sweet-smelling Persian violet preceded Pomeroy Locraft into my room. He held the plant like a shield, which was probably a good thing. Patty Sue was in a cast, but my arm was in good shape. I looked around for a suitable projectile. Luckily for Pomeroy, there wasn't one.

"Bees may like the smell of Persian violets," I said sharply as I whacked the pillows behind my back, "but I don't. Even if my nose isn't broken."

He smiled. "Actually, bees prefer wild daisies and clover. Patty Sue thought you'd like these."

"What'd you bring her, fudge?"

"Honey candy."

"I should sue your ass for negligence," I snapped, "or gross incompetence as an instructor, or something along those lines."

He placed the plant, a pale purple-and-green cloud of fragrance, on the movable tray near my head. Then in one slow motion he unfurled his lanky body into the room's only chair. His face was pinched with stress. His hand cut wavy furrows through his dark hair. Finally he looked at me.

"Goldy, I'm sorry. The school insurance ought to cover the repair to your van. Patty Sue, I don't know. I really didn't think she'd—"

"Be naive and reckless at the same time? Would you even recognize naive if you saw it?" I plopped back on the pillows. "Tell me, Pom. Do your students ever say, You are *driving* me crazy? You are *driving* me up the wall?"

He blushed, but for once I was impervious to the charm of vulnerability.

I said, "And while I've got you to myself, tell me what Laura Smiley's science text was doing in your backseat."

Now he turned really red. My guess as to the ownership of that book had paid off.

He said, "We used to work together sometimes."

"You were friends, or what?"

He let out breath that was deeper than a sigh. "What difference does it make?"

"A lot."

He said, "Friends, yes. We'd started working together on that spring project for fourth and fifth grades. Some of the students enjoyed working with the bees. Answer your question?"

"She and Arch were close," I said. "You know that. He's taking her death real hard. You know anything else about her?"

He paused. I waited.

"It doesn't matter now, I guess," he said. He looked

out the window. "We were in Al-Anon together. You know what that is?"

Sundays, noon, Episcopal church. Of course. I nodded. "Sure. It's the support group for relatives and friends of alcoholics. Can you tell me what she said in there?"

"No."

"Can you tell me anything about her?"

"Like what? I don't want to betray her—whatever you'd call it—memory."

"She's dead. I don't believe it was suicide, mainly because things just don't fit." I adjusted myself on the pillows. It felt as if the pain pill had turned my bed into a kind of boat floating in a big tub the size of the room. I said, "Do you know anything about her relationship *with* or *to* Fritz Korman?"

"Why?"

"Because of that mess with the rat poison, I'm suspected. The health department closed me down. No cooking, no income."

"Aren't the cops looking into it?"

"For heaven's sake, Pom, they're slow." I stopped talking long enough to take a whiff of the plant. "I'm trying to get myself cleared before the holiday season. Here's this nice teacher gone, my catering operation down. I'm trying to open a cleaning business instead, needing for Patty Sue to learn to drive . . . and then Patty Sue does one of her spaceout routines and my van gets destroyed. So yes, I'm interested in knowing as much as I can about both Dr. Korman senior who somebody tried to kill and Laura Smiley who somebody may have. Which includes anything you might know," I finished, again out of breath and with my head swimming inside the bed-boat.

Pomeroy said, "What are you looking for, background?"

"Anything."

He said, "Laura Smiley's father was an alcoholic. It's what killed him, finally. He drove himself and Laura's mother into the back of a pickup over near Conifer. Alcohol level in his blood was three times what they consider to be intoxication."

"What does this have to do with—"

"Just hold on a sec," he said and readjusted himself in his chair. "By that time Laura was long gone. She had moved to Illinois to go to school. She had some family, that aunt who was at the funeral, there. She taught high school when she finished at the U. of I.—that's how she met the Kormans. She came out with them one time on a ski vacation, while they were friends, to be their sort of guide and babysitter, even though she was only twenty-one or -two.

"Not long after," he went on, "the Kormans left Illinois. Moved to the spot Laura had shown them."

"Did she know they were here?"

He shrugged. "She knew they had moved to Colorado. She didn't know they'd moved to her hometown. When her parents died they left her their place, and she moved back. A big coincidence which probably didn't feel too great to anybody."

"When she moved back here," I said, "did she see the Kormans? Have contact with them?"

"Not socially, as far as I know."

"What do you mean?"

He thought, then said, "Laura avoided the Kormans because there was bad blood between them."

I said, "Bad blood from what?"

He was still looking out the window. After a minute he said, "That's something you'd better ask Vonette, I think."

"Great. What about Patty Sue?" I asked. "Apparently she and Laura had at least one earth-shattering chat."

"Yes," he said, "they did."

"About what?"

"You talked to Patty Sue?"

"I tried, Pomeroy, but that's not saying I got any answers."

"Yes, well." He shrugged again.

"Why would *Laura* avoid the *Kormans*?" I asked. This was the real puzzle to me. "It's too small a town to try to do that. Did she actually use that word, *avoid*?"

Pomeroy's head turned. His brown eyes met mine. He said, "You asked what she was doing in Al-Anon. She had a lot to work through, her parents dying in an accident, her relationship with the Kormans going from closeness to alienation. She had sorrow, a ton of it, and a lot of grieving to do. She, yes, said that she needed to avoid these people, that being involved with them in any way caused her pain. She said that for her mental health she needed to keep her distance."

I stared at him. I said, "Okay, first, she belonged to the athletic club, to which they also belong. Second, she became very close pals with their grandson, who just happens to be my son. Third, right before she died she went to see Fritz Korman. She made an appointment, Pomeroy. She had an office visit the day she died. The office sent her a bill, for God's sake. Explain how all this adds up to avoidance."

Pomeroy was quiet for a minute. "You know, I don't have all the answers." He shifted his weight in the chair and crossed his arms across his plaid flannel shirt. "It seems to me," he said thoughtfully, "that if you really want to know who would be wanting to get Korman out of the way, you ought to think of who would benefit from his being gone."

"I've already thought of that."

"In a will, it's usually the next of kin who inherit."

"You mean like my ex-husband?"

"Or his mother."

I said, "Vonette would never have the guts to do the old guy in. Besides. I saw her at that reception. She was as drunk as a skunk."

"She had a flask."

"Aren't you the observant one."

"Korman was cheating on her."

I said, "Why, you're just a fount of information. With whom?"

"I shouldn't be the one to say."

"Do it anyway."

He stopped talking and looked out the window, then he seemed to have an idea.

"Goldy. Didn't you say you were out of honey?"

"Yeah, so?"

"Why don't you come out to my place in the Wildlife Preserve and get some. Next week." He stopped to think. "On Wednesday."

"Why Wednesday?"

"You come on Wednesday. If the weather's still warm, you'll get answers to some of your questions."

CHAPTER 17

With Pomeroy gone the room was temporarily quiet. Privacy in a hospital, like silence in a library, is what one expects but only rarely gets. I looked out the window, now filled with the gray light of dusk. Had Laura been involved with Pomeroy? What difference would that make, anyway? I shook my head, which felt as if it was filled with the somber light of painkiller. It was hard to make sense of the whole thing.

The note!

When I leaped out of bed my body buckled. Soreness climbed my legs. My arms felt and looked as if they'd been stretched on a rack. The pain pill had apparently only entered my head. I hobbled across the room, reached into my bag, and found the letter.

It was crumpled, leading to the conclusion that Arch had read it before stuffing it in his desk. The beige stationery crackled. Inside were perfect, looping, black letters, the writing of a teacher. It read:

Dear Arch,

Thanks for your latest idea, dungeon master! I do like the idea of being a troll. Does that mean I can cast spells? I can't wait!

Unfortunately, we won't be able to play this Saturday as we'd planned. I have something very important I have to do. In a way it's like the thing you talked about in your last letter. Remember how you said most of the kids in sixth grade didn't seem to care about Halloween anymore, how they called that and your role-playing and trivia games kids' stuff? I remember how bad that made you feel. And now you don't know what to do? I have something like that in my life, too. And Saturday I have to do something about it.

How about next weekend for our game? That'll give me a whole week to get ready! Let me know on Monday, okay?

Hugs,
Ms. Smiley

But he had not let her know on Monday. Nor had he let me know that he'd had plans with Laura Smiley for Saturday, the day the deputy coroner had indicated she had died.

October the third was beginning to look quite complex.

There was a gnawing in my stomach not brought on by the van accident. I felt uncomfortable with, jealous and suspicious of, the relationship between Arch and Laura Smiley. She had been too close to him. And perhaps to the other student that Schulz had mentioned, the deceased Hollenbeck girl. These relationships smacked of impropriety, somehow. The note brought Arch into a world of adult problems, even if the reference was vague. This in turn might account for his inability to talk about the letter or to deal with Laura's death in an appropriate way.

I looked at the piece of paper in my hand. On Saturday, October 3, something had gone wrong after Laura had walked into town to do something, and then returned by car. But what? This letter raised more questions than it answered.

Arch. I could imagine him cycling over to her house and ringing the bell. Hearing no answer, he would have come back home. But why had he mentioned none of this to me or to Investigator Schulz? What was he afraid of?

Maybe Laura Smiley hadn't been all there in the upstairs department, after all. Maybe this desire to help students she liked had flipped her out. The problem was, whatever this drama was we were involved in, it wasn't over.

"My little Goldy," Vonette said after she walked in the next morning and gave me a smooch on the cheek. She smelled of Estée instead of gin: a good sign.

I said, "Thanks for coming, Vonette. Another meal of hospital food and I would have taken over the kitchen by force. Patty Sue know you're here?"

"Oh yes," Vonette replied as she checked her creamy orange lipstick and curly same-hue-of-orange hair in my bathroom mirror. "Got that arm set and everything. She's going to be great. Six weeks she'll be out of that thing, good as new, able to help you with the catering."

"Cleaning, Vonette," I corrected, "until we or the police figure out what happened to Fritz."

Vonette sauntered out of the bathroom. "Let's not get into that again. Gives me a headache just thinking about it."

"Tell me," I said while gingerly pulling my slip over my head, "since I'm still mulling that funeral over in my mind. Did you get to know Laura Smiley well when she was your vacation nanny?"

Vonette sat down in the room's only chair, brought out a pack of Kools, and inserted one in the newly lipsticked mouth. So much for the hospital's *No Smoking* policy.

"Yes and no," she said. She paused to light and inhale. "Anyway, I can loan you a car. That old station wagon of ours. Used to use it to pull the boat down to Lake Powell. Before the engine gave out. Boat engine, that is. I don't know about the wagon, probably been a year or more since it's been started, might need a jump."

"Do you know if Laura Smiley had any enemies?"

She laughed quietly and took a deep drag. "More enemy talk."

"Do you know someone who just plain didn't like her?"

She said, "Well, there again, yes and no." She raised one thin penciled eyebrow at me. "I did know her for a long time, though. I mean not that we were close. Nothing like that. You know."

Dressed by then, I sat down on the bed. "No," I said, "I don't."

"Well," said Vonette. "Well, well." She stood up. The cigarette drooped from her mouth. "I'll tell you all about it sometime."

"According to Fritz," I said, "John Richard would inherit the practice if he died. Doesn't that bother you?"

Her eyes narrowed. "You sure?"

"No."

"Well, I don't really know either, I guess. I thought if something happened to old Fritz, like he had a heart attack while he was doing an abortion, God punishing him, y'know . . ." She raised her eyebrows at me.

"Vonette!"

"Well? That's still a hot issue in the church, after all."

"It's too bad they worry about that more than they do adultery," I said evenly.

"Now, now," she said. "Don't start in on John Richard. Let's not get into that again, please. I'm beginning to feel a headache coming on. Anyway." She crushed the cigarette underneath one of her open-toed sandals. So much for hospital *hygiene*. "You know his daddy isn't much better. I try not to think about that. Although," she said as she felt around in her purse, "I have to admit, sometimes I've thought about killing the old lech myself."

"Really."

"Yeah." She eyed me sadly. "But you know I don't mean that. What the hell, I've made it this long, I can take it, right?" She gave me a confused look. "Oh yeah, the practice. I thought in that kind of situation, it was split between John Richard and me. I mean the Accounts Receivable. I don't know what happens to the equipment and the patients. Who'd want to kill him to get his patients?"

I had been putting on my makeup; I paused to look at her.

"You mean, the good ones are all gone?"

She sighed. "Well, you always lose a few. You know babies die sometimes before they're born. The patients blame Fritz. Now and then they sue, if they can stand all that agony."

"Anybody sue lately? That you know of?"

"Nope." She looked around the room. "My head hurts. S'pose they'd give me something here?"

"What are you taking for your headaches now, Vonette?"

She said, "Demerol."

"Demerol? With your orange juice?"

"Don't laugh, Goldy. You don't know how bad the pain is. I have to have injections when I just can't stand it."

"Sorry. I know how much you've suffered."

In truth I did not know the extent of her suffering. But I was determined to find out.

The hospital wouldn't give Vonette any oral meds, as they called them, so she contented herself with something out of a prescription bottle that she fished from her voluminous purse.

We drove up 38th Avenue in silence. Patty Sue was hushed with what I hoped was contrition. Vonette wasn't talking because she was deep in thought or pain or both. I was quiet because I was trying to figure out what Vonette was thinking.

"Gee, you guys," Patty Sue said thinly into the silence, "my hospital breakfast was awful."

"Mine was better than the other meal I had there," I said truthfully.

"You girls want to stop and get a bite to eat?" asked Vonette. "My treat. I could use something myself, anyway."

"Goldy," Patty Sue said in a husky voice, "are you mad?"

I said, "What? With no business? No car? No money? Me, mad? Yes. Mad as in *angry*. Heading toward *deranged*."

"Now, girls," came Vonette's soothing voice, "let's not get all upset. We'll have a little brunch. Couple plates of huevos rancheros and you'll both be doing a lot better."

She signaled to turn right. Her Fleetwood, which maneuvered like a road-bound yacht, glided into the parking lot of a Mexican restaurant built in the shape of a sombrero.

Vonette invited me to join her in a margarita, but I opted for a fruit smoothie. Patty Sue ordered a Coke. She asked the waitress if it was true that the Mexicans had chocolate sauce on their eggs and if so, could she? The waitress gave Vonette a questioning look.

"Oh, sweetie pie," Vonette assured her, "don't you worry about my girls here. Just bring the three of us your huevos and we'll be fine. Oh yes, and make that a pitcher of margaritas. Okay?"

Fine and dandy. It was clear I would be taking the helm of the Fleetwood after lunch. Which reminded me.

I said, "Where is the station wagon you're loaning me, Vonette?"

The pitcher of margaritas had materialized in front of us along with Patty Sue's Coke, my smoothie, and a single salted glass.

"Now remember," Vonette said as she poured and then

took a long swig. "We haven't used it as our family car for a long time. We bought it a few years after we moved here."

"Moved here?" I asked. Information might come after Vonette's first drink but before her fourth. I said, "You know, John Richard never talked to me about his life before Colorado. About how you and Fritz met, what your early life was like in Illinois."

My ex-mother-in-law pondered the crust of orange lipstick she had left on her margarita glass.

I said, "Please tell me."

Finally Vonette said, "Oh, well."

She began slowly. "We used to work together," she said. "I was Fritz's secretary. Sometimes he'd take me out in the country to help with a delivery. We became very close, but it was all proper, I wanted it that way, being a divorcée and all."

"What?" I said.

"Oh yeah," she said, "I'd been married before, right out of high school in Corpus. My first husband was in the navy. Then I got pregnant, had my baby, and the navy moved us to Norfolk, where Joe was from anyway. You know, in Virginia. There Joe got involved with first one call girl, then another. Then he left for good. I was awfully young, just twenty when Joe moved out." She sighed. "So when I met Fritz I'd been on my own for a while anyway, trying to make do for myself and my little baby girl." She sloshed a large measure of the green stuff into her orange-and-salt-lined glass. "Just breaks my heart the way people don't care about marriage these days. Or those days either. Anyway, there were hundreds of navy wives looking for clerical work in Norfolk, so off I went with a girlfriend and my three-year-old little daughter to Carolton, Illinois, because my friend had kin there." She paused for a few swallows. "We had some tough times, let me tell you, living in first one and then another trailer court, men always thinking I was available, as if I was . . . loose."

I said, "So how did the doctor fit in?"

"Oh, he was so nice to me when I was looking for work," Vonette gushed. "Treated me so nicely. It was my first regular job. Then after I had worked for him for six years, well, his wife died of cancer. A few months later he asked me to marry him and it took me about two seconds to say 'You bet.' "

"Colorado is a long way from Illinois," I mused.

"Yes, well." Vonette took out her mirror to do a little damage control on the lipstick. "Let me tell you, being a doctor's wife is not all it's cracked up to be." She thought. "We got married in a little chapel and then started to try, no matter what, to be a family. After I had John Richard I thought everything would settle down but it didn't." She stopped to look out the restaurant window. "My daughter, she, well, she had some problems in school. Not too bad at first, but things got so much worse when she got to be a teenager. John Richard was just about ten then, and I guess I wasn't paying as much attention to her as I should have. She had started out liking Fritz, but their relationship . . . sort of got bad, if you know what I mean."

Patty Sue excused herself to go to the bathroom. Vonette let out a very long breath.

"My daughter . . . got involved with a fast sort of gang. She had gone through a lot, and she was only seventeen." Another swallow. "Then one night, she drank too much. The kids dared her, is what came out afterwards. She drank a whole bottle of Southern Comfort, then keeled over dead. Seventeen years old, and everything to live for. It was just awful."

I reached out and held Vonette's hand.

I said, "I'm sorry."

"Yes, well," she said, "you wanted to hear this story and now you're hearing it. Just let me finish, maybe it'll do me good to talk." She gripped my hand. "Anyhow," she went on, "that's when I started getting my headaches real bad. Life wasn't good for Fritz then either; he was, well, he couldn't really practice, so we decided to make a clean break of things and move out here."

"Couldn't really practice?" I said. "Why? From grief?"

"Oh, no," said Vonette. She ran her finger over the orange lipstick on her glass.

"Couldn't practice," I prompted.

Vonette signaled the waitress for another pitcher of margaritas. She touched her fiery hair and began to talk slowly again. "It was such a mess." She sighed. "You keep asking why we left Illinois, Goldy. I'll tell you, but the beginning of it goes back even farther, to when my daughter was sixteen. It's awful, so please, don't go around talking about it."

I nodded, although I certainly didn't like the idea of keeping whatever bad news was coming to myself.

"We *had* to leave," Vonette said in a voice just above a whisper.

The huevos arrived; we ignored them.

After the waitress left I said, "*Had* to."

"Yes." She drained her glass. "The year before my daughter died, a couple of Fritz's patients reported him to some state board. Not only that, but there was a trial coming up. That's when Laura Smiley first got involved. Oh, hell." Another sigh. "My daughter . . . said they'd had relations."

"Who had?" I asked.

"Fritz and my daughter," she said, just above a whisper. "She was sixteen."

"What?" said Patty Sue as she returned to the table.

Vonette's voice turned fierce. "I thought about divorcing Fritz then, when John Richard was nine. But he kept saying how much he needed me, and I already felt so guilty about my daughter. Well, I just couldn't leave my son without a father. I felt so confused, and then my daughter began to run with that fast gang and to drink a lot—I thought, you know, to forget—and then she passed away. I was having these terrific headaches, and Fritz was so helpful with that pain. He was so eager to make amends. It was real tragic. He said he could get certified in another state with no problem, so a month after my daughter's funeral, we came out here."

We were all silent for a moment.

I said, "What was the trial going to be about?"

Vonette shrugged her shoulders. "It doesn't matter, does it? He helps so many women with their babies, and with their problems. I don't like to think about the bad." She nodded benevolently in Patty Sue's direction. "He does seem to be such a good man that usually I just don't know what to think, so I don't. You know."

She gave me a helpless look.

She pressed on, "I don't want to know. It gives me too much of a headache, having a lot of hate inside me." She stopped talking, then started again. "Sometimes I think, *Vonette, just leave*. I hate staying. But then, I don't know."

Patty Sue and I looked at each other. Her bottom lip was trembling.

The new pitcher of margaritas arrived. Vonette gave the waitress a grateful look.

Vonette said, "I don't want to burden you girls with this." She picked up her fork and leaned over her plate.

"It's okay," I said.

Patty Sue slowly began on the cold eggs. I started to do the same but stopped when I saw tears falling onto Vonette's plate.

"Vonette," I said, "listen. Come over to my house on the thirtieth, after dinner. I'm having some friends over to talk and have dessert. We can talk some more then. You might feel better."

She sniffed and said, "The thirtieth? I don't know. Call me about it." Patty Sue reached over with her good arm and patted her on the shoulder.

"Oh girls," Vonette said, "it's okay. It was all a long

time ago. I'm all right now." As if to demonstrate how all right she was, she lifted her glass in a mock toast.

I said, "Just tell me one thing. You never told us your daughter's name. What was it? I'm curious. John Richard never mentioned her."

Vonette put her glass down and looked at me. Her cheeks sagged; her mouth turned down at the edges. Her eyes were solemn and tired and indicated a sadness belied by the wild orange hair and made-up face.

She said, "Joe and I had thought since my name was French we should give her a French name. She was such a cute baby, that's what we called her. Baby. Only in French it's spelled different. So she was our Bebe. That's what I had put on her gravestone, too. Bebe Hollenbeck, 1950 to 1967."

CHAPTER 18

W ho said a little learning was a dangerous thing? Was knowledge dangerous, too? If so, what was a lot of knowledge, more or less dangerous? And if the knowledge was related but disconnected, what good was it at all?

I clutched the keys Vonette had given me and slumped behind the wheel of the Kormans' old green Chrysler station wagon, trying to put things in place. Vonette's first child had been Bebe Hollenbeck. Bebe had also been a student of Laura Smiley's when the Kormans and Laura had lived in Illinois. According to Vonette, Fritz Korman had seduced Bebe when she was sixteen. And Bebe had drunk herself to death.

Then, Fritz Niebold Korman had moved to Colorado, bringing with him Vonette and a young John Richard. Was the practice the reason? According to the torn newspaper account in Laura's locker, there had been a mistrial. I had to get home to get the article and give it to Schulz. He'd be able to follow up on it. Whatever Laura's involvement had been in all this, it had ended in her feeling alienation that had not subsided in twenty years of living in the same small town. But why had Laura overcome her alienation—or had she? This was the most puzzling aspect of all. What did she have to say to Fritz Korman that morning? And even if hostilities had erupted, how could she have put rat poison in Fritz's coffee after she was dead?

And how and why had Laura died, anyway?

"Um, Goldy," said Patty Sue. "What are we waiting for?"

I stared at the keys. It looked as if the only thing that was going to go into place was one of them. Vonette said she had cables if we needed a jump. I had had my share of bad luck with American cars and thus had no hope for a Chrysler. I thrust the key into the ignition, pumped the gas, and turned the key.

It started right up. For once, something went right.

Our first stop was Aspen Meadow Drugstore. The hospital had given me a prescription for pain medication. George Morgan, the pharmacist, looked as old as Gabby Hayes in his last picture. He was reputed to have been in Aspen Meadow since the gold rush in nearby Central City. I noticed with some satisfaction that he finally had hired a new female assistant. As I handed George the prescription I had a thought.

"George, did you fill any prescriptions for Laura Smiley?" I called after him as he was about to disappear between shelves. He turned and shook his head at me like a wise gnome.

"This'll be ready in ten minutes," he said.

I went off to call Arch, whom I had missed more than I would have thought possible. One night away from home felt like weeks. Worse, the doctor had recommended that I spend the rest of the weekend in bed, and that Arch stay elsewhere at least until the end of school Monday.

"Not to worry," Marla assured me over the phone. "He loves it here. He keeps telling me how cool all the insects are in my greenhouse. He wanted me to help him with this crazy Halloween costume, but you know sewing's not my thing."

"What Halloween costume?"

"Oh, something from one of those crazy games. Sounds like leech. Wait. Lich. Anyway, I told him to forget it, his mother could handle the seamstress routine. If you pick hi n up Monday afternoon when the bus comes, I can tell you all the latest news. And not just about bugs." She laughed and hung up.

Back at the prescription counter the new assistant eyed me vaguely. She said, "Did you say your name was Laura Smiley?"

I blinked. "Did you hear me say that?"

She wrinkled her nose at me and looked through the *S* prescription box. Then she punched some keys on a computer. "Penicillin?" she asked. "That's what you had last time."

"Really," I said, "what did I have the time before that?"

"Can't you remember what your prescription was for this time?"

I shook my head.

This soul sister of Patty Sue punched some more buttons. "Organidin? You had a cough?" I shook my head. "Ornade?" she asked. "Colds?"

"Don't have one now."

More punching.

"Looks like that's all you've ever had. Let me go find George."

"No, no," I protested, backing away. "Let me call the doctor. He's sure to clear this all up. I'll have him give you a ring."

She shrugged. Of course, it was not the doctor who would be able to clear any of this up. Maybe now Schulz would listen to me, even if it had cost me my own prescription to relieve pain.

————

Monday morning I had the article in my hand and dialed Schulz. He was away from his desk; the clerk took a message.

"Don't forget I have a doctor's appointment today," Patty Sue reminded me.

"I haven't forgotten," I replied. "How's your arm? You sure you want to keep up with this other treatment when you're in pain?"

She said, "It's not too bad."

I looked at poor, thin Patty Sue and felt a surge of pity. "How long's he going to treat you for not getting your period?" I asked. "I don't understand why pills don't work."

"He says they will," said Patty Sue. "It just takes time. I don't question him. He *is* a doctor, you know."

I shook my head. Several hours later I revved up the wagon and drove over to Korman and Korman to deposit my charge. Indian summer weather was holding, and already the sun was lightening a deep blue sky. I did not see the doctors' twin Jeeps, with their license plates that said OB and GYN, when we arrived in a cloud of dust. Patty Sue might be in for a long wait.

When I warned her of this, she said, "It's okay, since it's warm enough to sunbathe."

"Go right ahead," I said, "just be ready after I pick up Arch. I need you to look after him while I try to do a little more digging on this thing with his teacher."

"Oh, no. Not more school trouble."

"No. His other teacher. Laura." I looked at her. She frowned back. I said, "Just sun yourself on the benches outside the pastry shop until I come back."

She nodded and turned away.

I headed toward Marla's, down Ponderosa and up Blue Spruce, roads named for the tall trees whose velvet-green arms hugged the occasional bright gold stand of aspens. I rolled down the window. No early snow had trampled down the thick, rebellious field grass or stripped the blood-red chokecherry bushes of their summer splendor. Soon the little kids in town would be dressing up for Halloween and traipsing from house to house demanding sweets. So Arch was not too old for a costume this year, after all. I remembered the lich only vaguely from our role-playing night. Researching the costume might be a pain, especially if the sewing was either complex or expensive. As it was I would be tied up getting ready for the athletic club party and molding my caramel-corn balls for the trick or treaters. The balls were wrapped in cellophane, labeled GOLDILOCKS' CATERING for advertising purposes. I knew how irresistible Halloween bags were to adults.

My eyes avoided the brass plate on the door of my ex-husband's other ex-wife. Marla and I had become allies in our dislike of John Richard, but not in our decorating taste. The plaque read Chez Marla.

"Darling," she said expansively when she came to the door. "I have just made some coffee. Until your son arrives we can have the solarium to ourselves to enjoy it. Then he's bound to run us off so he can study those damn bugs. Honestly, Goldy, I don't know how you take the strains of motherhood."

Tires of flesh rolled and swirled beneath her peach satin robe as she padded in front of me toward her sun room.

"How'd it go?" I asked after we had flopped onto overstuffed green-and-white cushions covering what I hoped was sturdy wicker. Around us were all manner of sweet-smelling plants that Marla took great pride in cultivating. "Did Arch behave himself?"

"Listen here, Goldy," she said as she handed me a china cup and saucer and poured from a sterling pot next to a Rosenthal dish heaped with sticky buns. "He was great. Bugs and all. He's so easy to get along with, it's hard to believe he comes from a long line of bastards. Sweet roll? I took Arch to the pastry shop for breakfast and stocked up."

I shook my head and glanced at the china dish Marla had filled with goodies. Next to it was a crystal pitcher bursting with stems of fragrant Cape Jasmine. Apparently John Richard had not had as loose a hand with Marla's breakables as he had with mine.

Marla, resplendent in her queen-size robe, settled back into her cushion.

"Well," she said, "I'm just going to have one of these." She paused for a dainty bite. "So," she went on, "the rumor is that your new roommate is this great driver."

I said, "Don't. Don't even start."

"Obviously you've managed to get other transportation."

"The Kormans' old station wagon." I changed my mind and took a sweet roll. "Politics may make strange bedfellows. But it's nothing to what poverty makes."

She grunted and leaned forward to slice another roll.

I said, "I'm dying to know what you've learned about everybody I've been trying to track down lately. What have I missed? I'd rather have you than the paper."

"Well. Trixie is making noises about looking for a new job. She called and asked if I knew a lawyer, and I said what for and she said never mind and I said criminal or civil and she said criminal, I think. So maybe Hal is doing more than just making her pay for the mirror. She asked about Friday night, were we still going to meet, and I said of course, if you're not in jail, and the bitch hung up."

"Hard to believe that club has put up with her for so long," I said.

"It's hard to believe the athletic club puts up with a lot of other stuff."

"Meaning?"

"Oh, you know," she said. She picked dead leaves from a plant. "I really hate to gossip."

"Bull."

"Speaking ill of the dead, you know."

"Laura Smiley?" I asked. "What did she do at the athletic club? You were going to check out some theory of yours."

"Last month I stumbled, and I do mean it was by accident, into her having an intimate tête-à-tête with Pomeroy Locraft, in the hot tub, no less. Talking in hushed tones, mind you, so that I made a crack about it being too bad we had to wear suits in the hot tub, it being coed and all."

"What does this have to do with anything?"

She said, "I just figured, you know, that she was trying to put the moves on him. He didn't appear to be responding, so I thought, Unrequited love. She killed herself. Tragic."

"I don't buy it," I said. "He and Laura were friends, that is a fact. But as far as I can tell, it was friends, period. And maybe they were talking in low tones to avoid some of the gossipy people in this town."

"Yeah, well. After he'd gone, Laura started talking to me about the Jerk, like all of a sudden we're pals in hating him. She said, 'Did he ever go after girls?' I didn't know what she was talking about."

Good God. "Did she mention any names? Like Fritz, or someone named Bebe, for example?"

"No. I told her John Richard and I were divorced and I didn't think about him anymore, which was a lie, but I didn't really want to get into it with her. Her eyes were bugging out, like it was more than just being nosy. More like—"

"More like . . . ?"

Marla said, "More like she was furious."

I said, "But about what? It sounds as if she was *wickedly* furious."

"Please don't use that kind of language," said Marla, as she poured us more coffee. "With Halloween coming up and all."

One hour and a dozen pastries later the sound of Arch's raised voice came through the solarium windows.

"Oh, yeah?" he was screaming.

Two boys bigger than Arch were squaring off against him.

"Wimp!" yelled one. "Faggot!"

One of the big boys pushed Arch's shoulder and Arch swung back. The boy ducked, and the other boy gave an underhand punch to Arch's stomach.

"Hey!" I yelled through the glass. No one turned around. "Hey!" I yelled again.

"I'll show you," Arch was hollering. "I'll hit you with a fatal curse!" He was bent over, holding his stomach. With his free hand he was feeling along the ground for a rock to throw.

"Hey, stop!" I yelled again and looked around wildly for Marla, who had gone into the kitchen for more coffee.

The boys fell on top of Arch. The three of them squirmed and punched and thrashed. I turned, hit my head on an ivy geranium, then tripped over an exotic orchid, and cursed being lost in an indoor jungle for the second time in a week. Finally I made my way out to the front door.

"Arch! Arch!"

"You'll see!" he was yelling. "Just wait!"

"Na-na-na-na-na-na!" the boys mocked back. They disappeared down through the evergreens.

"What in the hell—"

"Let's just get out of here," Arch said without looking at me. He dusted off his shirt and rubbed his knee where his pants were torn.

"Just tell me why you're having so much trouble," I said.

"I don't know, Mom," he said. "They hate me. I'm small, so they can pick on me. Can we go home? I need to call Todd. It's *very* important."

After hasty thanks to Marla, we swung down toward Korman and Korman where I prayed Patty Sue was waiting on the pastry shop bench engaged in the peaceful activity of sunbathing. No luck. I went into the shop. No Patty Sue and they hadn't seen her. We drove back up to the front of the building and the office entry.

"I'll go in and get her," Arch volunteered.

He returned in a few minutes with the look of a young canary-swallowing cat.

"No Patty Sue," he announced.

The nurse-receptionist whom I had disrupted when I went searching for the files came charging out the front door of the office.

Arch and I both groaned. I said, "Patty Sue's probably dead."

"I hope she is," muttered Arch. "Then she won't be able to wreck any more cars."

The nurse banged on my car window.

"I want to speak to that young man," she said. "I want him to give back what he took."

Arch moaned and climbed out. He and the nurse stepped away from the car and began a low-pitched but heated discussion. Then Arch withdrew a packet from inside his shirt and handed it to her. The nurse stomped off and Arch skulked back to the car.

"You want to tell me what that was all about?" I asked.

"Oh," he said in a bored tone, "I just wanted to borrow one of those surgical packs from Dad's office for Halloween. Big deal."

"Why?"

"I thought I could use one of those tools for, like, a weapon. Not to really do anything, but to scare people. That dumb nurse wouldn't let me take it. I even told her my father was one of the doctors but it didn't work."

"Judas priest," I said, "that nurse is going to think we're a bunch of nuts." I got out of the car and went into the office, demanding to know from the loony-detector if Patty Sue had finished her appointment.

"I don't know," she said crisply. "Here's her bill. If she went out I didn't see her." She gave me a withering look and I left.

"Damn that Patty Sue," I said when I slammed back into the car.

"Why don't you check around the other side?" asked Arch.

"I already did," I said. "You were just thinking so hard about what you were going to lift from your father's office that you didn't notice."

"Not down below," said Arch. "On the deck on the other side. By the back door."

"Where, smarty-pants? I've only been coming to this office since before you were born. There is no back door."

Arch gave me his exasperated look. He said, "Mom, you can drive to it."

"How?"

He pointed. "Don't you even know where Dad and Fritz park when they get here early? There's a little paved part over on the right side that goes through to the back." He laughed under his breath. "Dad says sometimes he plays hooky that way, going out for a snack or something while a patient waits."

A *snack* or something. I started the car. All this time, and I had never known about this other parking area. Perhaps the Jerk had not wanted me to know how he got out for his *snacks*. I pointed the Chrysler in the direction Arch had shown me.

The OB- and GYN-plated Jeeps glistened in the sunlight. And there was Patty Sue sitting on a bench, her chin lifted to the sun.

"You could have told the receptionist you were leaving," I said as I walked up. "You haven't even paid your bill."

"I don't have any money to pay a bill," she answered me. She got up.

I said, "How'd you get out here, anyway?"

"Through there," she said. She waved a hand at the back doors of the office.

"Well, how about that," I mused softly as I studied the exits. There were two doors, one coming out from John Richard's side, one from Fritz's. I remembered now from my visit to Fritz's plant-bedecked office. There had been a back door, but it had been draped with ivy.

"He usually lets me out that way," Patty Sue offered. "It's like a secret."

So that explained how Patty Sue could get down to the pastry shop without my seeing her, as had happened a number of times before. I looked at the doors. A secret. I wondered who else the doctors might have escorted out this way.

CHAPTER 19

"Pluto to Mom. Come in, please."

We were home. How long I had been pressing the button on the coffee grinder I did not know. The beans were pulverized, fit to make hot mud.

In the distance Patty Sue was running a bath.

"You okay, Mom?" came Arch's voice again. "I need to talk to you about Halloween."

I looked at the would-be surgical-pack thief.

He said, "You want me to make you some coffee?"

"Sure."

Arch dumped out the dust I'd made of the beans, measured more, whirred the grinder, lined the filter with paper, ran fresh cold water. Then I remembered that I had not talked to him about what I had taken from his desk. He had been to school today. Had he noticed anything missing? And what was the bigger picture of my son and Laura Smiley, anyway? I studied him.

"Arch. Halloween. I heard you," I said. "I need your help to do the party at the athletic club that night."

"You look half-dead, Mom." He grinned. The coffee maker bubbled and popped. He said, "Coffee will be ready in a sec. Raising the dead is my favorite spell."

Right, with surgical packs. I said, "You're not going to go stealing my knives, are you? For some curse or something?"

"No."

"Did you ever play raise the dead with Laura Smiley?"

"Mom!"

"Well?"

He looked out the window. Then he said, "You're hassling me again."

I opened the cupboard. John Richard had given me one of those mugs that said BITCH BITCH BITCH on it. Why I had kept it all this time I did not know. I dropped it into the trash and picked out one decorated with rainbows. Then I turned to my son. His gaze was fixed on the pine trees outside.

"Well," I began as I filled the mug, "you wrote letters to her. You're into those fantasy role-playing games. You were her special friend, her special student ... I just thought maybe she would be interested in your game spells, especially if she had someone important to her who had died—"

I stopped to sip coffee. Arch turned slowly from the window to face me.

"Mom. What do you think she was, weird?"

"Well, yes, as a matter of fact." We were both silent. Then I said, "I found the note she wrote you before she died."

Arch snorted. "Great. You get mad at me about borrowing something from Dad's office, and then you go snooping through my desk."

"Arch, this is different. Your teacher called. She's worried about you, writing stuff like your grandfather has no respect for human life. Why would you write such a thing?"

He shrugged.

I said, "You're too involved in these games, you're not getting along with your classmates, you're getting into fights—"

"You know how you're always telling me to say what my feelings are? Okay. Now I'm telling you." He eyed me fiercely and dug his hands into his pockets. His voice broke with the promise of tears. "You're making me angry," he cried.

"Arch. It's just because I'm worried about you—"

He turned to walk out of the kitchen.

"Now where are you going?"

"To the car. I left the rest of my game stuff out there."

"Please don't leave. I don't want us to have a big fight."

He turned and glared at me. "You don't want to fight?" I nodded and he went on. "Just make that costume I marked for Marla. Okay? It's in here." He riffled through a book of fantasy characters he had left on the kitchen table. "Then after Halloween we can talk about worrying. Okay? I just need to finish this thing that I'm doing right now."

"Look, just sit down and cool off for a sec, will you? Tell me why you're so angry."

He sat, then crossed his legs and arms.

"Mom, why is it okay for *you* to go through *my* stuff? I thought you only cleaned for people who wanted you to do it for them. And I don't."

I dropped three ice cubes into a Coke glass for Arch.

"Archibald," I said, "listen to me, would you, please?"

He stared at me from behind the rimmed glasses.

"You can help. It's like being a detective. After this we can talk about Halloween, I promise. Maybe we could get your Dad to buy a costume."

"Oh, sure."

Arch poured his soft drink and slurped the bubbles that climbed the sides of the glass. He wrinkled his nose, brought the glass down with a bang. Upstairs Patty Sue was splashing and singing in her bubble bath.

"She invited you over that Saturday," I began, "and then said she couldn't get together after all. Did you go anyway?"

He said, "Yeah, I rode my bike over later. She had company."

"How do you know?"

"Her blue car wasn't there. She was having it fixed. She was always having trouble with that stupid car. Anyway, somebody else was there."

"What kind of car? Foreign? American? Pickup? What?"

"I don't remember. I just, like, heard the engine."

"Arch."

"I don't. And don't ask me what time it was because I don't remember that either. You're just like that policeman, acting as if I'm guilty of something."

"Sorry."

"I got the Good Citizen award in fourth grade, you know."

"Okay, okay. You went to her house. Did you see anything unusual?"

"No, Mom," he said, exasperated. "I don't even know what was usual."

I paused for a minute. "Do you know about a student of hers named Bebe Hollenbeck?"

"No. Can I go now?"

"Bebe was her special friend," I said, "as you were."

"Right."

"Maybe," I went on, "Bebe was shy, like you."

"Maybe they wrote letters," he said, "and maybe they played D and D. Who cares? I wish you would just stick to cooking."

"If you want to eat supper, mister, don't be difficult. I can't cook until I get this figured out, and I can't make any money cooking until I get myself cleared in this rat poison mess."

Arch sighed.

"In her note to you, she said she had something important to do. Do you know what it was?"

He chewed his bottom lip. "Not really."

"What?"

He looked out the window again.

"Arch," I said slowly. "Maybe she didn't commit suicide. Maybe she was—"

"I gotta go, Mom."

I looked at him, and pain filled the area behind my eyes. How much adult eccentricity could he take? From a screwball grandfather, an alcoholic grandmother, a philandering father, a suicidal teacher, and a demanding mother? Poor Arch.

He stood up and gave me his most bored look.

He said, "Can I go?"

"No."

He let out a gust of air and flopped back into his chair. "Now what?"

"Just tell me if you know whether for some reason you think someone wanted Laura Smiley dead."

"No."

The phone rang.

"No," I said, "no one wanted her dead, or no, you won't tell me?"

The phone kept on ringing; Arch glared at me.

"Arch!"

A sob exploded from him. Then another. Tears sprouted from his eyes.

"Leave me alone!" he yelled. "I don't want to talk about Ms. Smiley anymore! Can't you see that, Mom? So just stop this! Stop!"

The phone insisted on ringing. I reached out for Arch's shoulder only to have him whack my hand away. He ran out of the kitchen.

I grabbed for the phone receiver and yelled, "What is it?"

"What is what?" asked Tom Schulz.

"Sheesh."

"Well, well, Miss Goldilocks, I can see you're in your usual sunny mood."

"Why are you calling?"

"Man," he said, "it is a good thing that I am such a patient kind of guy. I mean, a very good thing. And that I can inquire how you're coming along on talking to your mother-in-law—"

"*Ex*-mother-in-law."

"Sorry there. *Ex*-maw-in-law. Tell me what she said about her daughter who died. The one who drank."

"How did you know about that?"

"I've been on the phone to Illinois. Finally getting some answers around here."

I could hear Arch thrashing about in the nether regions of the house.

I said, "I'm going to have to call you back."

"I thought you were interested in solving this."

"I'll call you back," I said. "I have to work something out with my child."

I followed the noise from Arch.

He had not gone directly to the car to get his equipment, as he had indicated he needed to do. I had heard him clomping down the stairs to the basement, which was the laundry and storage area. Now with the door cracked I could hear him rummaging through boxes and papers. After a few moments he came traipsing back up and I darted into a bedroom I used for filing, sewing, and storing table linens for banquets. On the bed I spread out several yards of unbleached muslin for the costume, in case he came in. Then I heard him clattering around in the kitchen. The noise sounded like the clank of butcher knife blades.

I prayed. After a few more minutes of racket he slammed out the front door. I crept back to the kitchen and counted my knives, every one of them. They were all there. Whatever it was he wanted, he apparently hadn't found it yet.

I hurried to the front of the house and scanned the driveway. Arch had left the station wagon door open and was throwing the books and bags of stuff he had amassed at Marla's onto the ground. He was closing the door when he stopped and bent in again, as if he'd seen something he'd forgotten. His head emerged from the car. He looked in all directions to see if he was being watched. I leaned back from the front window. After a few seconds I looked back: he was reemerging from the car, tucking something underneath his shirt. Then he gathered up his paraphernalia from the ground and started back toward the house. I trotted out to the kitchen, picked up the character book, and slipped into the sewing room.

After a few minutes I had the bobbin filled with beige thread and I went to knock on his door.

"I'm getting started on your costume," I called in. "Want to take a look at it?"

"No, Mom," he said. "Just go away. Please."

CHAPTER 20

It certainly is a good thing you've got a crack civilian detective working on this case," I greeted Tom Schulz when he answered his phone. "Although she can be difficult, she comes up with remarkable info."

"Goldilocks? 'Zat you? Must be."

"Such enthusiasm."

"Hey," said Schulz, "besides close you down, what did I ever do to you? Except be nice? Don't give me a hard time. Let's start over."

With as much patience as I could muster, I told him about my conversation with Vonette. Then I asked, "What did you find out from the neighbor and the doctor? About the day Laura died?"

"Not a whole lot. She saw the doc when she went into town."

"What did he see her for?"

"Routine visit, so he says. Not much more I can go on than that. The neighbor heard a car, not a gunshot. But I did find some things out from Illinois."

"Such as."

"I found the guy who worked the case. Twenty years ago there was this huge brouhaha over Korman."

I said, "But it all ended in a mistrial."

"Did you call Illinois, too?"

"No, it was in this article I told you about. I found it in Laura's locker, but I ripped it trying to get it out." I read him the fragment.

"That's what I like about you, Goldy—you're not bothered by technicalities like search warrants."

"What was the mistrial about?"

"Sex."

"Gee, copper, thanks a lot. Even Vonette told me that."

"Korman was brought to trial on charges of having sex with a minor. Our Bebe Hollenbeck. This guy said that Korman was then also under investigation by the Illinois Board of Medical Examiners for taking liberties with patients, which would explain the rest of the article you ripped."

"Sorry about that."

"That's the difference between you and Laura Smiley," said Schulz. "She was careful with evidence, that cop told me. She was going to be a witness against Korman. She was a young woman, then, a new teacher, in her twenties this guy thought."

"So why the mistrial?"

"It was 1967. Supreme Court passed down the Miranda ruling in 1966. Cops weren't used to it yet. They forgot to advise Korman—of his rights, you know." He paused for a minute, and I could imagine him drinking coffee, shaking his head. "Anyway," he went on, "Korman was under a cloud. Then this young Bebe, on her seventeenth birthday, mind you, drinks an entire bottle of liquor and dies on the spot. More bad publicity, so Korman moves out here to get a fresh start."

"And how did Laura Smiley get involved after that?"

"Now that's what the cop remembers, clear as a bell.

After the mistrial, the D.A. decided not to attempt another trial. So this young teacher comes strutting into his office and throws one holy fit. Turns out her father is an alcoholic. Bebe's mother is headed that way, so Laura wants to protect her student."

"What happened?"

Schulz said, "Laura screamed that Fritz Korman was a menace to all women. Said she had evidence that could curtail his practice of medicine permanently. Said if the cops wouldn't get him, she would. She tried to get the Board of Medical Examiners to do something too, but Korman decided to move out here, and rather than revoking his license, the board said, Just don't come back to this state. Are you ready for this? Our friend went back to the cops, banged on this investigator's desk. She said this will happen again over her dead body. Then she marched out. Laura Smiley."

I said, "But then the Kormans, not knowing her feelings, you'd have to assume, picked Aspen Meadow to live in. Vonette told me back then there was medical licensing reciprocity with Illinois. They liked the place when Laura brought them here, back when they were all getting along." I thought for a minute, then went on, "Nobody figured on Laura's parents being killed. She moved back. Her parents were gone, Bebe was gone, and the Kormans were already settled in her hometown, where she had a house and friends. She must have decided to put it behind her."

"Appears that way. Then after twenty years, something snapped."

"If she had something on him, why wait? Maybe she was blackmailing him." I paused. "I don't think so, though. She wasn't that type. And it goes against what she said in a note she wrote just before she died."

"Oh God. I don't even want to hear how you got that. Why don't you just tell me the rest of what you've been up to."

I dug out the note to Arch and read it aloud. Then I told Shulz that Laura had been friendly with Pomeroy, that they had been in an Al-Anon group together.

"And speaking of that, there was this weird thing with the drugstore," I said.

"You break in there, too? If somebody's listening in on this line, you're going to have to get back into business. Then you can hire me as a caterer after they fire me from being a cop."

"Are you interested in the drugstore or not? This'll go a long way toward getting that body exhumed."

"Don't tell me," he said. "You found the murder weapon on aisle B."

"Your new deputy coroner said Laura had a foreign substance, Valium, in her stomach. She didn't have a prescription for Valium or any other tranquilizer. And if she belonged to one of the AA organizations there's a good chance she didn't drink or take drugs at all." I hesitated. "Come to think of it, there wasn't any liquor in her house, either. Odd stuff like flour in a flower box—"

"What?"

"Just her sense of humor. Puns."

Schulz clucked his tongue.

I said, "I'm wondering if that person in Laura's house the day I set off the alarm . . ." I was thinking. "Was, maybe, looking for that evidence?" I stopped. "In the living room—" I began, remembering something. "Vonette—"

"She was in there?"

"No. She had a flask. At the reception. She added something to her drink."

"You're thinking she may have fixed Fritz's drink, too? Remember any pellets, Goldy, or just a flask?"

I said, "Pomeroy Locraft says Fritz was cheating on Vonette. If she knew he was up to his old tricks, maybe she'd take some kind of corrective steps."

"Hmm."

"Pomeroy saw the flask, too. Maybe she spilled her guts to him the way she did with us." I chewed my nails for a second. "I'm going out there tomorrow—I'll see what I can dig up."

"I wish you'd quit saying dig up to a homicide investigator," said Schulz. Then, "You still going out with me on Halloween?"

"Saturday night? Oh yes." How was I going to hide the food for the athletic club party from him? I didn't want to have to explain illegal catering. "I was wondering if you could pick Arch up and I'll meet you there. I have a late cleaning job," I fibbed. "But what made you think of Halloween?"

"I've seen the way you go goo-goo eyed over this Pomeroy fella. I want you to remember our date. Just in case he flirts with you when you go out there investigating."

"Aha," I said, pleased. "The jealous sort."

"Maybe so," he replied evenly. "But look at it this way. It's better to be with a great investigator than an incompetent driving instructor."

The road to the Wildlife Preserve was actually a wide, bumpy, mud-and-rock affair that was not officially open to the public between mid-September and the beginning of June. The altitude was about a thousand feet above town, and it snowed in greater abundance there, both early and late. I already knew how to lift and pull the swing gate to enter in the off season, since it had only been last April that Arch had done his beekeeping project with Pomeroy.

Before leaving I had written a note for Patty Sue:

Gone to see Driver Educator. Back late. Please give Arch nonchocolate supper.

And one for Arch:

Am out at Pom's getting honey. If P.S. not back by supper, have tuna casserole in refrig. Lich costume needs cotton batting. Please ride bike to Aspen Meadow Drug and charge some. I need to make costume tonight because tomorrow I have to cook for party.

Love, Mom

Arch, Arch. I swerved to avoid a pothole full of snow melt and remembered how it had been even muddier in April when he had jumped up and down in enthusiasm each time I'd picked him up after working with Pom. That effervescence, that love for his teachers and for learning, was all gone now.

"The bees are so neat, Mom," he had said. "They swarm once a year, and they usually come back to the same place. They come back to Pom's because of all the great wildflowers out in the Preserve. And they know where all the flowers are! You see there's this, like, navigator bee who goes out and finds bushes and stuff and comes back and tells the other bees how to get there. It's very complicated. Bees are smart."

"Bees? Smart?"

"Oh yes," he said enthusiastically, "they are very intelligent. Pom and I wear white because the bees like it. They're afraid of black because that reminds them of bears. It's way back in their memory. Sort of like how you hate snakes, and in the Bible somebody says women don't like snakes? Bees know that bears steal their honey so they all learned to hate the color black and to attack big black animals on two feet. So we have to wear white."

"I thought honeybees didn't sting."

"Of course they sting," he protested. "Why do you think we have to wear those nets over our faces? Actually, what makes them sting is if they get scared. You know, somebody invades the hive or something. That's why you've got to smoke them out before you go in for the honey. You see," he concluded in his patronizing tone, "there's really a lot to learn if you want to become a bee-keeper. You'd better not try it, Mom."

I rolled down the window to look for elk or deer trying to get into the Preserve before hunting season began. The day was warm, but a cool breeze buffeted the stands of pine that bordered the road. From a distance I could see the stone chimney of Pom's cabin. Although I knew his honey shed was large enough to also serve as a garage, he had left six vehicles in varying states of abandonment parked every which way on the surrounding property. Growing up in New Jersey, I had noticed that the natives accumulated hydrangeas. Coloradans, on the other hand, collected cars. And parked them in their garages and yards so they could use the nearly new four-wheel drive to get out in the snow, the old pickup to haul stuff, the old Scout with the plow to do the driveway, the station wagon to take everybody skiing, and the gutted VW and Chevy because they had such great parts.

"Glad you could make it," Pomeroy said and gave that heart-melting half smile before stepping aside for me to enter.

I said, "I kind of miss coming out here. Arch loved doing work with you."

"And I liked working with him. He's a great kid. You're lucky."

I sighed in spite of myself. "Being a parent is not all roses, Pom. It's almost as hard as being married."

He blushed an absolutely purple hue. Then I thought again of what Marla had said. Was he that hung up on his ex? Even Marla and I weren't that bad about John Richard. Whatever the reason, I already felt I'd blown it.

He said, "Why don't you sit down and have some herb tea? Got some great honey for it."

I looked around the one-room house. It had probably been a hunter's cabin before the area was declared a preserve. In front of the picture window were two telescopes. These I assumed could be trained on the beehives, which I knew to be upwind of the cabin, at a small distance in the meadow.

"Watching the birds and the bees?" I said while he was filling the teapot. I peered into one of the scopes.

"No."

"Watching wildlife?"

He didn't say anything. Maybe he still felt guilty about the driving lesson. In any event, his mind was elsewhere.

"I got a car," I said. "Vonette's loaning me one."

"Great."

More silence.

I said, "Are you coming to the club's Halloween party?"

A nod.

I said, "Don't tell anybody, I'm making the food." He snorted. "Cleaning the place, too. Hey!" I had moved the scope to focus on the area just below the hives. "You have a garden."

"Yeah," he said, "in springtime. Want your honey now?"

I took three large jars from him and gave him a check. Then I looked around the room for something else to talk about.

"Has it snowed up here yet?" I said brightly. "Do you see more or less wildlife when there's snow on the ground?"

Pomeroy reached for two mugs, placed a teabag in the pot, and cocked his head at me.

"You want to see wildlife, Goldy? Look through the other telescope. This is Wednesday, lunchtime, warm weather. Should be right on schedule. This is what I wanted you to see."

I gave him a sideways glance and stepped over to the

other scope. Without moving it I looked in. Far out in the meadow there was movement. My skin went cold.

It was people. One on top of the other. One was Patty Sue. With Fritz Korman.

Nobody had to tell them about the birds and the bees.

CHAPTER 21

I don't believe this."

No response from Pomeroy.

I looked at him. "Do they come here often?"

He poured the water into the teapot and steam clouded his face.

"Twice in the last couple of weeks. Weather's been nice. You know how people like to do it out-of-doors in this state. The hikers generally save it for summer, though."

My eyes scanned the room. He set the tea tray on the table. It was disconcerting to be witnessing the sexual activity of another couple while in the company of a man to whom one was attracted.

Pomeroy filled the mugs with tea. I couldn't help noticing the way his shoulders moved under his soft flannel shirt. I wondered who did his laundry, and looked around the room for a washing machine. His couch, tables, and chairs were rough-hewn pine scattered with store-bought pillows. The furniture looked homemade. There were no modern conveniences besides a refrigerator and oven in the open kitchen. In the living area were several lamps, and by his bed in one corner were a radiophone and alarm clock. So he had electricity and water, anyway. If Patty Sue and Fritz had wanted a cool drink or piece of toast for a postcoital snack, they could have marched on up. Right.

I looked again at Pomeroy, this engaging hermit in the middle of his homemade couch in the middle of his homemade cabin in the middle of nowhere. I ran my fingers over the green-brown coffee table made from pine beetle-killed wood.

He said, "Well?"

I moved a ceramic pot filled with ivy from one side of the table to the other, and thought.

"It makes sense," I said finally. "I was in his office last week looking for some files. Patty Sue had gone in to see him, but I never saw her come back out. This Monday I was over there and Arch showed me the back door to the office, which I never knew existed. So."

Pom said, "What were you looking for in his files?"

I stood up and went over to the window. Patty Sue and Fritz were walking through the tall grass toward the trees where the Jeep was just visible.

"Oh," I said dully, "you know I'm trying to get my catering going again. The cops aren't making much headway so I'm looking into things myself. Trying to figure out what the connection between Fritz and Laura Smiley was, why someone would try to poison him at her funeral. Trying to answer big questions like that while he's banging away on my roommate."

"Find anything?"

"No."

He stood up and walked to his cooking area, then came back with a plate of hot biscuits and a bowl of honey.

He said, "I made these for you. The honey's from a new batch of bees I sent away for from a catalog. South

American. Mean as can be—sometimes they chase me off. Good producers, though."

He split one of the steaming rounds, plastered it with honey, then handed it to me on a paper napkin. It was delicious.

He said, "Surprised at a man's cooking?"

"For heaven's sake, Pom, will you get serious? Even the police have told me more than you have, which is that Fritz cheats on Vonette, which is something I already knew from his past, thank you."

"What do you want to know?"

"Do you know why Laura went to see Fritz? If you two were such pals, why wouldn't she tell you something as important as that? She left an article in her locker. She was going to show it to Patty Sue and Trixie. It was about a mistrial. Was she trying to warn them about something?"

"I already told you, she didn't tell me everything. She had known a student, Vonette's daughter, who was her friend. Since Laura was the daughter of an alcoholic, she relived the whole scenario by seeing this neglected teenage daughter, who then had a stepfather coming on to her. She tried to stop it. When that backfired, and Laura's parents died, she tried to let it go in Al-Anon. But she was shocked when I told her what was going on out here."

"That was recent, wasn't it?"

He looked at me and nodded. "Last few months."

I said, "Was it at the athletic club, and Marla stumbled in on your conversation?"

"Yeah. Laura said, 'He told me he'd cleaned up his act.' " Pomeroy looked at me. He said, "Those were her words. 'After twenty years,' she said, 'I can't believe he's up to his old tricks.' " He paused and bit into a biscuit. "After we talked, she came out to work with me. She saw them out there in the meadow. She was angry, seeing this again after all these years, him going after a younger woman. 'I can't believe it,' she kept saying, 'he swore to me when I first moved back here that he'd changed.' " Pomeroy cleared his throat. "I do know this. She had something on Korman besides what I'm telling you. She said, 'This time there will be justice, you can count on it.' She was beside herself. I had to drive her home. That's when she left the science text in my car, by the way. Anyway, maybe seeing them was what triggered her. The next thing you know, suicide."

"It must be convenient for Fritz," I mused, "the women in his life just offing themselves when the going gets rough. First Bebe Hollenbeck, then Laura Smiley."

"Better keep an eye on your roommate," added Pomeroy.

Suddenly I was exhausted by it all. Now that the landscape was empty of people I turned my attention out the window. Several gently sloping acres in what could roughly be termed Pomeroy's front yard eventually met the creek, one of the high tributaries of the Upper Cottonwood. The white hives where Arch and Pomeroy had worked so diligently last spring ranged along the hill.

"What are the bees doing now?" I asked. "Still producing honey?"

"When it's warm in October like this, they'll fly. Not many flowers now, of course, so the production's real low."

A series of posts jutted along the creek front, with rope between some of them. The rope led to several of the hives.

I said, "What's all that heavy twine?"

He laughed. "Old-fashioned burglar alarm. Arch just loved it, said he was going to use it in one of his dragon-adventures, or whatever they're called. Somebody comes up from the creek trying to break into your place, trips over the rope, the hives topple over and you've got yourself a swarm of bees that'll do more damage than a shotgun."

We were quiet for a few minutes.

I said, "Arch really thought you were the greatest."

"I enjoyed him. I like all the kids. With Laura gone, I don't know if the teachers will be willing to let the students come out here for projects. I'll miss them. A lot."

"Did you notice anything strange about Arch? I mean last spring, was he secretive or—"

"No." Pomeroy waved his hand at me. "We had great talks, he was always very serious about everything. I could see why Laura got such a kick out of him." Pom gave me a long look with those brown eyes, full of sadness and pity.

My voice was hard. "I've been thinking that she shared too much with him. I'm not convinced it was healthy."

He shrugged. "I loved to talk to Arch, too. Sometimes it was like talking to a little adult. Maybe Laura felt the same way, I don't know. But I know she and Arch did admire each other." He paused. "Something else you should know, if you're worried about your relationship with Arch."

"I'm all ears."

"Arch said his mother was pretty tough. He even said one of the reasons he wasn't cool was that all the kids complained about how bad their mothers' cooking was, slime and worms and mold and so on. But to be perfectly honest, he would tell me, his mother's cooking was pretty good."

And with that shred of good news amidst all the bad, I said goodbye to Pomeroy and smiled all the way down the dirt road through the trees, back toward town.

"Mom, I got the batting," Arch announced when I strode into our house and banged the door behind me. "I opened the book to the lich illustration, so you can see what I need to look like. I'm going to wear it to the athletic club. Maybe some of the people will think I'm a midget and not a kid."

I hugged him. "Not likely. Midgets aren't as neat as eleven-year-olds."

He patted my back. "Did you have a good day or something?"

"Do I have to have a good day to give my own kid a hug?"

"Sorry. You just haven't seemed happy lately. Neither has Patty Sue."

No kidding.

"Did you have a snack?" I said.

"Well, they had burritos for lunch at school and I hate them, so I ordered from the Chinese place when I got home because I didn't exactly want tuna casserole. I charged it. Hope that's okay. Patty Sue came in a little while ago and she was hungry, too." He paused.

"Go on."

"Well," he said as he pushed his glasses back up his nose, "when the guy came with our order and we opened all those little boxes, I said, Hey, this is like the boxes I used to get my goldfish in from the pet store. I felt real bad because then Patty Sue went into the bathroom and threw up."

"Oh, God. Is she sleeping now?"

"I think so," said Arch with a rueful twist of his mouth. "I knocked on her door and asked her if I could bring her some sweet-and-sour pork on a plate, sort of like breakfast in bed, but she said the smell of it made her sick, and please don't talk about the goldfish."

"Any more good news?"

"Vonette called. She sounded real upset. Said she's a wreck and wants you to call her about the car."

I shook my head and headed down toward my sewing room. I said, "That can wait."

"Good," said Arch as he retreated, "because I need to use the phone and I didn't want to use the business line."

We parted and I reluctantly plugged in the Japanese sewing machine I had bought from a traveling salesman who had failed to mention the all-Japanese instruction booklet. But I had been smart enough to figure out how to go forward and backward, and, staring at the illustration for the lich, I figured that was all I needed.

A robe like a Druid priest's with batting in the shoulders and sleeves like a magician's, the description said; the costume should have a ragged but costly aspect. The lich face was terrifying, like a skull. I drew on the material with a tailor's pencil, then cut and sewed until the hood and shoulders were done and all it needed was a hem. Arch could paint the muslin any colors he wanted, and knowing him, he would.

The picture in the book was black and white. My gaze wandered to the caption, which read:

> The lich specializes in vengeful activity. It uses spells, charms, traps and poison potions to punish the wicked. One spell of particular use is raising the dead. By communicating with deceased victims, the lich gathers evidence against evildoers. It carries out its plan of vengeance using small sharp weapons and clerical spells such as deep sleep, fireball, and scaring its victims to death. The lich stops only when the wicked one is dead.

I set aside the costume. *Jesus wept,* I remembered, before he raised Lazarus. I had no such grand plans. But I wept anyway.

CHAPTER 22

Todd?" came Arch's whisper over the phone, "I can't talk long. I've been trying to reach you since yesterday."

"Our phone's been broken. What's wrong? Does she suspect something?"

"No, she's sewing," Arch replied. "But I've still got to be careful."

I'd wiped my face, blown my nose. Now I breathed oh-so-shallowly as I cupped my hand over the mouthpiece.

Todd said, "I can barely hear you. Do you want me to come over?"

"No," said Arch, "no time before dinner." He paused. "Listen, you're not going to believe this. I got it."

Todd asked, "Got what?"

"A weapon, silly," Arch said with an impatient hiss. "It's better than a knife too, because it's just like in the book. Small and sharp. I found it in a plastic bag in my grand-mother's car. We'll have to clean it later. It's under our woodpile now."

"Great!" replied Todd. "What spell are you going to use?"

"How about fireball?"

"Ever done it before?"

"Well," admitted Arch, "not in real life."

"Easy," said Todd, "you could just make a Molotov cocktail. Get yourself a bottle, see, and fill it with gasoline—"

"Who're you talking to?" asked a sleepy Patty Sue as she slouched into the room.

I pressed the receiver back into the cradle.

I said, "Nobody. Just checking to see if the phone's free so I can call Vonette."

She tilted her head at me. "What are you making for dinner? Arch ordered some Chinese stuff but it didn't look that great to me. I am hungry, though."

I said, "You've had a big day."

She nodded, yawned again.

"Sorry we don't have anything to eat," I lied. "In fact I need you and Arch to go to the store for me before dinner—"

"But I haven't even gotten my regular license yet," Patty Sue protested, "and I don't know how I'd drive with a cast." She wandered out of the room toward the kitchen. I turned off the sewing machine and followed her.

"That's okay," I said, "I'll drive." I grabbed a pencil from beside the phone and hastily began to write. Patty Sue was fishing gherkins out of a jar with her pinky. "I have lots to do," I went on, "and you guys can help me out while I do other errands." I called to Arch, and he came clomping down to the kitchen while Patty Sue read the list over my shoulder.

"Now what?" he demanded.

I looked at the two of them and tried to imagine myself as a patient person.

"I have two parties this week, one day after tomorrow for my women's group and one at the athletic club the next day. This means a lot of shopping and cooking. You two," I went on, "will please buy groceries while I pick up pizza and do errands, and then we'll all come home and discuss the news of the day. Okay?"

"Oh, guess what?" said Patty Sue. "Speaking of news. Dr. Korman's treatments finally worked."

Arch groaned and left to get his jacket.

I stared at her. "What do you mean, his treatment worked? You want to tell me what that treatment was?"

Patty Sue's face turned quite pink.

"Oh, that's confidential, Goldy. All I can tell you is that as of this afternoon, I'm, um, normal."

I shook my head. If the North Pole was normal, then Patty Sue was living in Antarctica.

"The thing is," said Patty Sue, "it's been a long time for me. Since I was normal, I mean. Anyway, I don't feel so good."

Neither, I reflected, did I, as I swung the boatlike Chrysler wagon into the parking lot of Aspen Meadow's grocery, one of a western chain of food stores. The store's dairy selection was pasteurized to the extent that everything tasted scalded; the produce was whatever could make it to Colorado from California without rotting. Nevertheless, I had made the list long enough to keep both Arch and Patty Sue occupied for at least an hour.

Under the woodpile. In September I had stacked a half cord of firewood beneath the house's old deck. Once back home I put on garden gloves and began to dig and scrape out bits of bark and grass from beneath the freshly split yellow logs. The sky was beginning to darken and the sharp smell of wood smoke was already in the air. I hoped that snakes of all genres had begun to hibernate or whatever it was snakes did in the winter. Black widows, of course, were notorious inhabitants of woodpiles.

A plastic bag crackled in my fingers and I drew it out. Inside the bag was the soft towel covering for a surgical pack, the kind I knew Fritz and John Richard kept in the storage closet in the room where the nurses drew blood. It was similar to, perhaps even exactly the same as, the one Arch had tried to steal from the office. Had he succeeded after all? I opened it carefully. Rolled up wads of latex, which I guessed to be surgical gloves, were at the top of the bag. They weren't usually in the kit. Tissue forceps, suture set, two-by-two's, other stuff I recognized.

A scalpel, one of the kind that used disposable blades. The blade had dried blood on it.

Now I really had something to tell Tom Schulz. And a few things to discuss with my son.

"Tom," I said into the phone, "I have to talk to you."

"I barely recognized your voice, you sounded so friendly."

"Tell me about the weapon Laura Smiley used on herself."

"Well now, I don't know whether—"

"Come on," I pleaded, "you told me yourself that a suicide case was closed unless some evidence was found—"

"And so far you've given me theories, a torn article, a note, and a missing prescription."

"Tom!"

"Okay, okay. One of those twin-bladed ladies' razors. It had a lot of blood on it, I know that. From the depth of the wound on her wrists, the deputy coroner figured she could have done it with that. Although he's not a terribly sharp guy."

"Not too sharp," I said. "That sounds like something Laura Smiley would say."

"I don't get it."

"Forget it," I said. Then I asked, "So the theory was she was shaving her legs?"

"I guess."

"Dumb. Stupid. Imbecilic."

"It's good to hear you sounding like yourself. What'd

you find out from Pomeroy? Did he know anything about Vonette?"

I said, "Hold on. Laura Smiley didn't shave, I'll be willing to bet anything. She was a feminist—"

"Is that like socialist? I don't think they shave either."

"I know it's a challenge, but try to take me seriously. Look at it practically. Have you ever cut yourself with one of those Good News razors? Or some other twin-bladed kind?"

"Strictly an electric man, myself."

"Well," I said, "it's almost impossible, I don't care what the deputy coroner says. You'd have to be trying real hard, because you can barely nick yourself, much less cut, wound, stab, or slash. I'd say your deputy coroner has got a hole in his head."

"Well," Tom said apologetically, "he's new. So you're saying you think she used something else?"

"She or someone else." I fingered the surgical kit. "You'd better come on over. I've got something for you."

Within fifteen minutes he had picked it up. He looked dubious. Wanted to know if this was some kind of kid's joke. Asked if I touched anything, and where I found it.

"Arch got it out of this station wagon, which belongs to the Kormans," I said. "You know Laura's blood type and all that?"

He said, "Yes, we do, Goldy. Now listen. I know it's hard for you to leave the police work to me. But just for a couple of days, try."

Then it was time for me to do the picking up, first pizza with extra cheese, Arch's favorite, then assorted goodies from the pastry shop for the women's meeting. When I arrived at the grocery store both Arch and Patty Sue were shuffling down an aisle wearing fatigued, irritated faces. It was, after all, past dinnertime. I checked their cart for the avocados, carrots, celery, cherry tomatoes, Belgian endive, apples, assortment of cheeses, chicken, eggs, chips, ground beef, cups and crepe paper, and decorative squash and pumpkin I had ordered. Plus Coke and chocolate soda. I was thankful for the fifty dollars from Hal.

"Mom," whined Arch, "this is boring. I'm tired and hungry."

"Just need frozen bread dough," I mumbled, claiming the cart.

"I saw your ex-husband and his new girlfriend over a couple of aisles," whispered Patty Sue, "with the older Dr. Korman and Vonette."

I turned to her as we headed toward the frozen-food section. "Oh, that's just great. What're they doing here?"

But I didn't have to wait for Patty Sue to come up with an answer, for at that moment the Korman entourage came wheeling around to frozen foods.

Patty Sue moaned. She said, "I'm not feeling too good."

"Just do me the favor of not asking for a medical consultation right now," I said.

"Why, look who's here," said John Richard. "Goldilocks shopping for porridge. What are you going to put in it?"

"Hello, Vonette," I announced, as if the girlfriend and two doctors were not present.

"Ho Arch! How's my boy?" asked John Richard as he pinched his unsmiling son on the cheek. With his tall, hunk-type frame, John Richard looked like a benevolent defensive end talking to a young fan. Only Arch was not acting properly adoring. John Richard responded by turning to his girlfriend. "I told you she was a bitch," he said between his teeth. The girlfriend bobbed a head of streaked hair. "Goldy," he went on, turning back to me, "meet Pam Mosser. She teaches geometry at the high school. She's my, er, fiancée."

I was so proud of myself. I smiled politely and said, "How do you do?" The virtue of an eastern upbringing.

"Patty Sue," said Fritz, "how are you getting along?"

"Well," she began, "not too—"

"Please be quiet, Patty Sue," I ordered.

"Now Goldy," Fritz warned. "Don't start up."

"Start up with what?" I asked and gave Vonette a knowing look, from which she shrank.

Fritz turned to stare at Vonette.

"Mom," Arch moaned beside me, "I'm getting tireder."

"I still don't feel so—" Patty Sue began.

My ex-mother-in-law looked at me guiltily and cleared her throat. Patty Sue had disappeared down the aisle.

"Oh, Goldy dear," Vonette said nervously, "I need the car back. I'm sorry, I forgot something, ah, it needs to go into the shop. Sorry," she said again.

I wasn't ready for another loss of vehicle. I turned to beat a retreat past orange juice and toward ice cream, where Patty Sue had arrived and was filling her arms with Fudge Swirl, Double Chocolate Chip, and Rocky Road.

"Couple of days," I promised over my shoulder. "At the club Halloween party. My van should be ready by then. Then I'll give you the Chrysler. See you Friday, Vonette!"

We were almost at the checkout stand.

To my utter delight, Arch turned around and yelled, "What's geometry?"

CHAPTER 23

I got into the car feeling light-headed. But I congratulated myself on one thing: I had survived the encounter. Every little success helped.

"Have some pizza," I said to Arch. "It's either next to you or you're sitting on it."

Patty Sue found the pizza box. She and Arch began to tug out hot triangular slices stringy with mozzarella. The smell was inviting, but I wasn't hungry. The last two hours had been too draining. Arch opened the soft drinks and offered me one. When I refused, I noticed that my hands were shaking.

I said, "Let's go home."

After getting Arch to bed and carefully placing the food supplies onto the pantry and refrigerator shelves, I still felt unsettled. It was bad enough to have to live in the same town and hear of John Richard's many exploits. Bad enough to have to endure his arrogance and new wealth. But to have to endure him at the grocery store was almost too much.

The next few days were going to be hectic. There was cleaning the club, cooking for the meeting Friday and the party Saturday, plus trying to follow up with Schulz on the scalpel and Arch and his eccentricities. If that was all they were.

The key to the athletic club beckoned. Work. That was the ticket. It had helped when I was preparing for Laura's wake. With decorating supplies and heavy-duty cleaners I could do something useful and work off industrial-strength stress at the same time. Friday night, I could make a recheck for a spot cleaning before the party. Even athletes couldn't completely mess up a place in a couple of days, could they?

My key turned in the latch and echoed loudly in the darkness. I flipped on the lights. The empty Nautilus machines sprang into view like a chamber of horrors. They flashed silver in the mirrors. Without jocks pumping iron and exercycling and running in place, the air between the club's cream-colored walls and gray and burgundy carpet expanded, thinned out.

I shook myself. The place had a new life when one was in it alone. The walls, shelves, machines seemed to undergo a metamorphosis at night, like toys in nursery stories. I gritted my teeth to haul the vacuum and bags of supplies across to the front desk.

Standing in the middle of the open area, I puzzled over where to put the table with pumpkins, punch bowl, and party munchies for Halloween. I could put the long tables by the walls overlooking the racquetball courts, then cover them and the columns in the dance area with orange and black crepe paper.

The closet next to the bank of mirrors flanking the Nautilus equipment, when I had found its one light, yielded four long tables that would work for the snacks. I placed all the chemicals on the closet floor and started setting up.

During a break I peered down the stairs and saw that all traces of the exercise-room mirror, the one Trixie had shattered, were gone. Oh, how replacing the old mirror with fun house–style trick ones to make all the skinny people look fat would have been hilarious. But I was not in the practical joke business.

I dusted, vacuumed, decorated. It was after midnight when I mixed the solutions for disinfectant and tub-and-tile cleaner and trotted downstairs to start on the locker rooms.

There were some jogging suits and open lockers on the men's side, and despite the staff's once-over on the sinks and showers, the vague odor of sweat still hung in the air. I sprayed the diluted disinfectant into one sink and heard music go on in the aerobics room.

"Just give me money . . ."

It was a jazzed-up version of a Beatles hit. I knew I was the only one who was supposed to be here. Was this a burglar with a sense of humor? One who needed rock and roll to steal hand weights and towels?

I pushed back fear by reasoning that the music camouflaged any noise I could make. I crept out of the locker room. Looking around the corner I could just see the movement of someone . . . exercising?

It was Trixie. She was kicking her legs out and shrieking along with the singers.

"Muh-huh-honey . . . that's what I want!"

I waved my spray bottle to indicate my presence.

"Hey, Trix!"

She gave the startled cry of a person discovered naked. Which, of course, she was not.

"Goldy! I thought you were coming tomorrow."

"What are you doing?"

She began to cry and crumpled onto the rug. I hurried over.

"I just wanted to be alone," she said finally. "I just

wanted everybody to quit bugging me. You ... don't understand."

"Try me."

She took deep breaths to try to calm herself, then hiccuped. "You can't, because you have a child."

"I am sorry about your loss. You know that."

Her voice was bitter. "That man took mine away from me."

"Fritz?"

"He knew I had high blood pressure. That the placenta could break down. It did. I lost the baby while I waited for him. What was he doing? Why didn't he hurry? Now everybody just feels sorry for me. And he goes on with his practice."

She began to cry again. I hugged her and eventually her sobs subsided. The tape ended; we were enveloped in quiet.

"Are you still coming to our group the day after—or I guess"—I took a look at my watch—"it's technically tomorrow?"

She gave that harsh laugh. "You really think that'll help?"

"What would help?"

Trixie gulped and said, "If Laura were still alive. She had some information on Korman she was going to show me. I told her my whole story one day after class. She said it wasn't the first time he had messed up. She was planning on doing something—"

We were interrupted by a noise upstairs, someone walking across the open room I had just cleaned and decorated. I put my finger to my lips.

I whispered to her, "Are there any weights down here?"

She nodded.

"Could you throw one at a burglar, if that's—?"

She nodded again. "I have a very strong arm."

"Let's go."

We crept upstairs. Trixie had picked up some weights

and was warming up her triceps with two-pounders in each hand. To my chagrin the intruder had turned the lights off. Only the outdoor parking lot lights cast a pale neon glow on the room.

"Where is—" Trixie began.

"The closet," I whispered back.

The closet door was partly open. A wedge of light shone out its door, casting a huge triangle of gold-gray on the carpet. The wrapped pillars looked ghastly.

"Can you hit the closet door?"

"I think so," she hissed. "Hold this one." She let go of one of the weights and damned if I didn't drop it.

"Eeyah!" I shrieked when it hit my toe.

The closet light went out.

"Uh!" shouted Trixie as she heaved the other weight through the darkness.

CRASH! went the Nautilus room mirror.

"Oh no!" screamed Trixie.

Someone rushed past us in the blackness.

I tried to run but fell over on my pain-wrenched toe.

"Turn the lights on!" I commanded Trixie. "Hurry! Run outside! See if you can tell who it is, or see their car!"

Trixie cursed and careened through the dimness. She hit the light switch and then stumbled out the front door.

Across the way the Nautilus room mirror looked like an avant-garde glass sculpture. I would have to remind Hal of this when he sued me. What the hell. He hadn't exactly provided a high-security place to work in, had he?

"I saw the car," Trixie gasped when she came trotting back.

"And?"

"Kinda weird," she said. "It looked just like Laura's old blue Volvo."

CHAPTER 24

Hopping down my well of sleep came frog-faced doctors holding scalpel blades. Hot on their trail were gargoyle-faced liches in unhemmed robes, and behind them roared a phalanx of honking blue Volvos. The Volvos crashed against the well walls; the liches and frogs in robes scampered down toward me to escape the wailing horns. I had the frantic thought: Have I disinfected those walls yet?

Br-r-ring! Br-r-ring! went the Volvo horns.

Br-r-ring!

The phone.

I sat up. My right toe was throbbing. What Laura would have said: Call a toe truck.

The clock read ten-twenty. I'd gotten home at two-thirty, I remembered, after finally driving an exhausted Trixie home. Except for this ringing, my house was quiet—a sure sign that everyone had decided to let me sleep after my wee-hour janitorial stint. Everyone, that is, except this nut calling me.

I said into the receiver, "This had better be good."

"Ho-ho!" came Tom Schulz's too cheerful voice. "In your usual good mood, too. What'd you do, tie one on last night?"

"Please."

He said, "I thought you might be interested in helping us investigate that scalpel. Because that's what it was, you know."

"A scalpel. I told you it was a frigging scalpel. I passed Med Wives 101, you know. Did you have a blood match?"

"Easy now. They're working on the blood match. It's coming. Right now I need more to go on than what you've given me. Including why your son would have that scalpel stashed."

"I told you. He found it in the Kormans' car, and my theory is that someone put it there after using it on Laura."

"Theory?" Tom Schulz yelled. "That's what I'm supposed to go to the D.A. with? A caterer's theory?"

"Seems to me, Tom," I said, "that you need to find out who would have access to Just One Bite."

"That's easy. Anybody can get it to kill rats."

"Lots of folks think Fritz is just that. A rat." I told him about the creekside activity with Patty Sue.

"Incredible," said Tom Schulz. "He's irresistible even to a woman with a broken arm."

"You don't understand," I said in Patty Sue's defense. "My housemate respects authority with a capital R. That's how people like Fritz get their power."

Schulz asked again, "Are you going to tell me what your kid was doing with that scalpel?"

"I don't know what he was doing with it," I replied truthfully. "I'm going to try to find out. But there's more. I got into a mess with Trixie last night." I told him about the intruder, the mirror, and the Volvo.

"Trouble just follows you around, you know? Be careful. Because whoever our guy, or gal, is, they're going to try again to do in Fritz. You don't want your kid to get in the middle. And chances are our culprit won't mess with a few pellets of rat poison this time."

"Why not?"

"Bright little Goldy can't figure that one out?"

"Excuse me. Let me go get a cup of coffee and my brain will get into gear."

"Our murderer will probably use something else, and there will be a next time," Schulz said, "because the first time, he or she flunked Poisoning 101. Just watch it."

"I plan to," I said, and hung up.

I spent the next day hustling around the house to get ready for the Amour Anonymous meeting. Looking at the treats from the pastry shop made me wonder if we might need more. I could always use any surplus from today on the Halloween party. I slathered fudge frosting on brownies for Patty Sue. I stuffed crêpes with sugared ricotta cheese and smothered them with apricot sauce for Marla ("I spent the last two days in Vegas," she'd called that morning to tell me. "I thought it would be a good break. Ended up spending the whole time with a glass of Jack Daniel's and bag of peanuts in one hand and a roll of quarters in the other. Pretty soon the coins sounded like peanuts and the peanuts smelled like coins and I thought, now I'm really crazy. Guess I need the group, Goldy, don't you think? I'll bring the dessert sherry, you just make lots to eat.")

The phone rang again. Alicia couldn't come: she'd had a blowout on I-70. Her load of pumpkins had exploded like grenades when they hit the concrete. Two dozen cars had spun out in orange slime . . . no one was hurt . . . the road was closed so it could be cleaned . . . traffic had backed up for six miles. With significant understatement, she added, "You can't imagine the mess."

A couple of other women called with excuses, none so

spectacular. When I finally got back to cooking I melted sugar into a dark syrup for Vonette's favorite, Burnt-Sugar Cake. Pondering what Trixie would fancy, I decided she could manage with cookies. Marla would finish them if Trixie was holding out for health food.

And speaking of which, I could use Pomeroy's honey to make my marvelous Honey-I'm-Home Ginger Snaps. This was my very own tasty invention. They were popular with the station-wagon set. Plus, they kept well.

The spicy scent of baking cookies filled the kitchen. When I was done I surveyed the spread. If we were going to be involved in telling all our sad stories we could do with a few sweets.

Marla arrived first. She swept in wearing a bespangled tent-type dress and a long scarf that said Club Mediterranée.

"God," she fumed, "I'm exhausted. It's a good thing I don't take drugs. Someone could have sold me some speed and I would have spent another six hundred bucks on those slot machines and put Planter's out of business. Tell me you've made something fabulous to eat."

"In there." I gestured toward the dining room.

"Where is everybody?"

"Coming. They're eating dinner."

"I ate dinner," she said as she picked up a dessert plate and attacked the brownies. "I just saved room for dessert."

"Did I hear someone mention dessert?" asked a yawning Patty Sue as she descended from upstairs, where she had been napping.

"You bet," said Marla, "come quickly before I eat it all."

Running suit–attired Trixie trotted in carrying hand weights. I begged her to leave them by the door, which she did.

"Hoo-hoo!" yodeled Vonette from the front door. She was already tipsy. Her orange hair looked like an abandoned robins' nest.

Honey-I'm-Home Gingersnaps

2 cups all-purpose flour (high
    altitude: add 1 tablespoon)
2 teaspoons baking soda
1/4 teaspoon salt
1 1/2 teaspoons ground ginger
1 teaspoon ground cinnamon
1/2 teaspoon ground cloves
1/4 teaspoon freshly grated nutmeg
1/4 cup solid vegetable shortening
1/2 cup (1 stick) unsalted butter
1 cup sugar
1 large egg
1/4 cup honey
1/4 teaspoon finely minced lemon
    zest

Preheat the oven to 375°F. Butter two
cookie sheets.

Sift together the flour, soda, salt, ginger, cinnamon, cloves, and nutmeg.
Set aside.

In a large mixer bowl, cream the short-ening, butter, and sugar until light and fluffy. Beat in the egg and the honey until well combined. Stir in the flour mixture and the zest, stirring until well combined, with no traces of flour visible.

Using a 1-tablespoon scoop, measure the cookies onto the cookie sheets, keeping them two inches apart. Do not attempt to make more than one dozen per sheet. Bake the batches one at a time, until the cookies have puffed and flattened and have a crinkly surface, 10 to 12 minutes per batch.

Cool the cookies completely on racks.

Makes 32 cookies

"Time to get started," I warned them as Vonette splashed dessert sherry into her coffee.

"What we do here," I began, "is talk, share, and give support."

Trixie said, "I just don't see how this can help."

I said, "Then why don't you go first? Tell us what's bothering you."

"I hate doctors," she said evenly, "and I don't want to talk about it."

"Aw, c'mon honey," coaxed Vonette. "I don't mind. And I'm married to one." She took a healthy swig from her coffee cup.

Patty Sue said, "I'm feeling sick."

"You see?" accused Trixie. "Somebody starts talking about doctors and right away, somebody feels sick. Why do we depend on them so much?"

"Chocolate's more reliable," said Marla, who was waddling out to the kitchen to replenish the brownie platter, which I had stupidly put within her reach.

Patty Sue said faintly, "I think we have to trust our doctors. Either that or the treatment doesn't work."

"Trix?" I said. "Do you want to talk or not?"

Trixie ground her teeth. "I did trust a doctor and look at where it got me."

Marla plopped back down at her place. Patty Sue gave me her wide-eyed look.

I concentrated my gaze on Trixie and said, "You feel angry."

"What do you think?"

"And so," I went on, "you throw—"

Marla said, "Oh my God. You throw up? What a waste."

"Please don't talk about throwing up," said Patty Sue as she stood to go out to the bathroom.

"This is great," Marla commented. "We say we're going to talk about men and all we talk about is food and barf."

Vonette cleared her throat. "Well, girls," she began, "I can talk about it without talking about food. You see, I know something about doctors. I can tell you—" She stopped to pour sherry directly into her cup, an action I felt I should stop, since she was already pretty sloshed.

I said, "Tell us, Vonette."

But Trixie interrupted her. "If you're angry too, Vonette, why don't you do something? Talk, talk, talk! How about a little action?"

"Temper, temper," said Marla. "Have a ginger snap." To demonstrate, she had one herself.

A limp-looking Patty Sue sat down again. I turned back to Vonette.

"So what do you want to tell us, Vonette?"

She took another long sip from her cup. "Do you girls talk about sex in here?"

Everyone was immediately quiet.

"Sure," said Marla.

"He's impotent with me," Vonette said finally, her voice dropping. "But not with everyone else. He says because I drink too much, our lack of a sex life is all my fault."

Patty Sue said, "I wish we could change the subject."

Marla rolled her eyes at me.

"Everybody thinks I don't know what goes on," Vonette was saying, "but I know. It's just that . . . thinking about it gives me these awful headaches. Thirty-six years," she muttered into her cup before draining it. "For what? Oh, my little Bebe." She started to sniffle. "I miss you. Bebe, Bebe."

"Do you think Laura had," I said tentatively, "something on Fritz, that she was going to confront him—"

"Confront?" yelled Trixie. "Confront? Why do we have to listen to shrink talk all the time?"

"She had something," said Vonette. "Of course she did. Oh, my." She reached into her purse and pulled out what I knew was her Valium pillbox, then downed one of the green pills with her newly filled coffee cup of sherry.

"You see," said Marla as she sliced a piece of the Burnt-Sugar Cake. "This is what happens when you abandon food for other palliatives."

"What palliatives?" asked Patty Sue.

"Forget it," said Marla, with her mouth full.

"This just makes me so angry," said Trixie, her forehead wrinkled into a scowl. "Yak, yak, yak. I knew it wouldn't do any good to come."

"Trixie," I said, "how else could you express your anger?"

"What's that," she said, "more shrink talk? How about having some of these doctors pay for the damage they inflict? I mean really pay?"

I said, "What would that look like?"

Trixie groaned and got up from the table, then flopped down on my living room couch with her arms folded across her chest.

"This is getting out of control," I said under my breath to Marla.

"Don't tell me," she said after swallowing, "I learned all about control when I had to deal with the Jerk's lawyer."

"Laura," came Vonette's drunken voice. In her stupor at the end of the table, she had heard little of the previous conversation. "Laura had something. But not just on him, if you see what I mean."

I said, "I'm not following you."

"You don't?" said Vonette with a confused look. "Don't you see that stuff Bebe wrote to her teacher about her home life said something about me, too?" She finished what was in her cup. "At that moment, when my Bebe died, my life was over. Laura had something on us, all right. It's not over, though. I'm going to get him. I'm going to go home and call him an impotent old ass. I'm going to tell him I'm going to turn him in to the Colorado Board of

Medical Examiners. Ha! That man screwed anyone, even his own patients!"

Marla and I looked at each other.

Trixie screamed, "You see what I mean?"

Patty Sue had her usual reaction to acute stress. She fainted.

CHAPTER 25

Halloween.

A thick shroud of October fog clung to the ground as I drove back up to the mountains at five-thirty Halloween morning. Already Colorado was in costume—a shroud mourning the loss of Indian summer. Or perhaps the loss of innocence.

Patty Sue was in the hospital. The doctor had said she was about two months pregnant. After the women's meeting she hadn't felt any better, even when I brought her back to consciousness with a little ammonia on a paper towel. She was in pain; a couple of pills "to relieve periodic suffering" did no good. It was late anyway, so I'd sent everybody home. Vonette was still babbling on about getting Fritz, even after we'd stuffed her into Marla's car.

About three A.M. Patty Sue's cramping from what she'd thought was her period had become so intense that even I became frightened. There was more blood. I scuttled the idea of an ambulance, figuring I could get her down to a

Denver hospital more quickly myself. After a quick call to the Emergency Room, we were on our way.

The on-call gynecologist was courteous, informative, and even sympathetic. Trixie should have been there to see a few stereotypes break down. He said they'd have to keep Patty Sue for a while. It looked as if there had been a small separation of the placenta. The fetus appeared healthy and had a good heartbeat. I was worried that the X-rays for Patty Sue's broken arm might have harmed the fetus, but again the doc said not to worry. Poor Patty Sue.

In her room I swabbed her face with a wet cloth.

Her eyes, dulled by the loss of sleep, fixed on my face.

"I feel awful," she said.

"First three months are the worst," I said. "I should have figured it out . . . the way you've been sick."

"Doctor Korman is the one—" she began, but tears started rolling down onto her pillow.

"It's okay," I said, and then stopped to take her hand. I said, "That's what you told Laura Smiley, isn't it? That he had been having relations with you."

She nodded. "He said it would help my condition. Laura already knew what was going on. She told me she needed to talk to me about it."

I said gently, "What did she say?"

"She said I had to get him to stop. But I told her I was afraid of him. What did I know about medicine? Maybe he was right. And he told me that if I told anyone about the treatment he would call my parents and tell them I was uncooperative."

She started to cry again, a miserable sobbing that erupted from her chest. I leaned over and hugged her until she stopped.

I said into her ear, "Can you just tell me what Laura said when you said you couldn't confront him?"

Patty Sue coughed before whispering back, "She said she could get him to stop. She thought he had changed from the way he was before, you know, from what Vonette told us. Laura said she thought Fritz had reformed. Then it was strange because she said she could ruin his practice. She said she had the power to do that."

"Do you know what she meant?"

"The next time I heard about Laura, she was dead."

I called Patty Sue's parents. Her mother answered. When I related my news there was a long silence.

Patty Sue's mother said, "She didn't tell us she had a boyfriend."

I told her Patty Sue would tell them all about it. She said she and her husband could be at the hospital shortly after eight that morning.

Now the mist clouded my windshield so thickly that I slowed to twenty miles an hour and pulled over into the far right lane. When winter approaches in Colorado, it comes like the poet's cat. It pads along the back roads and darkens the sky earlier each evening until finally, near mid-December, it plops on its ample backside as the cold sets in. During those months of early darkness, the residents take refuge by their firesides or bulk themselves up with Coors and ski stories to await the coming snows.

And it began this way, not with the ferocious onslaught of thunder and hail that mark spring's arrival, but gently, subtly, with a cold cloud of mist.

Fog swallowed the cars around me. I straightened up to peer through the glass and thought about Patty Sue. When she came to live with us she had worked hard learning to cook. She had asked questions about my life, and she had told me about hers. It was in September that she wafted off, first into indifference, and late in the month into distraction. The distracted behavior coincided, I now realized, with the confession to Laura and Laura's death.

My heart tugged for this twenty-year-old about to learn the rigors of motherhood. I would have stayed with her longer but I was worried about Arch. He had been very drowsy when I had told him of the impending trip to the hospital.

Arch, Arch. What was he up to with liches and magic spells and lessons in making Molotov cocktails? Worse than that, what were his plans for a used surgical kit?

I pushed open the front door. The house's air was warm and still, a place wrapped in sleep. Soon Arch's alarm broke the silence. I ground coffee beans, ran water, and turned up the radio news, which warned of clouds and wind and possibly snow in the mountains Halloween night.

The phone rang: Marla.

She said, "Vonette overdosed last night. She's really in bad shape. There's a possibility it was a suicide attempt."

"Oh my God. How'd you hear that?"

"Fritz called the priest from the hospital and the churchwomen set up a phone tree. I feel horrible. What do you think we should do?"

"Not sure. I have to get Arch off to school. How about if you call John Richard? We have to keep up with how she's doing."

"Thanks a lot," Marla said without enthusiasm. "Don't suppose it could wait until tonight, do you? I mean, if she's out of danger and they're still going to come to the party. I suppose that would be *beaucoup* crass."

"I wouldn't put anything past them. Call me later. I'll be up to my rear in chips and dip. Almost forgot. Patty Sue's two months pregnant."

"What? Expecting? I didn't even know."

"Neither did she. By Fritz, no less."

"Jesus," Marla said. "That guy never quits. If I were Vonette, I'd want to die too."

An hour later I had shooed Arch off to school wearing his lich costume. Asking him tough questions was simply not within my emotional repertoire after the events of the previous night. The house was silent. No clients calling for parties. No Arch sneaking about. No Patty Sue bumping into walls. Still. Questions hung heavily in the air.

Time to let the mind cook along with the hands. As usual.

First on the agenda for the athletic club party was the preparation of guy bow, an Oriental chicken-and-egg affair seasoned with soy and encased in a bread shell.

But as I folded and rolled out the dough, I could not get the image of Vonette out of my mind. She seemed a sudden absence. Prayer had been a difficult proposition since I'd stopped teaching Sunday school. But I prayed now for Vonette.

I set aside the guy bow and prayed. *Please, please.* Then I peeled, pitted, and mashed the plump avocados destined for my Holy Moly Guacamole. Once the rich dip was done, I set it aside and tried to think.

Why had Vonette done it? Had the headaches finally become unbearable? Had something not killed the pain?

Worst question of all was one that filled my mind like the bowls of silky guacamole.

Had the messy anger of our meeting the evening before triggered some deep mechanism that had been operating all along, only incrementally, with liquor and drugs? Instead of killing herself slowly, had Vonette gone over the edge because of what the meeting had made her think about? And what about her oath to confront Fritz?

About that I did not even want to think. But had to.

Before starting the deviled eggs and empanadas I called the hospital. Patty Sue was okay; her parents were with her.

A nurse who knew me said Vonette Korman was in a coma. I didn't ask if anyone was with her. I could imagine her face and her curly orange hair, but she wasn't there. It was as if the ground around our relationship had suddenly collapsed.

I tried to focus back on the party. My next task was to arrange concentric circles of the empanadas and deviled

Holy Moly Guacamole

1 large or 2 small avocados, peeled,
    pitted and mashed to make
    1 cup
1½ teaspoons fresh lemon juice
1 teaspoon freshly grated onion
¼ teaspoon salt
1 tablespoon picante sauce
¼ cup mayonnaise
Corn Chips

Place the mashed avocado in a non-metallic bowl. Mix in the juice, onion, salt, and picante sauce until well blended. Spread the mayonnaise over the top to the edges, cover the bowl, and refrigerate. At serving time, uncover the bowl and thoroughly mix in the mayonnaise. Serve with corn chips.

Makes 1¼ cups

eggs. With the eggs in the guy bow we'd have a cholesterol-heavy night, but what the hey. Eggs were cheap and looked good. Besides, they filled people up, a key concept in catering.

My phone rang: Tom Schulz. Yes, I remembered about tonight. I asked if he had heard about Vonette.

"Yeah," he said. "I heard the call for the 'copter. Why?"

"I don't know. I just feel real bad about it. She could have done it so many times before . . . Why last night?"

"Was she at that meeting you were supposed to have?" he asked, suddenly wary. "Your house, right? What happened?"

"Don't get suspicious, Mr. Investigator. We just talked. Women's stuff. Besides, it's confidential."

"Was she upset when she left?"

I let out a breath. "Well, yes. She was upset. But not suicidal."

"That Fritz sure has his problems."

I put all the bags of chips in one large bag. "Listen," I said, "I hope you'll stay on this case with Vonette."

"Take it easy," Tom responded, "she isn't dead. Yet."

"If she dies," I warned him, "I hope you'll get on it right away. Toxicology, the whole bit."

"Don't worry. That's my job, Goldy. And the coroner's back, too, no more new deputy stuff. Are the guys around here happy about that!" He chuckled. "You just concentrate on tonight. I'll be by at seven to pick up Arch while you finish your cleaning job. Then we'll dance the night away, and you'll forget all your troubles."

"That," I said before hanging up, "I seriously doubt."

CHAPTER 26

"How do I look, Mom?" asked Arch as he entered the kitchen that evening. Although he had not made up his face for school, he decided for the party to put on the full war paint of the superhuman lich.

I stopped packing the appetizers into plastic containers, took off my witch's hat and mask, and surveyed him in the painted muslin robe and hood. Around his neck was the heavy gold-plated jewelry Vonette had lent him earlier in the week. The eleven-year-old face glowed with white and black theatrical makeup painted like a skull.

"What am I supposed to say to a lich," I asked dryly, "you look dreadful? Sorry, lich, I didn't pack any worms for you to eat. And please don't get any ideas about installing an alarm system at the athletic club."

"Don't worry, Mom," he replied soberly, "liches are only satisfied when they suck the blood from their victims."

On that happy note, I whisked off for the club with the Kormans' station wagon full of food. The last thing I needed was for my soon-to-be escort, who also happened to be the police officer who had closed my business, to know that I was catering illegally.

Twenty minutes later I pulled the station wagon into the club parking lot, which held only two cars. Already the night was quite cool, and the rising moon glowed yellow on the eastern horizon. I shivered.

Pomeroy Locraft greeted me at the door and took one of the boxes from my hands. He was dressed as a bee-keeper, complete with mask.

"Now that's an original costume," I remarked.

"Beekeeper from another planet," he rejoined, looking over my shoulder. "Newest offering from Stephen King. Trixie's here with me. She's a little drunk, just thought I'd warn you. Seems things got kind of out of control at your place last night."

"Don't remind me."

"Where's Arch?"

"Coming with Tom Schulz. My date," I added.

"Bringing the cops to keep your ex-husband in line? Not a bad idea."

We set about arranging the platters and punch bowl. Pom said Hal was having a fit about someone breaking the big mirror in the Nautilus room. I had every intention of confessing to my part in that accident after I got through some of the more pressing crises.

Trixie told me in a whiskeyed whisper that she had thrown away all the shards on the floor. She was trying to explain more when Arch came bouncing in.

"Where's Tom Schulz?" I asked. "Please tell me he's wearing anything but a police uniform."

"You know, Mom," Arch said in his serious tone, "you aren't very nice to Investigator Schulz. He's not a clown. He's a magistrate. An enforcer of laws in the human order."

"Just remember not to mention that I made this food for tonight."

Arch was nodding doubtfully when Tom Schulz walked in, bedecked in costume and makeup that was somewhere between Bozo and Ronald McDonald. I looked at Arch, who avoided my eyes by surveying the tables laden with food.

"Patty Sue called while you were in the shower," Arch said. "Said she'll be back tomorrow. Her parents were going to bring her up. She said she wouldn't be able to drive for a while."

Tom Schulz, Pomeroy, and I all said together, "That's good."

When Tom and Pomeroy had sauntered off for a friendly glass of punch, I asked Arch, "Do you still miss Ms. Smiley?"

He nodded without looking at me. This was always a bad sign.

"On Halloween," I went on, "all the ghosts of dead people are supposed to come out, you know."

"Don't be weird, Mom."

"I was just wondering if you'd thought about that."

He returned my gaze. "Sometimes I miss her. She was the only teacher who ever liked me. But if she killed herself, then I guess she was crazy the way everyone says."

"If she thought you were a really great kid, and she did, then she was not crazy."

"Mom? I want some chips."

I reached for his forearm. "Just tell me, Arch, you're not taking this lich stuff too seriously, are you? Curses, violent revenge for dead souls, sucking blood, all that?"

"What makes you think that?"

How could I say, From your phone conversation with Todd that I wasn't supposed to be listening to? He sidled away.

"Arch, old buddy!" Pomeroy called out as Arch approached the tables. "What are you supposed to be, the label on a poison bottle?"

I looked around the club. The place still looked pretty clean. Trixie had done a passable job of cleaning the floor of the Nautilus room.

"A lich," Arch was explaining to the Martian beekeeper. Hal whizzed over on roller skates. He was dressed as a Blues Brother.

He glared at me from behind his dark glasses.

He said, "You want to tell me about that mirror?"

I said, "What mirror?"

He skated away. I took protection at Tom Schulz's side.

"Think the Korman doctors will be here tonight?" he asked.

I nonchalantly rearranged the deviled eggs and the crudités inside a hollowed-out pumpkin.

"Knowing them," I said, "they aren't going to sit by the bedside of a woman in a coma. It remains to be seen whether they're crude enough to come here tonight. They don't even know about Patty Sue."

"What about Patty Sue?"

I told him the story of my hapless roommate, and also about what Laura had said to her, indicating she had some kind of power over Fritz Korman.

Tom Schulz picked up two brownies. "She didn't use it for twenty years," he said. "But seeing Patty Sue with him, or hearing what Patty Sue had to say, set her off." He thought. "If the docs come, see if you can find out what Laura was threatening. That's our missing link. I'm still running the scalpel for prints and other tests, by the way."

"Glad to see the cops are doing their job. Don't eat any more brownies until more people get here." He gave me a quizzical X-ray look. I'd blown it. I said, "You see, I'm still a caterer at heart. And I don't know how you expect me to find out what Laura was holding over Fritz's head."

"Well," said Tom, licking his clown fingers, "you're going to be a detective, you figure things out. Detect."

At that moment the Jerk made a grand entrance with the teacher on his arm. He was dressed as a doctor. Not very original. She was dressed as a nurse. Poor thing, I hoped she was well stocked with bandages.

Trixie reappeared from the bathroom, where I assumed she had been either drinking or being sick or both, and for the first time I noticed she was also dressed as a witch. We could have passed as nonidentical twins. Marla swept in, despite the fact that John Richard was here. Maybe that meant she was getting over him. She was dressed as a Las Vegas showgirl, plump but very charming in her net stockings and low-cut leotard. She made a beeline for the food table.

Then, to my shock, came a stocky bald man dressed in black. His gait and swagger gave him away: Fritz Niebold Korman. I heard an explosion of laughter near him, as someone who had apparently asked what he was screamed, "Oh no! Fritz Korman's dressed as Zorro!"

I surreptitiously began refilling the punch bowl with ginger ale and fruit juice. No one was talking about Vonette, which was probably a good thing. She would pull through, I was sure.

In a little while the guy bow and guacamole were almost gone. The empanadas lay untouched. You never could tell what people were going to eat. I resolved to pay no more attention to the status of the food and drink. I didn't want to get into more trouble with Schulz, and Hal had treated me rudely enough that I felt justified in not doing any actual serving.

One of the club staff put on an aerobics-class tape and men, women, witches, wizards, doctors, nurses, clowns, and showgirls all began to gyrate enthusiastically. Perhaps, like Pavlov's dog, they were used to working hard to this music.

"Where's your date, the cop?" Pomeroy asked when I was munching the last of the guy bow.

I waved my hand. "He's out there somewhere," I replied. "I'm not keeping tabs on anything or anyone tonight."

"Poor Goldilocks," Pomeroy said, "nothing is ever just right. Why don't you come dance with a lonely bee-keeper?"

The music had turned slow. One of the cool-down songs usually reserved for the end of an aerobics class moaned from the speakers. Some astute staff member lowered the lights and as Pom took me into his arms to start dancing, I noticed that I was feeling anything but cooled down. Just the opposite, in fact.

Pom must have sensed my reaction. He pulled me in a little tighter, and even in the darkened room I could see the Jerk giving me the Evil Eye. Ha! Let him suffer.

"I wish you'd take that mask off," I whispered to Pomeroy. "Then I could give you a kiss and make my ex-husband feel terrible."

"Hey, please don't think of me as a sex object."

"You know what Laura would have said about that?"

"No," said Pomeroy.

"She would have said that a beekeeper should make a stinging reply."

"She had a way with words, didn't she?" Pomeroy said as he pulled me closer. My heart went *zing!* But I was determined to stay rational.

When the music finished he steered me back to the food table as the couples began to disperse to get refreshments.

"What did she have on Fritz Korman, though?" I asked as I ignored my own resolution to do nothing, opened a fresh bottle of fruit juice, and sloshed it into the punch bowl.

He said, "I don't know. I think maybe it was something from that student of hers."

The empanadas had disappeared during the last dance. Pomeroy was looking around the room.

He said, "Still don't see your date, sweets, so you're going to have to put up with me for a while. Here they come—your ex-husband and his father. Now you can kiss me." He took off his mask and put it on the floor while I pretended to be busy replenishing brownies.

"I'm not going to eat a thing you fix," the Jerk said defiantly when I offered him the platter.

Laura Smiley would have said, *Then no brownie points.*

Laura Smiley would have said . . .

Laura Smiley would have said . . .

I thought of jokes. Laura-type jokes. Why didn't the gunslinging prosecutor shoot down the defendant? Because he didn't have enough ammunition. Why did the little girl eat dynamite? Because she wanted to grow bangs. Why dynamite? Why not gunshot? Or some other kind of ammunition?

Ammunition.

I turned away from my ex-husband. Two people dressed as bats began to play racquetball. The ball thwacked against the wall with the same regularity that my mind was making one step, then another. Finally, I had the weapon to shoot the bad guy down. Now all I needed was to load that weapon.

But not yet. After the party, after everyone had gone home.

Tom Schulz was dancing with Marla. I slid up beside him and whispered, "I figured it out. What she had on him. I even think I know where it is. And I have an idea of who might have put the stuff in Fritz's coffee."

He shook his clown stomach and said, "At least give me until the end of this song, okay?"

Marla rolled her eyes at me.

What the hey, after all this time and effort. I took a deep breath and strolled back to the snack table where Pomeroy, Fritz, and John Richard were engaged in some uneasy conversation. I still hadn't kissed Pomeroy, and my chance was at hand.

"Better go get your girlfriend," I said to the Jerk, "looks as if she's trying to set up another date."

And indeed, there was the fiancée on the club's desk

phone. She had a serious look on her face. After a moment she came over and whispered something to John Richard, who turned to his father.

"Dad," John Richard said. His voice cracked. Fritz turned to look at him.

"Dad," he said again, "she died."

Fritz, who was drinking punch, brought his hands up to his face. But then, just as suddenly as John Richard's announcement had come, Fritz began to cough. It wasn't just regular coughing, but hacking and wheezing, and he was holding his throat. He slumped to the floor and John Richard knelt down with him.

"Dad!" John Richard bellowed. "What is it?"

"That stuff, that stuff!" he cried, pointing to his punch cup.

I was frozen, statuelike, still in shock from the news of Vonette, but there was John Richard sniffing Fritz's punch cup and giving me an unholy look of rage. John Richard ducked underneath the food table and just as quickly brought out my bottle of phenol-based industrial-strength disinfectant concentrate. There was my name in black marking pen, as clear as could be next to where I'd written POISON with the telltale skull and crossbones.

John Richard glowered at me. "You!" he screamed. "Again! Schulz! Get over here! Put this bitch under arrest!"

"Now wait a minute," I murmured, but Schulz was already there talking to John Richard, trying to get him to calm down.

Schulz leaned over the table.

He said, "You didn't do this, did you?"

I said, "You *know* I didn't."

Schulz said, "Did you fix this punch and this food?"

I floundered. I looked at my shoes. I said, "I'm not saying a word until I talk to a lawyer."

When I raised my eyes to Tom Schulz's silence, his look of disbelief and disappointment was much more difficult to take than John Richard's anger.

"I didn't know this was going to happen," I said fiercely.

"Now you listen," Schulz said, jabbing the air with his index finger, "you get over and stand in that corner by that broken mirror. I need to call the Poison Center again, get this man down to the hospital. The guys in my department aren't going to believe this happened while I was here. I don't believe it myself. But that's not what I don't believe most of all." He eyed me. "I think you know what that is."

I nodded.

"Get your things," I ordered Arch, who had materialized beside me.

Looking around the room I could see Marla and Trixie in a tête-à-tête. Pomeroy had picked up his mask from beside the table and was heading over toward his net by the jagged mirror. I walked behind him to catch up; there wasn't any way anyone in that room could have missed the interchange between Schulz and me. But maybe Pom would be willing to ignore it.

Trixie appeared beside us. She said, "This really pisses me off. I mean, again? Honest to God, doctors."

Marla bounced over.

"Jesus," she said, "Vonette's dead. Have you told Arch?"

"Not yet," I said. "And don't you tell him either. We've got to find out what's going on with Fritz first. But there's something else I need you to do. Call your lawyer. Get him started on extracting money from Korman and Korman for Patty Sue's maternity care. She's going to need it."

Marla's face lit up like all of Vegas. "You mean I get to take John Richard to court again? For money? Ha! I'm in heaven."

"Arch," I called, "we're going with Pom. Lots has happened."

Arch said, "That sure was a short party."

I touched Pomeroy's arm.

"Can you give Arch and me a ride home?" I whispered. "I want to go out the back and avoid all this mess."

He nodded.

Then when Schulz was leaning over the recumbent Fritz, I hustled Arch out behind Pomeroy.

I did want a ride. But I had absolutely no intention of going home.

CHAPTER 27

Outside, a sudden breeze swept over us. The moon was still climbing.

Pomeroy said, "Why do you need a ride from me? Why don't you just climb back on the broomstick you rode over here?"

"Because," I said impatiently, "I don't feel so good going anywhere in the car loaned to me by my deceased ex-mother-in-law, whose husband I have just been accused by my ex-husband of attempting to poison. Again."

It was lame, but it would get me started on what it was I wanted to do with Pomeroy.

He smiled and said, "Let's roll."

Arch pronounced Pom's four-wheel-drive vehicle cool when we climbed in. The tires spewed gravel as we wheeled out of the parking lot, and the wind picked up the dust and blew it into a whirlwind.

I put my arm around Arch and hugged him close to me. The sad news could wait.

After a few moments Pom said, "Tell me where you live, Goldy."

I took a deep breath. "Well actually, Pomeroy, I don't want to go home just yet."

He continued to drive, very cool, no emotion. "What did you have in mind? Or should I say, where?"

I said, "I want to go to Laura's old house. I've got an idea of where to look for something. Drive me to her house and I'll show you."

Laura Smiley's garage was dank and cold and smelled faintly of oil. Arch said he wanted to stay in the car and I didn't blame him. The wind groaned through the garage window jamb and swished the dry leaves outside. I flipped the switch for the single garage light bulb; it threw a dim light. Groping through the odds and ends on the work-table, I found the box I was looking for and pulled it out to show Pom.

I said, "The woman loved puns. She left all the clues for us. She put flour in a box with a flower, sugar behind a picture of Sugar Ray Leonard. She was obsessed with punishing Korman and she knew where to keep that ammunition."

I took a breath, then went on.

"She wrote letters to students she loved. And they wrote back. I'll bet she kept every letter. That was the evidence she had, what she never got to use."

I looked at Pom in the garage's gray light. I said, "I'll bet you knew she didn't drink or take drugs. Someone slipped her a little Valium, enough to calm a person used to drugs, but enough to put a non-drug user, a total ab-stainer, to sleep. Then that person slashed her wrists with a scalpel blade and put a razor in her hand, except she didn't shave because she was a radical feminist. She didn't kill herself, she was murdered for what was in this box. You figure it out."

"I can't."

I read the label on the box. "BB's. In Laura's handwriting. I doubt she was out shooting western long-eared squirrels, Pom. I'll bet she never used her BB gun."

"You're way ahead of me."

Arch creaked open the passenger side door of Pom's car. He said, "Mom. I'm tired. Why are we here, anyway?"

"Just a few more minutes," I told him. "Take it easy."

With hands quivering, I opened the box. Inside was what I expected to find, letters in a large scrawling hand bound with ribbons. I riffled through them. The return addressee was the same on each one: Hollenbeck.

I said, "You see, she even used puns to hide things. Bebe's stuff is in the BB box."

Pom looked into the box and shook his head.

I turned to him. "You were looking for it, too, weren't you?"

He said, "Yes, but . . ."

"I'm not going to worry about that now," I said. "Listen. She made an appointment to see Fritz the day she died. Saturday. The day I think he killed her. Knowing about Patty Sue, about him seducing a young girl again, made her decide to confront him, made her threaten to bring out the letters after all these years. She could have ruined his practice, a fact he knew all too well. He escorted her out the back door, brought her over here in his old station wagon, maybe on the pretext of talking things through. I'll bet he brought her in that car because he didn't want anyone to recognize his Jeep with its customized plates. Then they had tea or something, in went the Valium, and out came the scalpel that he used and the ladies' razor that she didn't use. He left the surgical pack in the wagon, never thinking anybody would drive it. But the nurse screwed up and sent Laura a bill anyway, even though she wasn't a patient. If she was dead, nobody would think to look here for evidence. I mean, if it looked as if she killed herself."

I touched the letters, then glanced up at Pom in the darkness.

"I just need one more thing," I said. "Please take me to Fritz's office."

He drove, fast but silent. At the office of Korman and Korman I heaved a rock to break the front window, grateful for the things I had learned from Trixie. I climbed in and went to the file I was looking for. I read it and came back to the car.

"What the hell are you doing?" asked Pom.

"Just take me out to your place," I begged him, "and we can go through these letters tonight and call Tom Schulz, maybe get him to arrest Fritz instead of me. Arch can stretch out on your bed. I just can't go home now, wanted for another poisoning and with a crazed John Richard on the loose."

He sighed. "First my car, now my house. Let me know when you want the bees."

The four-wheel drive jolted and bounced over the muddy road to the Preserve. In my lap I held the box of correspondence between two women, both now dead. The moon came out from behind a cloud and shone through the pines, which were thickening as we roared deeper into the forest. Maybe coming here hadn't been such a great idea. Impenetrable woods populated with deer and elk and other wildlife could not attract trick or treaters. I missed the little neighborhood mites with their bags and plastic pumpkins. They brought Halloween down to kid-size level. Out here, the Eve of All Hallows, with its promise of unleashed spirits, loomed as large as the stands of blue spruce that swung in the evening breeze. Branches of evergreen lining the road fingered Pom's windshield. I reached for Arch's hand.

"You okay?"

"Yes, Mom. I just don't understand why we're going out here instead of going home."

I said, "Just wait."

When we got to the cabin, I took off my witch's cape

and hat and tried to wash the paint off Arch's face. I considered waiting until morning to tell him about the death of his grandmother. But I did not under any circumstances want him to hear it accidentally or casually, from someone else. I decided to break the news after I had tucked him into Pomeroy's cot.

"I'm sorry, Arch," I whispered. "I have bad news. Vonette died this evening."

He was very still, his eyes locked into mine. The shadow of the silver greasepaint that had not yielded to the washcloth gave him the aspect of a ghoul. When his tears began I wiped his face on the sleeve of my witch costume.

"And," I went on slowly, "somebody's tried to poison Fritz again. Except whoever did it probably didn't put enough in again. That's what I think."

A few moments later he murmured, "Why are we here?"

"Well," I said with a sigh, "your dad's feeling really crazy right now. His mother's dead and his dad's sick. And you know how your dad can get when he's angry, throwing dishes around and all. So I thought we'd be safer out here."

He said nothing for a long time while tears continued to well up. He opened his mouth to speak, then closed it, opened it again.

He said, "Is Vonette in heaven? With Laura Smiley?"

I felt the tears prick behind my own eyes as I took my son into my arms.

I said, "Absolutely. They are up there together, taking care of each other, right now."

Within half an hour Arch was breathing the comforting shallow wheeze of a child asleep. Pomeroy placed a mug of hot chocolate in front of me and we began the long work of opening letter after letter and reading them in silence. Outside, the wind howled and groaned. The waves of air would start and stop, and once after the sudden cessation of sound I thought I heard a car engine being turned off.

"Did you hear that?" I asked Pom.

He shook his head. "Out here you hear all kinds of stuff. You learn to ignore it."

"Listen to this," I said. I kept my voice low so Arch would not awaken. "Bebe writes, 'He came in this morning when Mom was still asleep. After he did it to me again he wanted to know who I've told. He says this is just supposed to be between us. He says people who betray secrets die. I'm afraid.' "

"It's bad, all right," said Pom, who was slouched down between the cushions of his homemade sofa. His beekeeper suit was crumpled; he looked like a tired ghost. "I just read where she was bleeding and was afraid to go to a doctor, least of all her own stepfather. So she just waited for it to go away."

Now there seemed to be sticks breaking outside. Perhaps it was a solitary elk moving through the forest. Pom noticed nothing. He was intensely involved in reading the letters. I thought I must be getting paranoid.

I read again, " 'Miss Smiley, I have stopped going to church because I know God doesn't like me anymore. Fritz said—' " I paused and looked up at Pom. "You see, there she uses his name. I'm sure that'll help with laws about evidence." I looked back at the sheet in my hand. " 'Fritz said Mom knows. What does that mean, Miss Smiley? What does Mom know?' "

I shook my head. "Pom. No wonder this kid drank a whole bottle."

"Yes," came a voice from the door, "that's why she did it, all right."

And in walked Fritz Korman still in his black Zorro suit. He had a small gun in his hand.

"Put that thing down," demanded Pomeroy. "Goldy's kid is asleep over there."

Fritz's bald head shone in the soft yellow light of

Pomeroy's lamps. He was leering at us. A broad self-satisfied smile stretched across his handsome face. The devil's own, out on Halloween night. My heart turned to ice.

I said, "I thought you were so sick."

He brought his nose up in a wrinkle and kept the gun pointed at us.

"Goldy, honey," he said, "that's why we have ipecac. To get poison out of people's systems. And since I figured it was Pomeroy or you or one of your buddies who tried to do me in, I've come to find out. And look at what else we've found."

I said, "You bastard."

"Now don't go waking up my grandchild, Goldy. He's going to find your and Pom's bodies out in that garage shed after your little lovers' quarrel. Now let's all go out slowly." And he motioned us with the gun to move over to the door.

"Did you kill Vonette?" I demanded without moving. "She knew about these letters, didn't she? She threatened you, is my bet. How'd you make it look like suicide this time? And what about Laura Smiley?"

He gave me a rueful smile. "Well now, aren't you full of questions?"

I pressed on, "Arch found an opened surgical kit in the Chrysler. Is that why you wanted your car back so badly, because of what you had left in there? Was that the car a neighbor heard at Laura's that Saturday morning?" He smirked at me. "What I want to know is, how you got in and out of that house without the police finding any prints."

He raised his eyebrows, again in mock surprise. He said, "Amazing invention, surgical gloves."

"Look, Fritz," said Pomeroy evenly. "Cut the crap. Take the letters and go. You don't need to kill us, for God's sake, there's been enough dying already. Just go."

Fritz cocked his head at Pomeroy, the same leer fixed

on his face. For the first time, it occurred to me that my former father-in-law, a man I had liked for so long, was insane.

"Pomeroy Locraft, you are offending me. You have offended me already. You have accused me of immorality."

"You mean," I said, "for performing an abortion on his wife who was an alcoholic?"

"Well, Goldy. You've been reading those files," said Fritz. He turned back to the beekeeper. "Poor Pomeroy, wanted to be a daddy so badly. Came into my office all upset. But it was too late."

Pomeroy was shaking his head. He said to Fritz, "I wouldn't go outside in that outfit if I were you—"

"Fritz," I babbled, "where will you go? They'll catch you, you know."

He snorted. "By the time they figure out I'm gone, I'll be the proprietor of a little hotel in Mexico."

"What about Vonette?" I demanded, stalling, anything. "How much Demerol did you have to inject her with to kill her? Don't you think the cops are going to figure that out?"

Fritz looked from one of us to the other. "Vonette's better off now. The police will find nothing. I am tired," he announced, "of listening to you two. Walk."

And out we shuffled. I gave a last long look at the lump on the bed that was my son.

Halfway to the shed, Fritz called to us to stop.

"Almost forgot," he said over the breeze stirring the trees. "If you and your boyfriend here are going to kill each other, we need another gun. So turn left, boys and girls, and we can go to my car and get one." And then he laughed, a horrible high-pitched sound that made my stomach turn over.

We turned and marched through the dry grass toward what I could dimly see was Fritz's Jeep. The evening was still cloudy and the moon was high in the sky. Occasionally moonlight swept the meadow. Pom's cabin, the honey shed, the silvered grass would appear—and then be gone. I kept glancing back to see some movement in the cabin. Had Arch awakened? But if he had, what good would it do? Would he have heard? How could he get help? Would he be too terrified or confused to do anything? I had noticed a rural fire number posted on one of the trees near the cabin, an indication that someone had Pomeroy on a map somewhere. Fat lot of good that would do us.

Fritz was muttering and thrashing through his glove compartment.

"Goldy," whispered Pom, "when we get down to the shed, I'll try to hit him. If we're in the back of the shed, go out the back door. Then run back to the house and get Arch and take off in my car. The keys are in it."

"What about you?" I whispered back.

"Shut up, you two," hollered Fritz. He had come around the car and now held two firearms. "Turn around and get down to that shed."

We obediently turned and started back over the rocks and grass in the direction of the shed, Fritz behind us. I walked on tiptoe, trying to avoid holes. At one point I stepped on something that felt like eggshells. Then suddenly the clouds parted again and gray-white moonlight flooded the meadow.

Jesus God in heaven. There was a small figure making its way to the creek, and it was carrying something. A bottle? I couldn't tell. There was something else I could discern, but did not want to accept.

It was Arch.

CHAPTER 28

When the three of us reached the shed, Fritz ordered Pom to go in first and turn on the light, with the warning that I would be shot immediately if the light did not come on. Pom did as he was told and we walked in. Surprise. Between the shelves loaded with supplies there was just enough room for a car. A blue Volvo.

"I knew you had her car," I said to Pom.

"I was supposed to be fixing it," he said.

"I already figured out that you were looking for the evidence she had against Fritz. Just tell me what you were doing at the athletic club the other night," I said.

"I told you two to shut your mouths," said Fritz.

But then I scanned the shelves in the shed, and I knew what Pom had been looking for Thursday night.

"Okay, this is how it's going to work," Fritz announced. "Goldy, you get over—"

"FIREBALL, FIREBALL, COME TO THE AID OF THE LICH!" shouted Arch's young voice from outside.

"Shut up!" shouted Fritz. "Hey, who is that? Come out here! Hey!"

Through the air from the blackness came some kind of a projectile, whizzing, ablaze . . . It was a Molotov cocktail.

"Get out!" shouted Pom. He grabbed my arm and shoved me out the shed door. I heard the bottle shatter and explode. Pom was on the ground beside me. Fritz was nowhere.

And then I heard what sounded like a low roar, beginning slowly and rising, louder and louder.

The bees. Arch had pulled the rope.

"I've got to get one of the smoke pots going to get rid of the bees," Pomeroy cried into my ear. "They're going to sting Fritz to death. Go around back! Get Arch!"

The warm weather had dried the grass to straw. Already smoke was billowing heavily from one side of the shed, and flames were licking the grass.

"Arch!" I screamed. "Arch! Where are you?"

A gust of wind fanned the flames into a roar that swallowed my voice. The smoke stung my eyes and nose. My breath caught in my mouth. A bee landed on my arm and I screamed.

"Arch! *Arch!*"

The smoke was so thick that my eyes felt as if they were on fire. My own tears blinded me as I stumbled toward the meadow. The air was hot. I felt wildly with my hands for trees, bush branches, boulders, anything by which Arch might be huddled. Pine tree branches whacked and scratched my face. I fell over a clump of rocks.

"Arch!"

A thin voice called, "Over here, Mom!"

I jumped and ran in the direction of that sound. Branches again clawed my face. Twice I stumbled on snake holes and fell into black straw. The air was thick, unbreathable with the smoke. From time to time I would feel the brush of a bee. I ran for Arch, calling. His responding voice was my beacon. Finally I could see the cabin.

Then came the sound of vehicles cracking over small trees. Who? Twirling red and white lights flashed through the web of branches and pungent air. What was it?

Oh, God. It was the fire department.

"Arch!" I called. "Arch! Arch!"

Turning back to the shed I could see some flames, mostly smoke.

"Arch!"

"Here, Mom," came a small voice by a tree. I stumbled over to the sound.

I pulled him to me. "Arch," I said, "Arch."

He said, his voice muffled by my squeeze, "Is Fritz dead?"

"I don't know," I cried. I could hear men's voices shouting. Figures were running down to the shed. "What were you trying to do by throwing that bomb?"

Arch said, "I just wanted to scare him. He was acting so weird!"

I shook my head, hugged him tighter. "And did you call the fire department before you started this blaze?"

He pulled back from my chest.

"Of course," he said matter-of-factly. "Pom showed me how to use his radiophone once. The fire number is on it." His face was shiny with sweat. Despite his apparent calm, his voice was shaking. "And I told the fire department to call Tom Schulz."

At that moment, I was so glad to have him alive and with me that I did not care whom he had called.

"Thanks, Arch," I whispered into his ear. "You probably saved my life, you know. Pom's, too." I paused. "Hon, I've been so worried about you. Potions and revenge and weapons. It's not the same as life, you know, real life."

He let his head bob forward. "I know," he said, barely audible over the din from the firefighters. "But"—and now his eyes behind the thick glasses implored me—"it was just because of the kids at school. Todd and I were going to put a curse on them. But it didn't work. I mean we sort of chickened out. You know? We had a curse and a weapon, but the milkwort potion was too gross. I got to make the Molotov cocktail anyway, because I remembered where Pom keeps his extra gasoline tank. And I, uh, let the bees go by pulling the rope that warns of an intruder. Man, I can't wait to tell Todd about that."

What could I say? He was my son. He didn't cater to anybody either. Still. The games were his escape from reality. What he had done was brave, but much too hazardous for a boy of eleven. I hugged him again.

"You're really great," I said. "But when all this is over we're both going to go see the school psychologist. We need to have a long chat."

He looked up at me. The smoke stung my eyes to tears again when he said, "All I need is you, Mom."

By the time we made our way back up to the cabin, Tom Schulz, still in his clown costume, was sitting on a tall stool boasting about having the situation under control. Fritz, he informed us, was going by rescue squad to a hospital in Denver. He had stings over half his body. And Schulz had sent an investigator to the Korman house to confiscate the records of injections the doctor claimed to have given Vonette. He was going to see if it matched the toxicological report he was ordering.

"I've got a cop with Korman now," Tom said. "Because we don't even have to wait for those records. That doctor is under arrest."

"Finally," interjected Pomeroy, who had reentered his cabin, covered with soot.

I sank onto the couch and pulled Arch down next to me. I never wanted to let him out of my sight again. For the next few hours, anyway. The muscles in my legs and arms ached. A sudden wave of exhaustion swept through my body.

"And you, Miss G," Tom said as he wagged a heavy

finger at me, "are in one load of trouble for making that food."

"Tell me what you arrested Fritz for," I demanded weakly.

He puffed out his chest. "Investigation of first-degree murder. Man, I am so smart. I got that scalpel checked for blood *and* fingerprints. Lucky for us the record on Laura Smiley said she was blood type AB negative, which just happened to match the blood on the blade and the handle. Best of all, I found a right index fingerprint."

I gave him a questioning look. "I thought there were surgical gloves . . . ?"

"Oh, Goldy," Tom rejoined, "you got a long way to go before you become a grown-up detective. Not to mention that your ability to follow orders needs some work. Man wears surgical gloves, touches his forehead or something, picks up some body oil which has some kind of enzymes or something in it, hell, I'm not too sure myself. Anyway, then he touches something and some of that enzyme and oil stuff comes off and bingo, the print comes through the glove." He smiled proudly. "I sent that scalpel down to Denver for a laser picture, got a print, matched it with the Department of Motor Vehicles print of Fritz Korman's right index, and what do you know."

I closed my eyes and leaned my head back against the cushion.

"Well," I said, "aren't you something. Take that box of letters, too. They ought to help your case."

"Hey, you finally found something! How about that." He slid off his stool and looked into the box.

I said, "I think that's what Laura threatened him with. Vonette might have known about them too, but was too afraid or embarrassed to reveal what she knew. They both probably threatened him with exposure. In Aspen Meadow that would have been the kiss of death. Which it was for them."

"Sort of like closing down a catering business?" he said with a smile. He stopped talking for a minute, shifted his weight on the stool. "Well, Miss Goldy, after all this, I ought to at least rate breakfast with you," he said with a big clown grin. "Make that brunch. Soon's I get some of the work on this done." He eyed Pomeroy, who was finally removing the sooty beekeeper suit. Then he added, "I mean, since we never did get to finish our date."

I looked at Tom Schulz.

I said, "You bet. Give me five minutes and you can take Arch and me home, out for breakfast when the sun comes up, whatever. Meanwhile, I need to have a little chat with the beekeeper. Outside."

Pom gave me a rueful glance and said, "Let's go."

The two of us walked in silence down to the creek. Our feet swished through the grass. The clouds had left the night sky, but acrid smoke stench still hung in the air. Lights from the flashing fire trucks made Pomeroy's tired face look like a statue in a city square at night.

I said, "You had a predator who raided one of your hives a couple of weeks ago. A skunk, maybe. That's why you couldn't bring me any more honey before the funeral, right?"

"Yes, a skunk. So what?"

"Arch didn't forget the things he learned from you," I went on. "He talked about those facts, even used them in his games. When a wizard trespasses a secret lair, he is attacked by a straight-flying line of stingrays. Just like bees. You have to approach danger from the side. Just like bees. When you have unwanted animals, you call the Division of Wildlife. Just like bees. In a game, when you have problems with giant water rats, you crack open a raw alligator egg and mix in chopped-up electric eel. Just like bees. Only with bees, when you have a skunk or rat or field mouse getting into the honey, you crack open an egg and mix the yolk with poison, right?"

"Yeah. So?"

"A poison called Just One Bite, right? That you just happen to keep on the shelves of your shed. Still right?"

Silence. Then he said, "That's right."

"And when a caterer turned cleaning lady tells you she's going to be cleaning the club, you sneak over to look for the poisonous disinfectant, right?"

"Right."

"But you make the mistake of bringing the club cleaning woman flowers in the hospital, and you call her 'sweets' at a party, both of which are remarkably like the bouquet and note you sent her after you first tried to poison Doctor Fritz Niebold Korman, right?"

"Goldy, I wasn't trying to kill him," he protested. "I wanted to, to terrify him, make him sweat. I wanted him to get real worried about dying."

"Uh-huh. And you mention to your protégé, the one who is so easy to talk to, who sounds just like a little adult, and who just happens to be my son, that Laura didn't get along with Fritz and Vonette, and that furthermore, Fritz had no respect for human life. Right again?"

There was a long silence. Pom crossed his arms and stared at the black rushing creek.

He said, "After my wife had her abortion, she left. All I could think about was death. And of course, getting back at him for what he'd done. I know it's not grounds for a malpractice suit. She did what she wanted. But nobody thought about me. It was my child, too, even if she was an alcoholic and the baby probably would have had problems. I wanted Korman to think about death for a while. I'm sorry if Arch took what I said too seriously."

"It's his grandfather we're talking about."

"I am really sorry. Revenge makes you a little crazy. I'm sorry about your business, too," he said. In the moonlight I could see his furrowed brow, his earnest dark eyes. "That's why I wanted to teach Patty Sue how to drive, so she could help you—"

"All because of your ex-wife's abortion? I thought in

Al-Anon you were supposed to learn how to take care of yourself. Let go of the addict in your life. I wish I'd figured out earlier what you were doing in that organization, instead of just working on Laura." I paused. "Wake up and smell the coffee, Pom. You want to have children, get married and have them."

We didn't say anything. I crossed my arms. It was time to go.

I said, "You know what Newman says to Redford in *The Sting* when they first meet? 'Revenge is for suckers.' " I was quiet for a minute before saying, "I have to tell Schulz you're the one. Unless you're ready to 'fess up."

Pom turned away from me completely. He put his hands on his hips and stared at the creek. He cleared his throat. I let him have his silence.

"I'm ready," he said after a moment. "The person I wanted to hurt is being punished. You don't need to turn me in. I can do that myself."

I touched his shoulder. He headed back to the cabin.

Later, although I could not say how much later, Tom Schulz was driving me out of the Aspen Meadow Wildlife Preserve in a police car. We bounced along the dirt road in silence. Despite all the excitement Arch had fallen asleep in the backseat within minutes.

The night was very still. Overhead, a sea of stars glittered. The moon was crossing to the west and the wind had died down. Or, I reflected, since it was near dawn and already All Saints' Day, the wind like everything else had given up the ghost.

"Guess you'll be getting back into the catering business," Tom finally remarked.

"Guess so," I replied, "since I don't need to worry about people coming along and dumping strange chemicals into people's drinks at my functions."

"You know," he said, "I had a feeling it was Pomeroy. Quiet people make me nervous."

"How'd you figure that out?"

"I thought I saw him. Couldn't be sure. It was right after you were talking real close to him, he bent over to put that net hat down and brought out the cleaner. Sometimes you don't arrest someone right away, especially when Murder One and a bunch of other stuff are a possibility at the same time. Anyway," he said with a self-satisfied smirk, "when you followed him I figured you knew he'd done it too, and that you could take as good care of him as I could."

"I thought you didn't want me to leave the party! Was that all an act?"

"Course it was. If Goldy's the prime suspect, Pomeroy won't try to bolt before I've got some evidence. Or a confession, thank you very much. You mind?"

"I can't believe you! Pomeroy could have killed me!"

"Oh, I think you and Arch could've defended yourselves. It took three fire trucks and six smoke pots just to get the bees and Molotov cocktail under control."

I smiled in spite of myself.

Tom Schulz turned onto the highway.

Funny thing, revenge.

Revenge against Fritz Korman was what had motivated Laura because of Bebe and Patty Sue, Vonette because of Laura and Bebe, Pomeroy because of his baby, Arch because of his teacher and his grandmother. Nor was I above reproach, with my hatred of John Richard Korman, the jerk I used to be married to.

Ahead the highway stretched like a smooth gray ribbon pulling us into the day when we remember the dead. To the west the mountaintops were fiery with dawn's light. Schulz pointed to the pine trees, whose needles glowed silver.

Why do we remember the dead? I had asked my Sunday school class when we were studying All Saints' Day. So we can let them go.

Tom Schulz pulled up in front of the Aspen Meadow pastry shop. The warm scent of cinnamon rolls wafted into the morning coolness. I was happy to be there, happy to be with Tom Schulz, happy, period.

He said, "I love this place. Let's start with some rolls. Not as good as yours, of course."

"Flattery will get you absolutely—"

"Same old Goldy. Okay, this being the beginning of a new day and all that, you better let me start by just buying you a cup of coffee."

I smiled and said, "Sure. Black. You put anything in it, I'll kill you."

INDEX TO THE RECIPES

ABOUT THE AUTHOR

Diane Mott Davidson is the author of eleven Goldy novels: *Catering to Nobody, Dying for Chocolate, The Cereal Murders, The Last Suppers, Killer Pancake, The Main Corpse, The Grilling Season, Prime Cut, Tough Cookie, Sticks & Scones,* and *Chopping Spree.* Diane lives in Evergreen, Colorado, with her family.

If you enjoyed Diane Mott Davidson's delicious debut mystery, *CATERING TO NOBODY*, you won't want to miss any of the tantalizing entrees in her nationally bestselling culinary mystery series!

Available wherever Bantam Books are sold